Lily's Odyssey

Carol Smallwood

ALL THINGS
THAT MATTER
PRESS

ISBN 13: 978-0-9840984-5-3
ISBN: 0-9840984-5-3
Library of Congress Control Number: 2009907615

Cover design by All Things That Matter Press

Published in 2010 by All Things That Matter Press

"If the party could thrust its hand into the past and say of this or that event, it never happened—that, surely, was more terrifying than torture and death."
—George Orwell, *1984*

To
John Galsworthy: his unerring observations of society in
fiction has provided lifelong inspiration and awe
and
Dr. Judith Lewis Herman: her ground breaking books
provided invaluable insight into trauma of contemporary
women

Acknowledgments

Internet Public Library

Preditors and Editors

Foreword

Weight of Silence, and *Nicolet's Daughter* were considered as novel titles but it remained *Lily's Odyssey*. Odysseus, the epic hero from Greek mythology in *The Odyssey*, helped by the gods with his band of men, maneuvers the Scylla and Charybdis passage as one of his many adventures in ancient times. Lily, from the Midwest, named by a gardener mother she doesn't remember, struggles with a subconscious she fears will destroy her. Her narrow passage is between reality and disassociation, her time the latter 20th and early 21st Centuries. Her odyssey without help from the gods, reflects a passage through linear labyrinths women interpret as round. Lily's fragmentation is echoed in the writing style.

Readers will recognize Lily in this psychological detective story divided into three parts, as one of the many women who, today as in the past, strives to define what society blurs or ignores. The botanic name for the lily derived from a Greek word, is a symbol of purity as well as death.

I am grateful that AllThingsThatMatter Press did not shy away from *Lily's Odyssey* because many times publishers still view any type of abuse, despite its pervasiveness, as a topic unsuitable for fiction. There is no question the see no evil, speak no evil, hear no evil ceramic monkeys at Uncle Walt's—their paws over their eyes, mouths, and ears with gleeful smiles, remain popular among us. As Sherlock Holmes comments in *Silver Blaze* about the dog doing nothing in the night: "That was the curious incident."

—Carol Smallwood
2010

Table of Contents

PART ONE

"Denial, repression, and dissociation operate on a social as well as an individual level."
—Judith Lewis Herman, M.D., *Trauma and Recovery*

Death in the Family

Nothing moved in the hushed darkness except a few lazy snowflakes as I walked from the parking lot toward Nicolet Community Hospital, its roof outlined with Christmas lights. A car door slammed—probably someone returning from a night shift at Hammersmith Paper—the sound was distinct, reinforcing the cold.

The original hospital, a Hansel and Gretel gingerbread stucco, had been swallowed by a phalanx of additions when insurance companies had smiled on specialists, and now you had to follow colored dots like breadcrumbs to find your way. I rang the buzzer twice while looking at the giant Christmas tree in the yard. A few days ago, when I arrived in Nicolet City, I'd noticed the huge sign beside the tree inviting people to purchase a light in memory of a loved one, for a new X-ray machine: a green light cost twenty-five dollars, a blue one fifty dollars, a red one a hundred dollars. But if you wanted to truly honor someone, you bought a white one, and that someone's name was then included in a huge printed sign.

I was beginning to think I hadn't come to the right door, the one Aunt Hester had said I should use after hours, when it opened.

"Have ya been standin' here long," a woman asked.

Without waiting for an answer, she jabbed a thumb over her uniformed shoulder and said, "I was down the east wing moppin' up." She tucked some gray hair in her ponytail and added, "They never have 'nough people here after midnight. Ya didn't get too cold, honey? Wipe your feet—we don't need no accidents."

I still hadn't said anything, and she went on, telling me what color dots on the floor to follow and looking at my shoes disapprovingly.

"Now, ya have a nice little Christmas," she concluded, and left, humming *Jingle Bells*, trailing a scent of disinfectant.

It wasn't until she'd rounded the corner that I realized I'd gone to high school with her, a time now fondly equated with secure family life and innocence. She still wore her hair in a ponytail, smoked, and called people "honey," but her shoes were orthopedic now. We'd sat across from each other in study hall our last year, and she made sure I noticed her engagement ring—the first diamond I'd seen on someone my age. Since she was a junior, she'd gone with a boy with a caved-in chest, and they'd acquired that "couple look," even when they weren't wearing matching sweaters or shoelaces.

I followed the yellow dots through the maze of corridors to the ICU wing, trying to remember her name when I came to Uncle Walt's room. It had that awful closeness, warm and stale from too many bodies consuming too little fresh air.

Uncle Walt's sister Heidi was there, sitting at the foot of the bed, which was banked by poinsettias. She peered at me as I stood in the doorway, squinting a bit since she didn't have her glasses on. She nodded, and then her eyes returned to Aunt Hester, who stood next to the bed, clutching Uncle Walt's hands.

"I'm here, Walt," Aunt Hester was saying in her usual hushed voice as if in church. "I'm here right by you, I haven't left you, dear." In a louder voice, she said, "Can you hear me, Walt?" and bent lower. "Do you need another shot of morphine?"

She sounded irritated that he wasn't responding. "Are you in pain, dear?" she said, and turning to Aunt Heidi, said, "I think he can hear me."

Aunt Heidi looked at me again, saw I was still standing in the doorway, and motioned me to the empty chair. My aunt had white hair, large eyes, and a pink, almost red nose that gave her an affable, Easter Bunny look. Uncle Walt often said to her, "Heidi, sure you haven't been hittin' your cooking sherry?"

I smelled onions when I sat down next to her. She put her hand on my arm and whispered, "It won't be long now."

Uncle Walt, my father's brother, had been nearly forty when my father died in the Second World War; my mother perished a week later, when our house burned down. I was almost three at the time, and my brother Vincent was five when Uncle Walt and Aunt Hester adopted us.

I was retirement age but still steeled myself against something indefinable, staring at him lying in a blue pin striped hospital gown with his eyes closed. Uncle Walt had been an engineer in the largest company in town, and was often asked to model at fashion shows. I saw his mouth slack beneath the brim of his Stetson set at a rakish tilt, his swagger. He would automatically adjust his expression to fit whatever situation he found himself in. He adopted a respectful look for men who were richer, and one fit for those who were poorer than he was. With women, his expressions depended on their looks, age, and social position—and their tolerance for leering.

He was pretending. Lying in bed as if helpless, using his old ploy of the misunderstood husband to get his way. Yes—just one of his cons to look defenseless.

In the stuffy room I wondered, did people get to see each other after death, as Aunt Heidi believed? "Smile and the whole world smiles" reflected her cheerful full-steam-ahead attitude, and she was particularly pleased when people sought her advice on cooking. She was a cook before she was married, and was never happier than when trying something new.

The last time she'd made baked tripe, Bubble and Squeak, which Uncle Walt used to call a "double drinker," since it justified doubling his cocktails. I glanced to see if I could see the conspiratorial smile on Aunt Heidi's perennially flushed face when she'd beckon me to taste from a proffered spoon—I'd never been sure whether she was smiling because I dreaded to taste it or if she considered it a great honor.

Aunt Hester offered rosaries for her sister-in-law while staring with her one good eye, having lost the other eye when a milk truck ran into her on her way to early weekday mass. But no one knew more about the proper length of hemlines than she did. I think it gave her a sense of security, a reaffirmation that she knew the proper thing also in the material world, even if she wore her own hemline higher than what fashion decreed. With a Nicolet Lumber Company yardstick, her straight mouth full of straight pins, Aunt Hester made hemlines as exact as her beliefs: after ironing, they looked sharp enough to slice potatoes.

I opened my mouth to relieve my clenched jaw while looking out the window at the Christmas tree near the hospital entrance and moved my head until the window framed the tree evenly, like a Norman Rockwell Christmas card. Someone in the hall asked, "You check Room 201?" but the reply was muffled by a cart rattling by.

I'd just formed the outline of a star from the green lights on the tree and was beginning a bell when my brother Vincent came. I hadn't seen him recently but noticed that his hair still separated like paths through tall grass; the dim room made it impossible to see how much lint was on his black clothes.

Vincent didn't have any hair on his hands; it was as if his arms were his physical side, his hands the spiritual. I was outlining a wreath on the tree outside when Vincent soon said, "He's gone." It was the same tone with which he always said, "Go, you are dismissed" at the end of saying mass.

Uncle Walt's soul could now be poised before the gates of Heaven, Hell, and Purgatory—I couldn't wish him to Hell; nor did Heaven seem fitting. Yes, to have believed in the three choices would've been a comfort, but I fought against shaking him the way his hounds did newly shot rabbits.

After an aide came and wrote the estimated time of death, Aunt Hester suggested we go someplace and compose the obituary.

So, that's it? I thought. He didn't look any different dead then in a coma; there wasn't even a doctor present. No one threw himself or herself on him, fainted, tore their hair, or screamed his name. I bowed my head, ashamed at not being able to cry.

The lounge, painted a sunny yellow with an orange band around the middle, was empty at that late hour. One wall had been decorated by the high school art students with Disney characters: Snow White held a bird larger than herself, painted in the Nicolet High School colors; Cinderella in fluorescent pink slippers was followed by seven dwarfs, also in the school's colors; Bambi with a butterfly on his nose, however, was painted by a close observer of butterflies. There were several other characters from Disney movies on fast food toys.

We'd just sat down in the hospital lounge when my cousin Mary Elizabeth arrived. Born with legs were set far apart, she'd walked pigeon-toed after the nuns had said she wasn't ladylike. Before Father Benoit started catechism lessons, his face would flush as he ran his finger around his tight white Roman collar, before telling us girls "to close the gates of hell" by crossing our legs. Mary Elizabeth was sniffling into a lace-edged handkerchief. Her streaked hair was coiled severely, pulled away from her narrow face; no longer was it a wavy auburn unsuccessfully restrained by a bow at the nape of her neck.

Aunt Hester snapped open her purse, took out a legal pad, and said as she wrote: "Walter Augustus Alger served as a Nicolet County commissioner for twenty-four years…or was it twenty-two?"

Aunt Hester was Uncle Walt's last wife. I hadn't known the others. Whenever anyone mentioned them, he would twirl his index finger to his temple, indicating they weren't right in the head.

Aunt Heidi sighed and avoided looking at me until Aunt Hester settled on twenty-three and a half years as county commissioner. After Hester jotted the information down, she looked up—one of her eyes was glass, but there were always dark circles under both of them. When I was a child, I overheard a neighbor kid say, "She looks like a raccoon."

The sun was starting to come up, and I observed the lint on Vincent's sleeves as he said, "He founded the Walter A. Alger Organ Funds for St. John's and my diocese." He was stuffing his hands in his pockets as he spoke, as had been his habit for as long as I could remember. Uncle Walt often joked about it.

Aunt Hester added, "He was a trustee of the Nicolet County Bank and Trust."

"I often heard him say he started St. John's Credit Union," said Mary Elizabeth, lifting her black leather purse up high to adjust a buckle; whenever my cousin got something new, she made a point of it. She wore a simple dress, pumps, and pearls. A strand dared escape her tightly coiled hair. With an impatient puff from lips never cheapened by lipstick, she blew it back.

Awards from the Nicolet County Rifle Club, the Wisconsin Engineering Society, and others were duly recorded. Care was taken about assigning Vincent's title, and the residence of Mary Elizabeth and her husband. Aunt Hester said she'd confer with Father Mulcahy about a baptismal font bearing Uncle Walt's name.

I avoided looking at the aquarium in the corner to avoid worrying about whether the fish were getting enough food and if there was an air filter so they'd get enough oxygen.

On the way to Big Boy's for breakfast, I followed a truck with a red, yellow, and orange revolving cone on its way to a carnival; only months later did I realize it was a cement truck. When we were seated at a large round table, Vincent said, "If Uncle Walt had died a day earlier, it would've been on the Feast of the Immaculate Conception."

Aunt Hester crossed herself, saying, "Jesus, Mary, Joseph!"

I noticed how white my knuckles were on the red and white place mat, a fingernail bleeding where I'd torn it. Until we were served, I listened to the clatter of plates and tried to float away on whiffs of Belgian waffles.

One of the waitresses had taffy color hair hugging her head like sand ridges. She walked as if one of her heels were missing, and after reaching under a counter, gave her underwear a quick yank.

The next morning everyone assembled to agree with Aunt Hester on a casket with a memory drawer even before the assistant director had a chance to take off his Nicolet Explorer cap (his grandson was on the local team). At Floyd's Flower & Gift, the florist had bits of fern clinging to his Flowers Are Christmas sweatshirt; while Bing Crosby sang White Christmas, I kept my eyes down so I wouldn't see anything wilting.

The next few nights before the funeral, I heard bells toll the hours through the window I'd forced open. Staring at the streetlight, I wondered what'd happened to Uncle Walt's blood. How much was there? Did they just slit his wrist and let it drain like oil from a car? I'd gone to high school with the mortician/funeral director. Whenever he greeted me my eyes would drop to his hands. They bulged with veins like divining rods for blood, and when we shook hands at the last high school reunion I couldn't wait to wash mine.

Carol Smallwood

That night I dreamed of attending my funeral like Tom Sawyer, listening to guns of some indefinable war pound.

As I entered the house where I'd spent my childhood, the smell brought so many conflicting emotions that I had to steady myself against the doorframe. Each house has its own scent, as individual as a fingerprint, and Uncle Walt and Aunt Hester's house was so intertwined with who I was that I would have known it anywhere, anytime. I often tried to figure out why other houses smelled the way they did. Was it the type of heat? Or was it the dead skin cells of inhabitants which defied dusting and vacuuming. I read we get new skin every seven years and dust is full of them. When I saw a magnification of a dust mite, it was the one of the most frightening things I'd ever seen, and I regretted ever seeing it.

The familiar Audubon print, "Wild Turkey," greeted me in the foyer, the bird's neck, with its wart like growths, as scrawny as ever. I'd always believed that Aunt Hester tolerated the print because the leaves in the background matched the green in the Chinese bowl on the table below it. Now, at this get-together a day before the funeral service, the life-size statue of Aunt Hester's Virgin Mary looked smaller than I'd remembered, her blue robe a little faded. To get rid of a suffocating feeling, I recalled one of Garrison Keillor's narrations about Lake Woebegon's Lady of Perpetual Responsibility. By the statue was the large painting of Christ in a brown robe, knocking at a door. Aunt Hester said it was the authorized Catholic version. I don't remember now if it was the Catholic or Protestant version that had the halo. Aunt Hester never tired of saying the door had no outside latch so the person inside had to open it—and then she'd look and see if you understood the religious symbolism.

The living room, where people were already gathered, smelled of baked beans, ham, apple pie, and coffee. I'd brought a tray of cold cuts that I purchased at the C&C, as well as peanut butter cookies I'd made at my daughter Jenny's house.

Aunt Hester took my food offerings from me, saying, "Thank you, my dear," her familiar tone blending forbearance and atonement for my sins. Only it seemed there was something different now, a note of challenge in her voice, as if defying me after all these years to say anything against Uncle Walt. I could tell from the conversation that whiskey, gin, brandy, and vodka had been flowing liberally. Seeing my surprise, she said, "J.D. and Rachel brought all the liquor and are overseeing the bar for me." Rachel had been married to my ex-husband, Cal, until he died almost ten years ago. J.D. had been an engineer, like Uncle Walt, and worked with him at the paper mill. I followed Aunt Hester's gesture to the table, covered with white linen and liquor bottles. The linen didn't cover the legs, and I recognized them from when Uncle Walt would make me bend over as a child whenever I spilled my milk so he could swat me. Above the table was the Alger crest that'd been there ever since I could remember—I'd been proud of it until I saw one just like it in a mail order catalog with another name on it.

I'd steeled myself against similar recollections before coming, and avoided looking at the large chair in front of the TV that no one ever sat in except Uncle Walt, but I caught a glimpse of it and his jackknife beside it. I found myself regretting that I'd no longer hear him call me "Dolly." Then I felt hot air on my ankles from the vents in the floor, and that brought to mind the basement, with its furnace, and the spot where I retreated as a child under some shelves, clutching my slippery Christmas doll made of red-checked oilcloth. My heart began to race when the hot air carried the scent of the basement with an old illusive memory for some reason; I made myself relax my jaw and walked to the middle of the room to talk with the friends and relatives who stood in groups with drinks in hand.

I was relieved, and at the same time surprised, that even Aunt Hester didn't appear sad, and that there wasn't anyone shedding tears. Aunt Heidi was the only one I heard even mention Uncle Walt, and that was to reminisce about how he took care of the money that she'd earned as a child so she wouldn't spend it. And about how she never saw their mother cry.

Vincent, my brother, looked like he'd been there a while, and, as Uncle Walt would have said, he wasn't feeling any pain. He approached me with an extra drink in his hand. When I refused it, he gave the usual exasperated look that said he would never understand me. The smell of alcohol was tempting, but I knew I couldn't have just one drink, that I mustn't use it again to achieve oblivion. He did give me a hug, though—an awkward hug, the first one I could recall he'd ever given me before he moved on to talk with others. I thought him self-centered, using the Catholic Church as a men's club aiding his rise in the hierarchy. We were alike in one way, that being how we managed to overlook what we didn't want to see.

I watched him converse, and pictured the always neat room that had once been his and now had lighted cabinets to display Aunt Hester's well dusted chubby Hummel figurines, thin religious statues, and see-no-evil, hear-no-evil, speak-no-evil ceramic monkeys. One monkey had its paws over its eyes; the other had its paws over its ears;

the other over its mouth. The trinity had such gleeful expressions, though and always made me suspect they could see, talk, and hear everything.

My old room had been made into a guestroom. I slipped out of the living room and went upstairs to look around, saw a comforter at the foot of the bed that matched the color of the new drapes, instead of my mother's quilt, which was on the bed in my house at White Water. How many times had I looked out the one window and dreamed of the life I'd have someday when I was a grown-up and living far away? I'd carefully cut out pictures from catalogues and newspapers while in my room, pasted them into scrapbooks, and grouped the pictures into paper families. And I'd cut out pictures of dolls from the Sears and J.C. Penney catalogues, dolls in pink dresses and blond hair, extending their arms asking to be held.

On Christmas Eve I'd stay awake as long as I could and stare through the open door to the hallway at the trapdoor in the ceiling in hopes of catching Santa Claus descend in a flurry of snow and soot. Since we didn't have a fireplace, I figured that would have to be the way he'd come. I'd listen for any hint of reindeer patter or bells on the roof, imagining a chubby, warm, kind-eyed Santa in a red suit and white whiskers who'd tell me what a good girl I was and how he'd saved a special doll just for me. A doll that would have blond hair like mine, a pink ruffled dress with ribbons, though Aunt Hester said pink was a "vain, worldly color." A doll that would give me a secret smile and welcome my hug when I told her how pretty she was. At night, I would always be sure she was covered with a flannel blanket I'd made and tell her she'd been a good girl. In the morning, she would open her eyes when I picked her up, and I'd smooth her dress, make sure that her bonnet, frilled with white lace and pale blue rosettes, wasn't crooked. I'd tell her, "You're a pretty girl. Aren't you a pretty, pretty girl?"

When I left the house, part of me was glad that people had come to honor Uncle Walt, as they would any deceased person, even though I couldn't understand why they didn't see the man he really was. Outside, relieved by the silence and fresh air, I walked the circular drive which as a child, I'd roller-skated and played hopscotch and marbles. It had been resurfaced, so I couldn't find the crack where I fell so often that the bruises on my knees didn't have time to heal. The smell and feel of chalk, the sound of the wheels on the skates—I almost looked down to see if my knees were bleeding. But I didn't, and also resisted looking at the place where my grandfather's house had been. His fields were where I'd run as fast as I could with kites. Every spring I'd save my money for the most colorful kite

Woolworth's had and fly it as high my ball of string allowed as I ran over patches of snow, weeds, and furrows. Other neighborhood kids could get theirs so high they'd almost become invisible, but mine would fall and tear; patched kites are unbalanced and almost impossible to fly again.

But I did recall the frustration I'd felt trying to get around Uncle Walt's hunting dog who blocked me when I wanted to walk to my grandfather's and see his face light up when he saw me.

***

The morning of the church service, Aunt Hester's white Olds was behind the sleek black hearse in the procession, followed by Vincent's smoke window car. Jenny and I and my son-in-law, Scott, were next, in his Chevy Blazer. Aunt Heidi was there, of course, along with my son Mark and his family, Rachel and J.D., Mary Elizabeth and her husband, as well as other relatives, neighbors, and friends.

A patrol car's flashing lights led the way to church, allowing our flag-fluttering cars to ignore stoplights and signs. I wasn't sure if I was moving or if things around me were moving like in a car wash.

The kids had liked going with me to the car wash when they were younger. When it was our turn they'd squeal, pretending they were afraid; the swirling water, the foam, the mist, the green, hanging moving pieces made me think of the narrow straits maneuvered by Odysseus. I never knew if the Toyota was moving or if everything else was. When I became dizzy I'd watch the large sign, "A Clean Car Reflects You," or the attendants, resembling frogs, moving quickly in big green earplugs and black and yellow spotted uniforms. But I dreaded the part when soap covered the windows because it made me gasp for air.

I watched a truck transporting a huge rocket in garish carnival red and yellow probably destined for the mysteries of space. It wasn't until months later, when I saw another on the road, that I realized the spinning cone was a cement mixer. Jenny began crying in the backseat; I forced back my tears because I knew if I started, I'd never stop, which would upset her even more.

The procession ended at St. John's, the oldest church in Nicolet City. I recalled the article in the newspaper about the large white frame building being moved inch by inch by horses over several days in 1911 to its current location. After we got out of our vehicles, Scott guided us up the stairs past the white Doric columns.

My son, Mark, whom I hadn't seen since my granddaughter's baptism, hugged me. He felt as brittle as the first ice of winter, and I knew he was remembering his father's funeral. I sat in the front row on the right, between Aunt Hester and Jenny, near the black-draped casket. The pallbearers, sons of Uncle Walt's fellow engineers at Hammersmith Paper, sat to the left. The frankincense burned in the metal censer in front of me, and I imagined three grinning witches cackle, "Boil and bubble, caldron bubble. Cover, cover it all."

The seated people brought back a dream I'd had.

I was attending a play, but I didn't have a ticket, and so kept walking around. Everyone assumed I had the right to be there, and I did, too, because it was connected with the social position I'd once had as a surgeon's wife. I was afraid I'd have to show a ticket, and I hoped that, since I'd helped with the production, no one would think I couldn't afford one. The large gathering in the dream included a group that had long, heavy coat uniforms, and another group that wore metallic clothes, and still another wearing white cloaks. No one was watching the play, but watched those coming in and joining their particular group. I was interested in the play, but it was more interesting that everyone seemed to be locked into assigned roles. As I walked the aisles, I saw the groups and the division of the types plainly, like patterns on a quilt. They spoke only to others who dressed like and sat next to them. I was impressed with those who had the most money--they had seats nearest the stage and were the most self-assured.

At the service, drifting in and out of attentiveness, I wondered why the Church said death was a joyous event because you got to see God, yet everything at a requiem mass was black. If life was but a preparation for death, wouldn't bright robes embroidered with birds and flowers, like the Chinese robe the explorer Nicolet wore when he greeted Winnebago Indians, have made more sense?

Vincent stood before the congregation without saying anything. He surveyed the congregation and then lowered his head. I thought he might have been overcome with grief, but realized that he was merely pausing for effect. When you could hear a Kleenex drop, he began.

"This morning," he said slowly, "we have come to honor Walter Augustus Alger, a good friend, a trusted neighbor, a public-minded citizen, a fond relative, a beloved and devoted father to his adopted children."

It was like a speech from Julius Caesar; perhaps the Roman vestments he wore made me think of it. After another long pause, he rubbed his forehead with an index finger and in a louder voice said, "I had the good fortune to be one of those children. God had a plan for our brother in Christ, just like he has a plan for each and every one of us." He extended his arms like the statue of Nicolet in the park. "Walter was God's chosen, the salt of the earth. He let his light shine. May it shine as brightly in each and every one here this morning in this, His holy church."

Vincent lowered his arms and looked approvingly at a sniffling Mary Elizabeth. His voice trembled when he said, "Not one of us has failed to feel Walter's light upon us. He let his light shine. Not one of us can have doubted he was the very salt of the earth." He paused, looked up at the choir loft as if seeking inspiration, before adding with emphasis, "My friends in Christ, he was the very salt of the earth."

I stifled a smile at my brother repeating his own words like the Protestant evangelists he belittled for depending on the Bible so much; I could, however, see his point, because the Bible was so full of contradictions.

"Yes, my brothers and sisters in Christ, never doubt that God watches over us. He is the Good Shepherd. Yea, our Good Shepherd. We may ask ourselves, 'Why was I not born with wealth, good looks, good health, as my neighbor next door? Why don't I have a BMW in my garage, unlimited credit cards, fame and fortune waiting at my doorstep?'"

He paused and looked around, then frowned when a baby began to cry. He bowed his head in pained silence, remaining tight-lipped until the baby was carried out, then slowly raised his head and gave one of Aunt Hester's smiles of forbearance before continuing.

"My brothers and sisters in Christ, God gave Walter Alger the opportunity to prove he was a good shepherd when he adopted two young children." Aunt Hester sobbed louder. "What more perfect example of becoming his brother's keeper could there be than when he adopted my sister and I after we'd lost our parents?" With a deeper tremor, and drawing his arms as if in welcome, he added, "He took us in."

He nodded toward Aunt Hester, then continued as if returning from a long journey of vision: "He has been a generous founder of St. John's Organ Fund and various funds in my diocese devoted to helping needy children, as well as the Annual Catholic Relief Fund. A generous giver. A faithful supporter of God's work here on earth."

I wondered how much of my uncle's generous giving had to do with Vincent becoming a monsignor and then a bishop. I'd heard he was aiming at becoming an archbishop—maybe then he'd get the BMW he wanted, or rather, as Aunt Hester put it, "coveted."

Vincent raised his arms and the folds of his vestments flowed gracefully. "Now, Lord," he continued, "take your servant, Walter Alger, with you to eternal paradise. Bring your lamb into your fold." Aunt Hester and Mary Elizabeth were sobbing loudly and I missed some of what Vincent said, but heard, "…good and faithful servant. Heavenly Father, we ask…the beginning of time."

I tried to ignore the metallic taste of blood in my mouth. Aunt Hester had often told me that my real father was in Heaven with my mother, but I'd often wondered why she could be "with God in Heaven" when I needed her.

Mrs. Stoke, a friend of my mother's, would roll her tongue inside her cheeks, which pushed her mouth forward, and say, "Your mother was too good for this earth, and God in His wisdom took her to Him. If she had a piece of cake in her school lunchbox, she'd give it away instead of eating it herself."

I must have muttered something then, because Jenny put her hand on my arm and pleaded with her eyes for me not to make a scene. I forced my clenched jaw apart to move my tongue around before swallowing to avoid swallowing any pieces of teeth that surely must have shattered and was surprised when it didn't happen.

When I saw a ray of sunlight on the pew, I remembered another shaft of light, somewhere murky, primeval. To drown it out, I pictured the rows of greeting cards at Rite Aid in White Water, undulating with color. Rite Aid was where I went every Sunday now, since going somewhere filled my childhood habit of going to church every Sunday. I found myself looking at cards more often now, and picking the ones I'd most like to receive. The store looked rectangular from the outside, but, once inside, the aisles radiated in a labyrinth within angled walls with high porthole windows as on a ship. It gave me a dizzy feeling; the stores in Nicolet City only had up and down aisles. I learned to judge where I was by the merchandise.

I'd about decided on a card with embossed pink roses while waiting to hear that my prescription was ready. Waiting for a prescription to be called on the speaker (before federal law forbade it) was like in the movies when uniformed servants stood at the top of long stairs announcing your name. When picturing my majestic descent, I was pushed. It must be another woman trying to make me trip because the prince only had eyes for me; no, it was Aunt Hester, it was time to walk out behind the casket.

I dreaded facing the congregation, especially Rachel, whom Cal had married after our divorce. But determined that no one would see me cry, I jutted my chin even higher. I took a deep breath, and the frankincense almost overwhelmed me so I imagined riding a swaying camel, swathed in a saffron chiffon scarf touching the sand, followed by a caravan of princes competing for my hand carrying gifts. I stared at the choir loft starburst clock like a star on a distant horizon to block Rachel's Raggedy Ann red hair.

The caravan stopped in the bright lobby. When I shaded my eyes, I gratefully detected Elizabeth Arden's Red Door on my wrist. At Cal's funeral, I'd worn Estée Lauder's Beautiful; at Mark's marriage, Elizabeth Taylor's White Diamonds. Through the high, open doors was a cloudless sky and a pure world under newly fallen snow. The casket was carried to the waiting hearse by the six pallbearers, their dark legs moving in unison like a giant caterpillar.

Uncle Walt had survived so many of his contemporaries that he'd seemed indestructible. At any minute I expected him to walk up the salt-sprinkled steps in shoes shined with Kiwi shoe polish, the wax kind that came in tins, grinning, with the cigar in his mouth tilted like FDR's cigarette holder. He'd give his yellow plaid suspenders a snap and laugh about how we'd all thought he was dead. Then he'd tell one of his jokes. The older Uncle Walt got, the dirtier they got. I'd always known right away if it would be dirty because a certain look came over him, and the longer he hesitated, the dirtier the joke was; he'd stroke his extended cigar slowly, grin like a bad little boy, study his cigar and say, "Christamighty! I like 'em fresh, firm, and fully packed."

But Uncle Walt wouldn't be reappearing, and when I saw the pallbearers returning, talking among themselves after sliding the coffin into the hearse, I felt tears of disbelief running down my cheeks. He'd always been around. Without him, I'd have to reinvent myself and I didn't know how.

The parking lot fence looked like snaggletoothed cronies hanging on to dreams, the dried weeds at their feet tufts of fallen hair. I breathed deeply, grateful for the moist fresh air, the pure white snow, and drank in the graceful starkness of the bare trees, the vast calmness of the sky that saw so much but was always there without sentimentality. When I felt tears smarting, I looked down at my black coat that made me look like a drab crow, and reminded myself again that funerals were only ceremonies.

***

The tables for the luncheon brought back tables filled with people on Little Chicago Lake, the smell of the hot tar of summer, the satisfying plop of belly smackers off the dock. It got its name because people from Chicago had built summer homes when the Manitowoc & Nicolet Railroad skirted the lake in the late 1800s. The large log depot with boarded windows still stood as a testament to an era when railroads brought in people for the summer season. It seemed waiting for train whistles, still anticipating the bustle of families arriving after Memorial Day and departing before Labor Day. I could see people of all ages taking a last look at the lake, trying to remember the good times as they stared at the water that never looked the same, revealed its secrets, or stopped taking lives. A lake circled by narrow Indian trails to Lake Michigan.

At the Little Chicago Lake picnics, the people sitting at the sturdy pine tables by the lake resembled each other in the way they nodded, shook their heads, and managed to avoid looking at those whom they were talking about sitting at adjacent tables, who were doing the same thing. Uncle Walt had described them as "gussied up blockheads" or "muttonheads." People were careful to check each other's tone to be sure they stayed within the social boundaries they were supposed to follow. In contrast, my uncle's expression, as he nodded and greeted people, was genuinely benevolent. In his way, and on his terms, he liked people, and, as a child, it was from him I had felt human warmth missing in Aunt Hester. Before leaving those get-togethers, he'd usually walk around the park, his cigar planted in the corner of his mouth, to be sure he hadn't missed talking with anyone.

People would tell me, "Your uncle's such a great guy," and, "Walter Alger's the salt of the earth, and if someone speaks ill of him, they'll have to answer to me."

I recalled a conversation at one picnic, about a woman who'd been raped.

Uncle Walt snapped shut his jack knife and said, "God, having a wife like that sure as hell must make a husband feel like crap," and motioned for another beer. Aunt Hester handed him an Old Milwaukee from the cooler. "Why the hell did he let his wife go out wearing short dresses like that?" He took a swig of beer and said, "Sure as God made little green apples, she asked for it." And then in the thick voice I dreaded, "I hope she was satisfied."

Aunt Hester said in her church voice, "It's supposed to rain t—"

"Women have it all," he went on, "but are they satisfied? Hell, no." He motioned at the bench he was sitting. "Christamighty! If you lined up all the satisfied women you ever ran across on God's green earth, their rear ends wouldn't fill this damn bench. Women sure as hell hold the wealth in this country, but the potlickers say they haven't two dimes to rub together." He slammed his fist on the table, making his jackknife fall in the grass. "They should've gone through the hard times of living in the Depression like I did."

At the funeral luncheon in the church basement, relatives I didn't recall seeing before told me they didn't know whom I resembled. When I was a little girl, I thought a neighbor couple I liked were my real parents. They had no children and always talked to me as if they really saw me—in fact, the woman looked at me so intently that I was afraid she must've wondered about Uncle Walt. Aunt Hester called her "A misguided Protestant." Looking back, I'd probably have denied anything from a sense of loyalty and from being unsure if I'd be any better off. Still, I imagined that I was once theirs, and made up stories about why they had to give me up which never failed to make my eyes sting. I'd have lived with my grandfather if I could've, even if he wasn't able to send me to college. Uncle Walt often said how much an education cost, and I really wanted to go. I remember walking slowly in step at my high school graduation to "Pomp and Circumstance," smiling while my classmates cried.

A rubber tip on one of the chair's legs was missing, and when I sat down I had the sensation of being off balance, which continued when I got up. I avoided looking in the direction of Rachel and J.D. Whenever I saw them, I'd be reminded of Cal, even after all these years. Ironically, it was Cal who told J.D. about my first counselor's interest in me, and, after that, J.D. went out of his way to flirt with me while Cal and I were still married. When he married Rachel I was surprised; some had called him an opportunist. He was stocky, wore checked vests, and regarded people with a steady look as he spoke, which impressed them. J.D. seemed sincere. But the next time they saw him, they'd realize he looked at them the same way when he was merely shaking hands (which he did often), or passing them on the street.

Rachel and J.D. were taking turns pushing Mark and Becky's baby, my granddaughter, in her stroller. What was the name of that weave in the baby's blanket? I'd learned about weaves in Miss Dixon's high school home ec class. Herringbone, that's what it was. Miss Dixon had also taught us how to present pleasing meals, with contrasting colors and both hot and cold items of various textures, the importance of a freshly ironed tablecloth and napkins, and an appropriate centerpiece. And always to shower, apply deodorant, (we got samples of Mum), select attractive clothing from a closet scented with oranges covered with whole cloves, and finish with a powder puff and lipstick. When your husband arrived to a clean house and clean children, she said, you smiled when you greeted him at the door, then hung up his coat and offered him a drink and an array of tempting, colorful appetizers. You asked him about his day making sure the children were quietly playing. If asked about your day, you only mentioned pleasant things.

At the luncheon, I made as many trips as I dared to the restroom without causing people to wonder if something was wrong with me. Inside the unheated cement block room, my long deep breaths came out like smoke signals when I opened and shut my mouth to relieve my clenched jaw, shake my head in disbelief. Each time I went in, I saw cracks in the ceiling that I hadn't seen before. Some natural light came through a small casement window dotted with snow, and I recalled making dots of snow on windows into fairy tale pictures when a child.

When people had complained about the cold rest rooms to Father Couillard, who was the priest before Father Mulcahy, he'd say, "Enjoy the cold while you can, my friends. Where many of you are headed, it will be plenty hot."

Aunt Heidi had laughed about that, though Aunt Hester had frowned at laughing about God's representatives on earth. Father Couillard's stomach had hung over his belt like bread dough exceeding the volume of a pan, and I always wanted to prick it with a fork to see if it would make a wheezing sound before collapsing. I had a dream about going to see Father Couillard and screaming wildly when he started in about the love and wisdom of God.

My vapor breath in the basement rest room reminded me that the ground was frozen, which was why Uncle Walt wouldn't be interred until the spring. I saw the graves of my mother and father. When I went with Aunt Hester and Uncle Walt to their graves as a child, Uncle Walt would always sob loudly. A kneeling angel with wings over its face held the scroll:

IN MEMORY OF MY BELOVED BROTHER AND HIS WIFE
1942
BY WALTER AUGUSTUS WALTER

The angel's partially spread wings were the first to crumble on the sagging base, and each year it leaned more forward, like an aging boxer. As I grew up the angel appeared smaller, less frightening. It became less likely to feel the air it made from beating its wings while scolding me for not coming more often. I mostly avoided the cemetery, because I didn't like seeing dying plants or the dying grass from newly dug graves, the awful heavy silence squashing one into darkness to join those decomposing underfoot. And when the headstones were deep in snow, the finality was deafening.

I preferred the cemetery in the fall. Then, the wind coming off Lake Michigan made the dead leaves rustle, banking bunches of them against rectangular granite, making the headstones less stark. The leaves were raked by the caretaker, but thankfully some always escaped; when I listened, with my eyes shut, to the fantastic stories they told being chased by the playful wind, Aunt Hester thought I was praying. But I'd always leave my mother's and father's graves as soon as I could, mumbling apologies, terrified they might've been buried alive.

***

D.H. Lawrence had observed: "Different places on the face of the earth have different vital influence, different vibration...call it what you like. But the spirit of place is a great reality." I sensed this in an old bar by the cemetery. It always looked the same—peeling paint, missing shingles on the sagging roof. A tilted sign, Whipper Will's Bar, noted the current owner, who'd retained the name after his father gained renown by whipping an out-of-town customer. The whip, a relic from when it was a stagecoach stop, rested on deer antlers hung over the bar along with an assortment of bathing beauties calendars from 1946.

It had been called Hemlock Bar for decades because the tables, doors, and windows were trimmed in native hemlock bark. I doubted hemlock was associated by many regulars as being used in a drink to kill Socrates. The crooked floor made sober people stumble—newcomers were advised to "Grab yur drinks or they'll land there" by regulars, indicating the river following US-13 out of town. The highway was the prime reason the building was shifting—the vibration of large trucks caused the logs of the foundation to gradually settle in the clay.

The air was always heavy with cigarette, cigar smoke and stale beer, the murky windows guarding customers from "the old ball and chain" at home. Gnarled wood and old bottles from the lumbering era were stacked in corners for the occasional tourist, but when one asked about the cobwebbed relics, they got outlandish answers along with ill-concealed grins.

When the dim light got too dark, strings connected to bulbs in the high ceiling were pulled. The red neon BAR sign on the window sometimes looked like, DAR,, much to the disgust of Nicolet City's member of the Daughters of the American Revolution.

One of Aunt Hester's relatives had once owned the bar despite the fact she always denied it, calling it "A sinful place where no respectable person would be seen." And it did have a reputation— regulars kept a space free in the parking lot for fights.

Black bears visiting the nearby fields filled with blackberry bushes would make headlines when they wandered in through the back door. Their visits encouraged drinking because of the belief that bears "wouldn't pay attention to you when you had few," a belief that reached the status of gospel after a picture appeared in the paper of a cub lapping beer on the counter. Drinks like "The Hair of the Bear" and "Blackie's Kick" became popular, and bets were placed on when the next bear would come ambling in.

Hemlock Bar was in a neighborhood called the Tannery. A prosperous shoe leather-tanning factory had been there that'd used local hemlock bark in the tanning process until the trees were depleted in 1923 and the best paying jobs in Nicolet City disappeared.

A Catholic cemetery was nearby. Aunt Hester headed an ongoing committee to close the bar because as soon as a burial service was finished, many men rushed to Whipper Will's, cussing at the blackberry thorns. Uncle Walt laughed, despite Aunt Hester saying the thorns were "God's way of keeping men from sin."

At funerals, "When the Saints Come Marching In," sung off-key, drifted across the field. Aunt Hester pretended she didn't hear by further compressing her lips; Uncle Walt would grin and say, "Damn fools, they're three sheets to the wind. Joe's voice is always louder than the rest of them. He was the best damn softball player you'd ever meet."

***

When I got up the next day in my daughter's house, I couldn't take any more friends and relatives saying, "You had such a great uncle," and "They broke the mold when they made him." So I packed and called Jenny. I hadn't seen her that morning—she'd gotten up early to go to work.

"I've decided to go back," I told Jenny."

"You're leaving this morning?" She sounded surprised.

"Yes, there isn't much more I can do."

I wanted to get away from Uncle Walt in his open white satin-lined coffin from where it felt like he was exuding a glue so sticky that the more I tried to break free, the more sticky and elastic it got, until it stretched like utility wires, connecting me with him no matter where I was.

Back Home

When I got to White Water and pulled into my driveway, I sat in the car looking at the house I'd bought after retirement. I'd spent more money on it than I'd planned, but at least it was relatively new, with no close neighbors, and was a convenient distance from town.

The realtor had called it a stick house, built like a regular house, except in a factory. The house I'd lived in at Nicolet City—first with Cal, and then after the divorce by myself with the kids, smelled of mildew. It was built on land that had been part of Lake Michigan before the water formed by melting glaciers retreated. When I moved, my things retained that smell. The new house had white walls, white drapes, and gray carpeting with a gray roof and gray siding. It wasn't until I'd lived in it for some time that it acquired my scent—one it took me a while to recognize because it was the only house I'd lived in by myself. On its slight rise, built so the ground wouldn't be as wet, it looked a bit like a lady holding up her skirts; the houses some distance away were farm homes surrounded by corn fields and dairy herds.

My friend Caroline's red cardinal sun catcher, the first thing I hung, added a needed touch of color. The quilts I made from clothes Mark and Jenny had grown out of as kids lent color to the bedrooms.

And I had my mother's quilt, the one that had been on my bed in Uncle Walt and Aunt Hester's house. When I first saw it as a child, I'd asked Aunt Hester about it. She said, "I heard your mother liked to sew, but everything else went up in smoke when their house burned."

I'd bought a vase in a secondhand store, imagining it had belonged to my mother, and kept hoping it'd become a genie and grant my wish that my parents were alive. I'd dream of being in their nursery helping them grow flowers, shrubs, plants, and trees. A beauty shop and real estate agency now stood where it had been; when I passed, I'd stare as if trying to detect clues. I was born there with the aid of a midwife, and it was where my mother had died.

I wondered where my mother had gotten the velvet for the quilt. When I touched it, I could see my fingerprints. If rubbed a certain way, it became the color of fog before the sun broke when just the tops of trees, their lower parts obscured by fog, hovered suspended. I'd print messages on the velvet to her, and the next day run my hands over it as if it were in Braille, to see if there was any reply, being careful that tears didn't fall and erase any possible messages or harm the material.

The quilt stayed at the foot of my bed, but when I had to mend it by cutting open the backing, my anger at her dying welled up so that, in my haste to finish, the repair wasn't the best.

Aunt Heidi had told me, "When you sew, you're never lonely." Cutting, ironing, and sewing quilt pieces was comforting but you had to use an exact pattern made out of check or plaid material to guide you — if it wasn't straight the rest would come out right.

My grandmother always sat very straight and was never without a handkerchief. Her small delicate handkerchiefs were edged in tatting or lace. I never saw her use them to wipe tears — she saw tears as a lack of backbone. But of all the things she made, my favorite was a dresser scarf from a flour sack with faded black letters I was never able to read. The four sides had open drawn work like rows of hourglasses, or ladies with cinched waists. She'd died from complications aggravated by wearing tightly laced corsets. What had dried up her tears? But I envied her security, her freedom from panic that I assumed never jabbed at her.

Sometimes the urge to add color to my new house to make it mine would be chased away by feelings of disloyalty to my old house. I suppose it wasn't unlike having to treat my aunt and uncle as my parents, all the while knowing they weren't.

I'd been reluctant to walk outside after dark. There were no outside lights, and the croaking frogs in the woods, the swooping winged insects, lent a Devonian atmosphere, a return to a distant, murky past. The Paleozoic era when fish evolved legs, and other geologic periods still held the mystery as when I'd first discovered them in books as a child — the very short duration of humans on earth still as slippery to grasp.

I'd lived in my Nicolet City house for thirty years, and now had to get used to where things were again. It wouldn't be until a few more years passed that I'd realize how many other things I thought I'd left by moving had become a part of me.

The first time I went to the grocery store in White Water I headed to the baking aisle to see if it had Clabber Girl Baking Powder with its illustration of a girl holding a plate of biscuits. I could never tell from her Mona Lisa smile if she'd left the others in the picture and was going to eat the biscuits herself, or if she was on her way to share them. A kitten and toy horse were next to a woman who looked like she was making lace; when I used a magnifying glass it appeared she was plucking a goose. I made up stories about the scene, wondering how many other women had, too, and if they'd baked biscuits, never sure if they'd rise nicely and match those on the label. If I didn't have a can of Clabber Girl on my shelves it didn't seem a proper kitchen.

As I closed the door to my old house for the last time, I knew I'd never forget touching Mark's stick crayon figure on the door for the last time, that awful feeling of knowing I couldn't get in anymore because I'd left the key inside for the new owner. I'd known the moments I'd remember: Mark's and Jenny's eyes when they saw their first birthday candles; watching Mitchell, with whom I fell in love in Ithaca, walk away.

I'd asked the realtor how White Water got its name. He said the founders had wanted to remember the rivers they'd left. I'd expected to see a river with rapids, but the area was flat without rivers, streams, or lakes. There were cars with bumper stickers, RAFT THE RAPIDS, that played on the name.

There were large fields divided by straight roads, punctuated by prickly looking trees and stop signs; Ithaca had been hilly with roads running up and down like zippers on a plump woman. The trees in the back of my house were small and slim. The ground was too wet to support large ones; if trees got too tall or large, they'd topple, their mounds of upturned roots increasing the prehistoric look of the woods. Wind came up without much notice in White Water. It was seldom windy, but when it was, it descended with a frightening pent up fury. I didn't know it then, but in the spring I'd have a small pond in the back woods and parts of the lawn would stay soggy until the middle of July.

The Soil Survey of White Water County from the local Soil Conservation Service confirmed that when the last glacier covering Wisconsin began to recede about 14,000 years ago, it formed moraines, till plains, and glacial drainage ways. The few streams had deep, steep-sided drainage ways through till plains. Natural drainage was poor as a result. The black and white aerial photo on the survey cover showed flat land divided into gray squares, straight roads, square farms, and round silos.

The lack of tall trees gave the sky a wide, expansive look, and the appearance of a John Wayne western—leaving me feeling insignificant and without any cover. Even the clouds looked squashed, weighed down by the immensity of the vastness of unobstructed sky. When I let Kitty out she quickly crossed the lawn to the cover of uncut grass and weeds, parting them like the Red Sea, becoming one with her surroundings. It wasn't unlike what I did as a child when I looked, smelled, and listened—sometimes stretched on the ground to see the sky, sometimes downwards so my heart was nearer my beginnings. Sometimes, listening to comforting crickets, one felt the earth turn.

Sitting in the car, I rested my eyes on a cloud above the house, watching it change from a smoke belching train to a horse kicking up its heels. A flock of birds settled in a tree for a moment, took off, and began swooping up and down, stitching up the sky in long loops. How did they decide what direction to go? Did they have a leader or did they all know? I'd never seen birds like these that moved as a school of fish.

There were stuffed birds and squirrels on the walls of Uncle Walt's den, with eyes that seemed to move. I asked him if they could be still alive, and he said, "Christamighty! What kind of a half-cocked question is that?" I'd wanted to help them escape, but how could they live without anything inside them?

I thought I saw a stray cat, and my heart started racing, but then I realized it was only brown leaves. Sometimes weeks would pass without my heart racing like that, but when it did, I became hot and dizzy, and I steeled myself against paralyzing panic. At those times I'd tell myself it would pass, as it did all the other times; it would pass if I'd just hang on.

The panic often began when I got up in the morning, when something would surface that refused to stay totally submerged. At that time of day I was accustomed to dragging myself around on automatic pilot, concentrating on climbing out of the black hole. I plodded as if walking in sand, carrying a dishtowel on my shoulder for security, trying desperately to recover equilibrium, the way it was before. When the molten panic ran its course, I was greatly relieved, unable to believe I'd once again let myself be stunned and fragmented, praying it'd be the last of such stupidity. Uncle Walt was dead. He wasn't buried, but next spring he would be, and that'd be the end of it—wouldn't it?

***

As soon as I returned, I wrote the hospital that the poinsettia plants needed water, and I repotted the one from the Nicolet Women's Civic Club, which was wilting in Uncle Walt's room.

I remembered when I'd sung the hymns in church, part of me rejoiced that my uncle was dead, and then being consumed by guilt for feeling that way. But I'd remained calm. I didn't give his yellow plaid suspenders a resounding snap, or dump a bucket of excrement into his white satin casket. It did occur to me to do it, and imagined the exact smile I'd wear when they took me away as charitable people said "She couldn't stand the strain of losing such a fine uncle." The religious ones would say "She's headed straight to hell." Relatives would say "Who'd she inherit that behavior from?"

I remembered being so close to the burning incense in the censor that I saw its glow for the first time. I recalled the slight hesitancy in Father Mulcahy's voice when he said, "Religion was an important part of Walter's life," and recalling Emily Dickinson's lines

'Tis not the dying hurts us so
'Tis living
Hurts us more.

and how the downward lines on each side of Vincent's mouth resembled the stripes that extended from Kitty's eyes—to make her eyes look more ferocious, I assumed. In Vincent's case, the lines helped make him take on the gravity of a church official.

Uncle Walt had recently said, "By God, what'd you say if your brother became Archbishop Alger?" He'd fingered his pocket change and continued, "Even if he went into the damn Church, he's getting ahead, and that sure as hell makes me feel better. But I wish to God he'd do something with his hair."

My uncle had been vain about his hair. He'd had a standing appointment at Palmer's barbershop at the corner of Elm and Main since it opened in 1946. And when his red hair thinned, he'd used a special hair dryer to make it appear more full.

Had Vincent remembered that the funeral service was the day after our mother's birthday? She'd died trying to save a new strain of lily she'd been perfecting when their greenhouse burned, a week after my father had been killed at the Battle of Midway. After Vincent and I had hugged briefly, he'd avoided any opportunity to talk alone with me.

I'd made myself bake Christmas cookies the day after I got back, and went to the college library to look at the *Illustrated London News*, but the feeling I'd had of being disoriented persisted—like the time I'd gone to church one Sunday before realizing it was now daylight savings time and had to ask someone what day it was.

When I went to pick up a ring that was being repaired, a smiling girl with long hair said, "We haven't gotten to it because of the holidays." She was the type that, when she dropped anything, men would shove each other to come to her aid. I glanced at a nearby shelf and said, "That's beautiful lead crystal." I could see the smiling girl push her hair back and size me up as a sweet woman, a churchgoer, a member of the hospital auxiliary, who, when not spoiling her grandchildren, was clipping coupons. Yes, I was a respectable character, still keeping shoulder-length hair in place with an Alice in Wonderland ribbon. But what would she have said if I'd told her, "One finds a mystery at the bottom of everything?"

I'd confided that to my cousin, Mary Elizabeth, at the funeral. She straightened her pearls and said, "Why can't you just accept things and trust in God?"

As long as I could remember, Mary Elizabeth had always been sure of herself. Whenever I couldn't do simple things, like getting the wrap off Wendy's crackers or not being able to open a container of McDonald's half and half, I recalled how she'd made me feel inadequate.

I suppose the jewelry girl's long auburn hair reminded me of Mary Elizabeth. Afterward I found myself thinking about the left-side pews in St. John's where we used to sit at daily mass before school started, near the big blue statue of the Virgin Mary standing on a serpent and holding baby Jesus. The boys sat on the right side, near the bearded St. Joseph, in brown robes holding carpenter tools. The high ceiling made me feel insignificant, but at the same time secure. I liked to imagine stories about the saints on the vaulted fresco ceiling while Mary Elizabeth bent over her prayer book. But I didn't look too long at the ceiling in case the nun in the pew behind my class would notice. I'd select saints and imagine them flying gracefully in a flutter of robes and wings through clouds as azure as the robes as the statue of the Virgin Mary. Had any of them bought red cherry or black licorice cough drops during Lent because they couldn't eat candy? Smith Brothers Cough Drops with those dignified pictures of two bearded men on the boxes made it seem like it was medicine and not sinful. How long had it taken Mary Elizabeth to perfect her pause before entering a room, to give people adequate time to do her justice? Her smile that said, "Yes, I'm a snob, but don't I do it in a tasteful way?"

***

When I entered the McDonald's in White Water, a white-haired employee greeted me with, "You made it again, young lady! I'm proud of you."

I didn't know if it was his job, like a Wal-Mart greeter, or if he was just friendly. I smiled, said, "Thank you very much," and went to order.

Then I heard him say the same thing to someone else, another older woman, only she looked much older than the woman I saw when I looked in the mirror and wasn't sure then if I liked being called a young lady.

When had I begun receiving senior citizen discounts without asking? Of reminding people of their grandmother and not their mother? It was just another label, I told myself: daughter, wife, mother, grandmother, though that last label meant you were old. But it gave me pause to wonder. When had I begun receiving senior citizen discounts without asking? Or reminding people of their grandmother and not their mother? And being old, I was discovering, was like characters in a Greek play depicted as invisible. Sometimes I stood in the aisle just to see people walk around me—to prove I had form. But not being seen also allowed me more freedom from the rules imposed on younger women, and the leers of men.

McDonald's seemed to me like the village wells that had been communities' gathering spots. There were retired men, children looking for the latest Disney toys, teens looking at each other. Once when I was there, I saw an elderly couple who brought tears to my eyes. The woman carried the tray, and as soon as they were seated, she spread paper napkins on the table like they were linen. She then served a wrapped hamburger and plastic cup of coffee to the man, and bowed her head. He joined her by folding his hands to say grace. They both had such expressions of perfect peace and contentment that I envied them.

There was a pre-holiday edge in the air, people's uneven movements betraying frayed nerves, whining children off schedules, women tense and irritable no doubt from juggling job and family while preparing a *Good Housekeeping* Christmas, men glancing at their watches. I was grateful I'd gotten my Christmas cards done and presents wrapped, but the more of that I did ahead of time, the more time I spent baking and decorating.

A boy in jeans, with a backside so flat I wondered how his belt held up his pants, kept eyeing a girl at another table. His mouth was open; Uncle Walt would have said he looked "half-cocked." He had a red hairline, as if he'd just had a new perm, and I bet his Purdue jacket was mail order. Without the perm he would've looked like the boy in college who taught me to dance the twist.

Teenagers wanted their independence and individuality, and yet they tended to go out in packs like their hunter and gatherer ancestors; instead of skins they wore Big Ten sweatshirts. With their backs to me, I sometimes couldn't tell which were girls or boys. Even when they turned around, I often still couldn't tell, since both boys and girls wore earrings now.

But then, why was it so important for me to know if they were boys or girls? When I was in high school, if a boy had worn earrings, he would have been in serious trouble. When Jenny was in high school, she told me that if a boy wore an earring in his left ear he was okay, and she just grinned when I asked her what it meant if he wore it in his right. Now, when boys had earrings in both ears, what'd it mean?

There was a table with children and adults not far from me, probably a grandmother, daughter, son-in-law, and grandchildren. The grandmother looked worried and never said a word, but you could tell they cared for her. Her daughter and some of the kids had eyes like hers. The children were fresh-cheeked with dark hair. One had braids bound with rubber bands, reminding me how Aunt Hester would implore, "Jesus, Mary, Joseph!" when I'd wiggle and cry when my hair was pulled—though braiding wasn't as bad as having my hair rolled tightly in metal curlers Saturday nights for church. The daughter's husband had green eyes.

I remembered a dream of a man with green eyes and hairy legs telling another man that he had bedded his daughter often. The other man grinned and compared his daughter with what his friends related about their daughters. I felt repulsed but at the same time assured that it was so common. My eyes were the green of Uncle Walt's; what color were the eyes of Oedipus before he gouged them after realizing he'd married his mother?

A woman at the table behind me kept saying in a boisterous voice, "I had no clue," then gave a loud irritating laugh and asked, "Would you believe it?"

I knew what the loud woman looked like before I turned around. Her resentful eyes were on a man wearing a hat like Harrison Ford's in *Raiders of the Lost Ark*, but he had eyes only for a girl next to him. A blaring headline across the top page of a tabloid between them read, QUEEN ELIZABETH I FOUND ALIVE IN GREENLAND LOVE NEST. Pictures of Sir Walter Raleigh were beneath, both in seventeenth century clothes. At another table one teenage girl was showing another her belly button ring, telling her, "It tickles when I wash."

In the parking lot a shopping bag jerked like a puppet on invisible strings before disappearing under a car. Another sailed by until it was stopped by a curb and stayed there quivering.

I'd once seen a mouse quiver like that. It was when I wasn't sure if one was inside a heavy plastic can in the garage. Kitty's vigilance made me wonder, so I lifted a tin of Christmas fudge among the sacks of cookies, afraid it was trapped. When I saw it I put the tin down in surprise and it must have gotten under it—when I lifted the tin it quivered a few times and was still. After removing the tin and sacks I carried the can outside, and feeling like a murderer, tipped it on the snow hoping it had only been stunned, forcing myself not to look. I now saw the chew marks on the can and marveled at the force that made it fight to live; the same force that made weeds grow between the narrowest of cracks in sidewalks.

Forcing myself not to see things had become a part of me, of trying to scream, no sounds coming out.

But sometimes sounds did come out. One morning Mark said, "Gee, Mom, you screamed like you were being murdered," so I knew I actually had screamed aloud.

Then I remembered the mouse that came from under the hood of my car with its fur blowing. It looked at me through the windshield when I was driving, I slowed down, it turned around a few times, and went back under. I stopped to give it a chance to climb out. The next day when I drove it came out and disappeared again. When I got home I opened the hood, and saw a nest made from pink insulation with four tiny pink dead babies on the battery. I put them under a tree in their nest and the next day they were gone. There was a dead mouse near the tree a few days later. I wondered if it was the mother, but wouldn't let myself think about it because it made me cry. It too, was gone the next day.

A Visit From A Cousin

My cousin Polly was a little woman, a retired nurse with a receding chin that emphasized her birdlike look. When she arrived, I had to smile because her Ford pickup didn't coincide with my remembered image of her. She'd gotten my address from a relative who had told her about Uncle Walt's death. Although I hadn't seen her since we were kids, I had no trouble recognizing her: her diminutive size and brown eyes were as lively as ever even though her hair was an out-of-a-bottle shade.

"Oh, I love your house," she said after we hugged.

"Did you have any trouble finding my place," I asked before hanging up her coat.

"No, none at all. Your directions were super clear." Her voice had such a ring of unbounded optimism that I felt like extending my foot so she'd fall on her beaklike nose. Polly put her hands on her hips and twisted to one side until her "bones were heard from," and then did the same to the other side. She used to pop her knuckles, and I checked to see if they were oversized, like Aunt Hester said they'd be. When I saw they weren't, I felt disappointed, cheated.

"I'll put your boots on the furnace to dry," I said, recalling how as children, we'd pretend we were grownups visiting each other.

"Oh, that'd be super."

"Please have a seat."

I left her perched on the edge of the chair, patting her hair. When I returned from the utility room, I said, "You're very brave to drive from St. Paul this time of the year."

Polly dismissed it with a wave of her hand and said, "Oh, I asked St. Christopher to keep his eye on me." She said, "I have a super guardian angel," with such conviction that I glanced above her shoulder. I half expected to see an angel, as portrayed on the holy cards that'd been awarded to good children at St. John's Catholic School—barefoot in midair, in a white robe, smiling, and with perky wings. Polly looked at me closely and said, "You look well in green. And how'd you do it—you don't have any lines on your face."

I looked down at my green jumper. When we'd taken turns holding color swatches against each other's throats in home ec in high school, I was told that green was my color because it highlighted my eyes. Others had complimented my skin, but lately it'd been dubbed "youthful." My square chin had always contrasted with my fair skin, blond hair, and even features. In contrast, Polly's cheeks had a blotchy look some children have, and her nose was still pointed—when we were in grade school the kids had called her Woody Woodpecker.

"Would you like some tea," I asked. "I have apple cinnamon, mint, and orange pekoe."

"Mint sounds super."

After I'd put the kettle on I said, "I'll give you a little tour of my house, if you like," because she still sat on the edge of the chair like a bird anticipating a worm.

"I'd love one. You have a lot of privacy here, don't you?"

"It's almost too secluded, but I wanted a quiet spot."

"You have quite a bit of room."

"No matter what you have, I don't think you ever have enough closet or storage space—I've come to the conclusion, if you have space, you'll fill it."

The first room down the hall was my son-in-law's room.

"I see lots of blueprints." Polly said. "Is he a contractor?"

"Architect," I replied, and noted with satisfaction that Polly was impressed. "It's very hard for Jenny to be left behind. He got a phone for the room and uses a calling card—their monthly bill must be terrible. They're looking for a house, and he describes every one he sees in great detail."

"It's super that you have him around to help you settle in."

"Yes, he's been a great help. He's easy to have around." I waved my hand, "You can see he's pretty neat."

We went on to a storage room filled with things I couldn't part with—things I hoped someday Jenny and Mark, or their kids would treasure. I didn't have anything of my parents' except a quilt my mother had given someone, and so it'd been saved. Everything else had been lost when their house burned down, after their adjoining greenhouse caught fire. After that, I showed her my bedroom, guest bathroom, the kitchen, and utility room.

When we returned to the living room, Polly said, "You're as methodical as you were as a child."

She was probably right—my books were grouped on shelves like they were in Nicolet City.

"You always walked on sidewalks and never took shortcuts on the grass," Polly recalled. "Where'd you get your dining set?"

"I wanted a big family table, and found it from a newspaper ad when Cal and I first moved back to Nicolet City."

A few of the ebony and rosewood marquetry squares had been lost, but otherwise, the matching mahogany sideboard, hutch, table, and chairs looked the same. Suddenly, a dream resurfaced:

> *I was sitting at a dining table deciding what to do. I was to be married to a local boy but couldn't go through with it. Everyone belonged to the same church or was a relative, and I wanted my freedom. They all thought I was mentally unstable and doomed. I felt tempted to go ahead and marry the boy I didn't love to fit in, but remembered the words in Brave New World I'd read in college: "Orthodoxy means not thinking—not needing to think."*

"It's super," Polly said. "And I love your grandfather clock. Does it chime?"

I nodded. "I'm glad you got my address," I told her. "I've often thought about you. Tell me about your kids," I said, then wondered why women automatically asked each other about their children like two fencers saluting before fencing.

Polly began pulling her hair through her fingers, which she'd done as a child. If she'd been eating something sticky, she'd end up with hair like Medusa. "Eddie's in Colorado," she said. "He stayed in the Air Force, never married, and loves traveling a lot. Pattee's in Wyoming and has two girls. She married a realtor and became one herself when the girls graduated from high school." She opened her purse, and I knew what was coming.

After I made the proper comments on the photographs, I said, "Your mother showed me pictures of you when I visited her, but after she died I lost track of you."

"I'm glad we got in touch again," Polly said. "Even if it's the time in our life that we're the old fogies we used to make fun of."

I laughed and said, "Hey, we're not old yet! But I admit the last time I got towels, they were bright striped ones instead of plain beige."

She said, "Remember those days at girl scout camp?"

> *A dream came to mind—of mazes I went through with others at the girls' camp. We were told to follow each other in two rows through long tunnels, and I was terrified when the tunnel got very narrow and pulled me in like a vacuum.*

Polly adjusted her slipper socks and said, "My mother wrote me that she couldn't believe your uncle or husband didn't give you any help raising your kids after your divorce."

I stared at the red crickets on her slipper socks and replied, "I often think of your mother."

Watching Polly adding sugar to her tea, I decided not to tell her the situation I'd found myself in after the divorce: Uncle Walt had backed Cal and I had to live in Nicolet County or lose split custody of Mark and Jenny. So I returned home and drove over two hundred miles a day to my Rhinelander job until I couldn't any longer. What filled me with deep cold fear was that Cal would take the children away like he'd said he would if I couldn't support them.

Knowing I couldn't tell my cousin any of the most important details about my past, I changed the topic. "I hope it doesn't snow when you're on the road."

"The forecast is for three inches tonight."

"I'd love to have you stay."

"Thanks, but I can't." Polly twisted her back again a few more times till she heard her bones again—the creaking never bothered me, but I knew it had others. "How old were Jenny and Mark when Cal died?" Polly asked. I could see she wasn't going to let Cal go away.

"In their late teens."

"You have a picture of him?"

"I found one unpacking a box before the funeral. Just a minute."

I went to find it, and when I reentered the room, Polly quickly flipped over her tea saucer. Had she checked my silver too? Well, my silver and china were respectable even though I'd given Jenny the Wallace sterling and Lenox china I'd bought gradually over the years, in order to have something of value to hand down.

"This is Cal's graduation picture," I said, handing her the framed photograph. "I was going to give it to the kids but forgot to take it with me to the funeral." In the photo, Cal's hairline was already forming the M so typical of men's receding hairlines, but it was carefully in place so he'd probably already been using Brylcreem. His concession to casualness was to occasionally not use any, but I'd noticed that the more natural his hair appeared, the more abrasive he became as if not wanting anyone to forget he was a surgeon. His lips reinforced his look of purpose and rectitude. His lips had always been thin but the more surgery he performed, the longer we were married, the thinner they got. I'd also kept a little grade school picture of him showing the good in him before it faded.

Polly said, "He was nice looking."

"Thank you." But the most noteworthy thing I was realizing now was how little I knew him and what I was piecing together wasn't pleasant. I smiled politely and lifted my teacup, but returned it to the saucer without a sip. I'd debated what to do with the picture—my first impulse which had surprised me, had been to smash it to oblivion.

Polly handed it back to me and said, "I bet he knew his own mind."

"It was his sense of strict morality and purpose that first attracted me. And his lectures made me feel he cared," I said, and then remembered the cat would disappear as soon as it heard Cal's car.

I asked, "Did your professors call women students 'twig pickers' because they'd work until their houses were furnished?"

If women weren't married by the time they were twenty-one, it was assumed there was something wrong with them, or they weren't attractive enough to catch a man. The more attractive and innocent you were, the more marketable—that is, you'd get husbands with the most earning power to provide for you and your kids.

Cal had known what to do on our wedding night, but I thought it was because of the anatomy classes he'd taken.

Polly said, "Well, at least your kids had a father longer than you did. You were too young to remember your father when he was killed, and it was so fortunate that Walt adopted you. I'll always remember him as a Horatio Alger success story."

I smiled my "your uncle is so great" smile.

"I suppose it worked for him too," Polly said, "since he didn't have children of his own. He had such a sense of humor. I chuckle every time I remember him sending Aunt Susan that postcard saying: 'Dear Susan, Your drawers have been loosened. You can pick them up on your next visit. Love, Walt'"

Polly must've noticed my blank expression because she explained, "You remember he'd repaired some dresser drawers that kept sticking? Uncle Martin brought them up when they came for a visit. Aunt Susan was so embarrassed when the postcard arrived all bent like many people had read it."

When I didn't reply, trying to get rid of the blood from biting the inside of my mouth, Polly asked, "Where's your brother?"

After another swallow, I replied, "In Milwaukee."

"I heard he'd become a bishop." An odd look came over her face. She added, "So how've you been feeling?" Maybe she was trying to find out if I'd been in a rest home, the story that had gotten around when I'd gone to the University of Wisconsin-Ithaca.

"It still seems like I should be going to work," I told her, "and I'm not sure I'm ready for retirement. Still, things were stressing me more."

Polly switched hands, began twisting her hair on the other side of her head into corkscrews, and said, "Yes, I find I don't have the patience I once had."

"Do you ever have the feeling you're not contributing anything now that you're retired?" I said.

"Not one bit! I'm having a super time enjoying things I've never had time for before."

I didn't reply, recalling counselors telling me I didn't let myself enjoy things.

She asked in the same chirpy tone, "So, how're you adjusting to your move?"

"Oh, fine." With Scott around, preparing regular meals gave me some structure, since I felt that I should be home when he returned from work—he said I didn't, but it seemed the thing to do. I automatically picked up after him, but I was glad when he'd asked to do his own laundry, after seeing me put his whites and colors together to save soap, water, and electricity.

"It seems like you're pretty well settled here," Polly said. "You never expressed your feelings much even as a child. Mom said she never saw such an unemotional little girl and never saw you cry. I suppose divorce was difficult; still, it happened years ago."

But to me, it seemed only yesterday that Uncle Walt had come over after I'd begun divorce proceedings and said, "You'll be alone and will never marry again. You're damn lucky to have a husband like Cal who doesn't beat you."

Uncle Walt had sat at the dining room table, in Cal's captain's chair, arranging his pocket change, and said, "You're so thin you look sick." He hit his fist on the table and swore. "I don't know if you've been running around, I'm just concerned with your welfare. Cal has all the money I loaned him sunk into his new building, and you don't deserve any damn support anyway."

My uncle's voice quivered, and I prayed he wouldn't cry. "I can't understand it—you have everything you want and see everything ass-backwards. Christamighty! If Cal was running around or drank, it could create some problems, but by God, you don't know what the hell you want. If you don't want anymore kids, why don't you get your tubes tied and get off the damn pill?"

I tried to remember if he'd said that before or after the deposition Cal had arranged for me to state what Dr. Schackmann had said—that my uncle was a lover figure instead of a father figure.

"…hope you won't be alone for Christmas?" Polly said.

"Scott and Jenny are stopping by when they get back from his parents in Green Bay."

"That's super. You seem to enjoy having Scott stay with you."

"Yes. He's easy to be around," I said, and smiled, picturing his large pointed ears, thin triangular face, and mischievous look. He reminded me of a tall, thin elf in a children's book.

"Is he easy to cook for?"

"He likes more salt than I, but that's easily remedied."

When I heard Scott say to Jenny once, "This is the way your mother would do it," I was surprised and flattered.

Polly talked about her children then, until she looked out the window and said, "It's time for me to get on the road and see an old classmate. I'm so glad we had this visit."

When I walked Polly to her truck, I told her one of Scott's jokes: "A policeman stopped a car and said, Congratulations, you've the lucky driver to win ten thousand dollars for wearing a seat belt."

"Thanks, officer!"

After the officer left, the driver's son said, "That's great, Dad. Now you can get a driver's license."

His daughter said, "And rent cars instead of stealing them."

A muffled voice said from the trunk, "Get me outta here!"

Before I washed the dishes, I called the telephone company about the static on my phone and I was given seven options; I pressed one and got disconnected. I didn't want to hear anymore of "Joy to the World" so I slammed the phone. I saw one of Kitty's hairs on the counter and remembered the hair growing from a mold on Laura Spencer's chin at the funeral—how Chuck Belleborne's jutting head gave him a turtle look—how Marguerite Hull's sparse eyelashes and vacant smile encouraged Uncle Walt to say she had "nothing upstairs"—how Henry LeFebvre wore his long hair tied back in a rubber band, "like some damn Hippie," Uncle Walt had said. How Ben Whitworth's shoes squeaked.

Did they make white shoe polish anymore? The kind with the brush that is a part of the cap? I was brought up when white shoes were worn between Memorial Day and Labor Day, and if any female appeared in them a day earlier or later, people shook their heads happy with the thought none in their family would do such a thing. Come spring, I thought, when the ground was soft, Uncle Walt would be buried. I dreaded going through it again.

The water circling down the drain made me think of a rescue worker on a television documentary I'd seen. He'd said when a person falls between a passing train and a train platform, the body gets twisted like a corkscrew from the ribs down. When they're moved, they die because their guts fall out. When accidents like that happen, workers call their relatives, after telling the victims they'll have one or two minutes to live after being moved.

Dead, all dead. Cal, Uncle Walt, Dr. Schackmann.

I'd told Dr. Schackmann, "When I was growing up, I got rid of the ugliness of things by going outside. Even in the worst snowstorms, I've never felt the loneliness I've felt around others."

I swallowed the lump in my throat, and remembered listening to cowbells near my grandfather's place while spider webs hovered over the grass like lace. Each acre had a different look and feel as if guarded by a different pagan spirit, and the breeze carried with it the mystery of things only glimpsed in childhood. As a child, I'd sensed that every insect, leaf, cloud was one with something larger. Light, air, scent, and sound healed whatever was hurting, and I saw blue birds flying as if they were loosened fragments of sky. It was in my grandfather's fields my ashes would be scattered; hoping to copy Antaeus, I'd gain renewal by touching Mother Earth.

***

One day I ran across post-traumatic stress disorder in a book in the college library. I knew anxiety was connected with obsessions, so I'd been searching through psychology books. I read slowly at first, afraid of what I may learn. Then I bought a copy to highlight, underline, and read over and over. Holding it, putting it in a place I could easily see, and reading it, gave security to hang on to, an explanation finally that fit all too well and could not be ignored. The obsessions about abandoned animals had begun after Jenny was born, but I'd never connected them with postpartum depression.

I'd chosen my new house because neighbors were far away and I wouldn't see chained dogs or wilting plants. Now, to get out of the house, I went to McDonald's, Sav-A-Lot, Staples, Wendy's, and a few other places that felt safe. In places that had shopping carts, I'd rescue one in the parking lot and bring it inside.

One night I dreamed I was on a medical association trip with Cal on our honeymoon but we got separated going up an escalator that turned into a mushroom. I went into the rest room and a stream of warm urine arched from the next stall. I cried and smelled awful, and when I'd crawled out under the door, I asked

people where the surgeons were. When I found the
room, I saw people strapped down on conveyor belts.
Cal was there, and he looked at me like I was damaged
goods he couldn't stand to see.

The next day I woke up exhausted trying to resolve how much to tell Mark and Jenny about Uncle Walt and Cal. I'd be saying bad things about the dead if I told them. Also, nothing had been mentioned about the Will after the funeral, though before Aunt Hester would say that she and Uncle Walt had made changes and wait for my reaction. And I thought, if I said anything about Uncle Walt, couldn't it ruin my chances of getting money from Aunt Hester? Shouldn't I think about that for the kids' sake, if not for myself?

A Visit From The Avon Lady

I located an Avon lady to help me feel more at home. When I called, she mentioned how many years she'd been a representative. I looked forward to meeting a possible friend my age and a way to know others.

"Do you know you have a wasp's nest by your door?" she said when I answered the door.

"Oh, is that right? My goodness!" I said, trying to sound concerned.

The Avon lady extended a calendar to me and said, "I know it's late for a calendar, but aren't they delightful children? This year they did them in such lovely pastels." After a long sigh she added, "I always wished I'd had a sweet girl to dress in pink," and in a voice not quite regretful, "but I just got the most husky boys you ever saw." When she pointed to the pink skeins of yarn piled in a basket for the month of February, I saw she had faint whiskers like the woman in Nicolet City who pounced on bits of gossip—the Avon lady's round bright eyes were like hers, too. And I wondered again why women didn't support each other more instead of regarding each other as rivals. The Wisconsin Women's Commission newsletter I just received said that the U.S. Senate had 14 women out of 100 members.

When she was filling out my credit card receipt, I asked, "Is it this hot in town?"

The way she said, "Well, I think you have more of a breeze here," I knew she'd whiffed the neighbor's dairy herd as she sat very straight, her small feet together, her back not touching the couch. When handing me my receipt she said, "It's been warm at my grandson's baseball games. He looks just like my son." She looked around again and said, "I'm sorry your order's a bit late but my husband and I are going on vacation and I've had so much to do. You know how it is, my dear."

I could tell she was trying to figure out where I fit in the scheme of things and pictured her teddy bear cookie jar on a kitchen counter cleaned with antibacterial wipes—her husband wiping his feet on teddy bear doormats. It was hard not to feel at a disadvantage because I had no husband.

"I'm so glad to find an Avon lady. I've used Avon where I lived before."

"Where was that?"

"In Nicolet City."

When she tilted to one side and asked, "Why did you ever come here?" her hair didn't move—it had curls like the picture in a nursery tales book Jenny had about the girl with the curl in the middle of her forehead.

"Oh, to take classes," I said. "I guess I wasn't finished with school." I wanted to say that classes were the moveable feasts like Paris had been to Hemingway, that I believed in Reason and enjoyed the smell of rectangular classrooms with rows of desks facing a large desk. A projection screen that, when partially down, resembled Kitty's tongue washing her paws. Classrooms had blackboards with intriguing half erased words left from the class before.

When the kids were small, I'd gone to a Celebrate Fall Homemaker's Fair in Centerton with sessions like how to grow mung beans and make curtains from percale sheets. After lunch, I saw a film on Lee's carpets and a demonstration on cleaning Kenmore ovens. Mark had been in school and Jenny stayed with other kids with 4-H girls and I'd returned with lots of Wisconsin Consolidated Gas recipes with blue flames like tears in each corner.

She said, "Why, you sound like my sister. She's an X-ray technician and wants to change jobs at forty-four," adding, "she's still single." Her eyes fell to my ring finger and, as if she still couldn't pigeonhole me, she asked, "You work?"

"I'm retired from a community college."

She said with regret, "You probably never had time to bake cookies like I did."

After I ordered Friktion, Wild Country, Uomo after-shave and cologne on the phone she'd commented, "It sounds like you know what someone likes," and I almost said they were for myself to see her reaction. Truth was, most of them were—I liked remembering the solidity of men and belonging before things changed. Some were for my brother; I didn't know if he used cologne now but he did once. I didn't see the Honeysuckle in the catalog that I'd worn once even after telling myself I was wallowing where I didn't belong. Ah, its cloying sweetness, unfailing optimism of it! Yet I needed to remember what being in love was like and it brought it all back—its spell in the faraway look of the model dipping her hand in a stream glowing with anticipation and sunlight on her hair: "Every moment's to be lived. You rush to greet the dawn each day with laughter and love." You just had to rub your wrist on the sample. The next page showed a model wearing a gown sprinkled with rose petals the shade of the Avon Lady's nails and lipstick.

But the things I bought looked smaller than in the catalog: the shower gels that hooked on the shower weren't much bigger than tubes of toothpaste. Even so, it was reassuring to have Avon catalogs on hand and see that models still had curly hair, perfect teeth, and trailed filmy scarves on pale pink beaches. That children with chubby legs carried baskets of strawberries even if Avon sold cell phones now. I saw a woman walking toward something white and fluffy (it looked like Heaven); her hair blew one way and her gown went the other as if held by wires.

Still, I'd look at the next catalog—the Avon Lady said she'd hang it on my door knob if I wasn't home and give the bag an extra twist so the wind wouldn't carry it off; it gave a sense of belonging, of fitting in. It was as American as the *Reader's Digest*.

When I hung the calendar with its misty pastels, I wondered if the photographer had used a pink screen over the lens; even lotion pour le corps had pastel labels. The look of eternal romance was reassuring, nostalgic; like the Avon lady said, "Women like the pastel look. It's so delightful, so feminine and flattering. So comforting, you know, my dear." Part of me wanted to ignore that it was women who held Clarissa so Lovelace could rape her.

Yet it is probably not wise to examine Avon catalogs closely; one of the refrains in folklore class was not to go beyond the norm.

Dr. Bradford

It was when I was still married to Cal and my children were too young to be in school, that I'd begun to see Dr. Schackmann, a psychiatrist, because of my obsession with abandoned animals.

When I saw the mailperson bypass my neighbor's house, for instance, I felt panic that no one was there and that their dog had been left. Outside, I'd stare at the ground through narrowed eyes and hum to avoid hearing something abandoned; I wore certain pieces of jewelry, carried pieces of paper to ward off panic. When I couldn't catch a cat and her kittens in live traps, I couldn't rest until I left food outside, and I'd worry about what to do if I just caught the mother. Should I drop it off at the shelter, or let it go because of the kittens?

Dr. Schackmann saw more in my obsession about strays than I ever expected, but when we began to explore the underlying reasons, I thought at first he was completely wrong. He was the first to encourage me to examine Uncle Walt's behavior toward me.

Then, when Jenny and Mark were in high school, and Cal and I were divorced, I'd seen Dirk, who was a psychologist. That had also been because of my obsession with abandoned animals. And then I saw another other psychologist, Rebecca, after Dirk moved.

And now, with my children grown up and Uncle Walt dead, I wondered if seeing a counselor at the university where I'd enrolled would be different. The panic, jabbing at me until I could hardly breathe when I saw plants or animals I thought weren't cared for, had gotten worse.

The receptionist had a nice smile and didn't look at me like I had HIT ME stamped on my forehead. She said she'd let Dr. Bradford know I'd arrived and to have a seat. There were plants in the room that seemed healthy, but I wished they were artificial.

One of the pamphlets I looked at while waiting, "Common Anxiety Disorders," had blue stick people standing in the middle of a yellow highway with black cars whizzing by. On a page about post-traumatic stress disorder—between phobias and panic disorders—a soldier held a hand over one eye and the other over an ear, like a see-no-evil, hear-no-evil, speak-no-evil monkey. It was by a pharmaceutical company, so I was leery; I'd become hooked on the Delmane sleeping pills Dr. Schackmann had prescribed, and it'd been rough kicking them. Whenever the images on my dish satellite melted on the screen during a storm, it brought back the fear if I didn't keep taking them.

I'd recently tried various selective serotonin reuptake inhibitors prescribed by physicians, but the headaches and the impaired ability to think wasn't worth it. I tried Prozac, but by the second week I didn't feel steady enough to drive. I also didn't want to believe that my mind consisted merely of a bunch of chemicals.

A flyer said that three or four out of ten women have experienced some form of sexual abuse. I took one to look at later.

The magazine on the table, *Simple Living*, with an uncluttered cover, made me shake my head over people needing magazines to simplify things.

Dr. Bradford wasn't what Uncle Walt would've called a model for Stetson hats. His remaining rim of hair gave him the air of a monk; his eyes, under bristling eyebrow hedges, were so blue his gray hair appeared white. He guided me into his office as if walking on tiptoe and waved me to some chairs. When I'd called the university's counseling department and explained what I needed help with, the secretary had said they'd assign me to the one with the most experience.

Seated near the window farthest from more plants, I saw students outside on their way to and from classes. The room, like any associated with education, was a launch pad for the American Dream, with books, bodies, paper, pencils, sun, chalk, tile floors, cement block walls, and glass windows. When Dr. Bradford, behind his desk, leaned over to adjust the blinds, my index finger formed question marks; it eased my nervousness. As he read my registration form he rubbed the plump index and middle fingers of his free hand together in a scissors motion, his eyebrows seemingly making an effort to disentangle themselves. He wore a wedding band, and, for some reason, I pictured a tall thin wife.

"I see you're retired from the faculty of Centerville Community College, Lily," he said, his congratulatory beam revealing very white teeth. "It's good to see someone like you return to college."

He made me feel at ease and I hoped he'd be okay, not being able to forget my experiences with other counselors. Still, I was older now and out of the loop to attract.

"Thanks," I said. "I wish there were some students my age, though. Why don't more go back?"

"They probably feel out of place," he said, "and that they can't compete with the younger students. Have you heard of the Phoenix Club? It's for alternative, older students."

When he handed me their flyer, the coincidence of the name brought Father Teiresias to mind. His advice when I'd returned to Nicolet City was: "Don't be a Phoenix in the fire too long or you won't be able to rise in the updraft." He'd worn a Phoenix, rising amidst flames, on his sweatshirt, the kind of flame images teenagers used to decorate their cars.

"I'll have to go to one of their meetings," I said to Dr. Bradford.

"Where're you from," he asked.

"Nicolet City?"

"Oh, that's a beautiful part of the state."

He seemed to be paying attention; I could have told the last counselor I'd seen (once) that I'd killed a dozen people after he'd dozed off.

I smiled, but was distracted, recalling Uncle Walt telling the judge: "Child authorities say it's important to keep familiar surroundings for children. Nicolet County is God's country, away from the crime, pollution, and the fast pace of big cities where people would as soon run you over in their cars than stop. I raised my niece and nephew here in God's country after my brother and his wife were killed. It's so important to have children stay near close relatives who ..."

I'd closed my eyes, clasped my arms around myself and rocked back and forth, murmuring, "No, no, no," to help me not see his relaxed assurance with a toothpick in the corner of his mouth.

"I do miss the trees and the water up there," I said, remembering the lake where I'd go swimming with the kids in the neighborhood. When the water was up to your neck you felt disjointed—part of you belonging to the water, part still claimed by land, and with only your head above water you laughed at the others who looked just like you, resembling floating heads. After swimming underwater, your blurry eyes open to prove you weren't scared, you'd head, bouncing like a pogo stick, for the safety of shore, smelling and tasting invincibility. The water was always cold but got warmer as you neared the shore.

But my eyes kept being pulled to the plants, so I told Dr. Bradford apologetically, "I worry about plants not being taken cared for."

"I can assure you these are well cared for," he said with an assuring smile. "I see you want help with post-traumatic stress disorder," he said, referring to the form I'd filled out.

Nodding, I moved my chair so the plants were more out of my line of vision. I was finding that I was watching old black and white movies more and more because I didn't have to be afraid of seeing green plants turning yellow. From my recent browsing through psychology books in the college library, I'd concluded that I had post-traumatic stress disorder. Dr. Schackmann's diagnosis, over thirty years ago, of obsessive compulsive disorder, had never felt right to me. I didn't do things like wash my hands over and over again. Yet part of me still didn't want to accept I had post-traumatic stress.

Dr. Bradford said, "How are your classes?"

"I'm taking another one in writing," I said, "and I'm really enjoying it."

"Writing helps you express yourself, so it's good you have that kind of class," he said, and bestowed another smile on me. "Many people enjoy running but never reach the Olympics, so don't be concerned about having anything actually published. It's the doing that counts."

I was sure he was right, but it wasn't what I liked hearing after picturing myself in *The New York Times Book Review*, and being interviewed by Oprah when not autographing books in large stores smelling of exotic coffee.

"I see you've wanted help with obsessions," he said.

"They started with ducks in a pond a neighbor feed and then they left for the winter after my daughter was born," I replied.

"It takes time to stop thought processes so you must work on them being less and believe they will. Did you have any as a child?"

I didn't want to remember it but I said, "Well, I had something like them about closing the basement door. I'd get up and go down the stairs even in the middle of the night to see if I hadn't because Uncle Walt said it was my duty." I sighed and looked down. "I was afraid of being swatted by him and having to tell I'd been disobedient in Confession." Suddenly I could smell those cement stairs, see their spidery cracks so clearly that my heart began racing. After swallowing the blood from biting the inside of my mouth, I added, "They're worst when I first awake."

"That's the time when you feel most vulnerable," he said.

Dr. Schackmann had told me it was because the id was still partially in control—it was the same explanation of how the mind worked.

"Ask yourself what it'd be like if you were happy and enjoyed life."

I didn't know how he stood on religion, so I didn't tell Dr. Bradford the first thing I'd memorized was the question and answer in my catechism: "Who made me? God made me to love Him and serve Him in this world and in the next."

"You must learn to take risks to grow. It's a continual process."

It wasn't what I wanted to hear.

***

I was almost late for my next session. A writing assignment made the time go by so fast, an absorption that surprised me and for which I was very grateful since I was trying to forget a cat walking near the library that I couldn't catch. When I woke up worrying about that cat, the only thing I thought would help was to crumple a piece of paper and hold it as a physical link, something to hang on to until seeing Dr. Bradford. I pictured his index and middle fingers doing their scissors walk, and recalled the feeling of safety in his room, the smell of books, bodies, paper, pencils. There'd been a hint of Old Spice but I didn't know if it was Dr. Bradford's or someone else's.

After more sessions, he told me, "The uncle who raised you and your husband were sick, distorted people. They didn't know how to behave, but you're free of them now. They're both dead. Didn't you see them buried?"

It took a few moments to recover my surprise before replying. "My uncle died when the ground was frozen," I explained, trying not to remember that he'd called them sick, distorted. "When he was buried, it was when my son's baby was being baptized. My husband was buried where he went on his honeymoon, and I thought his wife would resent me there, so I didn't go."

Dr. Bradford leaned forward and his querulous eyebrows joined. "You must bury them," he said. "Picture their funeral."

I recalled Dr. Schackmann saying, "Your uncle's a magical figure with you."

How could I really bury them? Put their pictures in boxes, like those my checks came in, and bury the boxes in the backyard? I only had a grade school photo of Cal, and a small one of Uncle Walt with Aunt Hester in matching Christmas vests against a church Nativity mural. I'd given the rest to my kids.

The last time I'd gone to a cemetery to find my grandmother's headstone was when all the flowers were frozen so I wouldn't be upset to see any of them wilting. The smaller tombstones like the one inscribed 'Mary Ruyerton ?-1939 Beloved Wife and Mother,' were the most personal; several weren't legible or were in crumbled heaps. I could've been standing on my grandmother's grave and not known it. She died in her twenties after childbirth. But I often had conversations with her, absorbing the love and concern in her eyes.

Would burying Uncle Walt's picture keep him from grinning at me in dreams? If it didn't, maybe I could place his picture on my drive and run over it again and again the way I did now to a bird or animal on the road to save them from a lingering death in case they weren't already dead. I heard Dr. Bradford say, "They're dead, Lily. So is it you or them who's putting you through this? You set yourself up to be controlled by outside forces and then panic. You must move on and not let the past control you."

It was good that Dr. Bradford's plump hands didn't form steeples; Cal's thin hands had made steeples as precise as his surgical instruments—as sharp as his remarks.

"You are not constricted anymore," he told me. "The small pots for plants that upset you are reminders of your uncle and husband holding you in. But they can't hurt you anymore. You say that panic often hits you when you first awake, so make yourself a schedule: from seven to eight eat breakfast and get dressed; from eight to nine do housework; from nine o'clock to noon, do class assignments and so on. That way you control things."

I noticed the *Campus Review* on his desk had a phone number for students to call to be escorted on campus at night, which was comforting and at the same time scary. Even with the increasing casualness between the sexes, unisex clothes and rest rooms, sex discrimination laws, lowered professional barriers, rape still flourished. I was elated to read recently that state legislation, introduced by a woman senator, had proposed covering the $800-$1,000 rape evidence kit for victims, and that there was now no statute of limitations for 1st degree sexual assault.

That night before when I couldn't sleep, Kitty had come in with her tail straight up when I opened my bedroom door and I'd said several times, "You're a fine girl. Yes, you are. You're a pretty girl." I'd put new bells on her collar the day before, after brushing her nettles off while she stretched with her front paws over the edge of the deck, Sphinx-like. I'd gotten her from the Nicolet County Humane Society as a kitten. I liked cats better than dogs because they had more dignity; you had to earn the affection of cats and when you had, they acknowledged you like royalty granting favors. Kitty preferred napping on towels or sheets laundered daily that hadn't yet been folded.

I told Dr. Bradford, "I thought once I was out of Nicolet City that the obsessions would go away like when I went to college at Ithaca."

"Obsessive drives provide a sense of safety," he said.

"Then why haven't I gotten rid of them like when I went to Ithaca?"

"You hadn't returned to Nicolet City for the sake of your kids then. How many years was it before you got to leave?"

"About twenty."

Dr. Bradford said, "The longer one stays in a stressful situation, the more ingrained the trauma becomes but if you left, you saw that as abandonment, a repetition of your aunt abandoning you as a child to your uncle. Your husband also emotionally abandoned you." What he said was too much to comprehend—I'd deal with it later.

"I'm just glad that I didn't know what staying would do to me. If I had, I don't know if I could've handled things." A part of me had known, though, because I remember scaring myself thinking about Anna Karenina's fatal way out.

"The mind does a remarkable job of shielding us."

After biting my lip, I said, "I also haven't met anyone here," trying not to remember the statistics on marriage for a woman my age—not connecting love with aging and the ability to attract.

"Your uncle was a sick, distorted man and his problems were put on you," he said instead of reassuring me I'd find someone. "He was insecure and defensive, so he controlled people."

Dirk, the psychologist, had called Uncle Walt grotesque, but even after looking it up several times in the dictionary it hadn't sunk in what he meant. Perhaps it was fear that since he was that way, it meant I was also.

"The more things piece together," I told Dr. Bradford, "the more I relate to the sailors sailing with Columbus being afraid of falling off the edge of the earth."

He smiled and said, "You can just keep sailing. There are always options in every situation. You were a victim as a child and didn't have any choice, but now things are different. You aren't a child in Nicolet City anymore. You're free." Then he added, "Your greatest need is to quit running from the past. Trauma disconnects people from the present. Say with me, I'm free."

I said the words with him and then he had me say "I'm free" by myself, louder. I regretted not being able to understand what he meant and could only relate it to Kitty hugging the ground to make herself less visible when she couldn't run away. He was trying to help me and I really appreciated it. I realized he was a sound psychologist that I was very fortunate to have run across. It made me feel ungrateful and that I wasn't putting forth enough effort.

At the next session when I confided, "I often dream of seeing someone in the doorway of my bedroom and not being sure if it's Cal or Uncle Walt." I felt warm blood coming from my nose, grabbed some napkins from my purse and lifted my head to stop it. Dr. Bradford paused until I lowered my head and removed the yellow Wendy's napkins. I hoped there wasn't any blood on my face.

Suddenly I heard myself telling Cal, "I agree with Dr. Schackmann when he said you ignore what you don't want to see."

Cal flared up and said, "Sure, go ahead and join the pecking match."

"Pecking match?"

"When chickens see blood on another chicken, they join in and peck it to death."

Feeling Dr. Bradford's eyes on me made me pay attention. But when he asked, "Do you remember what happened with your uncle?"

"In a picture when I was four, my eyes were haunted." I studied the purse in my lap and said, "Recently, when I turned off the bedside lamp and the image of the bulb remained, I thought it was like my symptoms, burned-in images."

He must have sensed my discomfort because he said, "Did you find the Phoenix meeting room?"

"Yes, but the people there were in their forties, returning to become mostly technicians. At least I made them feel younger." He laughed, and I added, "I called the psychology professor you mentioned, and went to a play."

"I'm pleased you investigated and followed through so quickly."

I shook my head and replied, "It's still hard for me to think anything's wrong, because I've been told I had a perfect life," staring at a few of his books: *A to Z Handbook of Adolescent Problems*; *The ABC's of Stress*; *Abilities, Deviation, and Methodology*; *Abnormal Behavior and Personality.*

When he said, "Yes, the all-American Norman Rockwell life, when it really was out of Stephen King," I thought it was clever of him to put it that way to someone taking English classes.

"I haven't read Stephen King," I said. "His work isn't considered by many to be literature."

"He strikes major chords in people and is read around the world."

"How do I accept what's happened," I asked. "I know I have to, but I don't like the cognitive approach the psychology professor advocates because it sounds like brainwashing. The psychology professor said to practice behavior modification to overcome your fears, that getting to the cause didn't matter. But I want to know the cause, even if I can see how symptoms could become habits."

"You must find what works for you."

I nodded, reassured. "I often have dreams of being stuck to Uncle Walt with mucus that won't let go, of his hair falling over his eyes as he was leaning over me." When I clenched my hands, I winced. I'd forgotten my thumbnail; my fingernails started splitting from cuticles to the tips when the obsessions started. I'd tear at them until they looked like *National Geographic* illustrations of those bumpy plate tectonics that move in response to forces deep within the earth causing continents to drift. A part of my nail rose in the middle of my thumbnail like smoke from a volcano—I'd tried cutting it, since filing made it bleed.

"Why not write letters to your uncle and husband?" Dr. Bradford suggested. "Say what you feel and keep writing until the anger lessens."

It sounded silly, but I nodded.

"You'll see, it'll help you in your odyssey."

"Odyssey? It's more like those boxes inside other boxes."

"Chinese puzzles, you mean?"

I returned his smile and said, "I've started a list of things to help make White Water my home, like you suggested. And I remember what you said about my relatives thinking it's day when it's really night, to let them go ahead and believe it because I know differently."

But I didn't tell him how hard it was, that it left me without any foundation. He would know that anyway. *The Odyssey*, which was prescribed freshmen reading when I was in college, described Dawn with rosy fingers, but it now arrived with sharp claws of obsessions.

Afterward, I went to the Phoenix Room, but it was empty and a plant on the lockers made me uncomfortable; I wondered if it'd been potted in enough soil for the roots to grow as they should, and whether it had been watered recently. To keep from thinking about it, I went to get potato chips and candy.

I now had more freedom than I'd ever had. I had enough money to live on and didn't have to worry about supporting Mark and Jenny. But I often felt I had no business being on campus and I should go back to Nicolet City and keep the Norman Rockwell facade of the adopted daughter of a respected uncle and the first wife of a respected husband. My roots were there, and I'd never need to show ID since everyone knew me; it was where Maize, my cat for 19 years, was buried in her collar wrapped in my flannel nightgown edged in eyelet under a tall pine.

***

Jenny was born after Cal and I moved back to Nicolet City from Detroit, following the race riots. Shortly afterward, my symptoms started. I would eventually realize that my obsession with stray animals and then neglected plants had something—maybe everything—to do with what was happening in my marriage, with Cal spending more and more time away from home.

And that brought up something equally unthinkable: Cal's actions. When he saw me drinking and taking sleeping pills, he must have known the danger of the combination. Dr. Schackmann had said, "Cal had the right to choose whether to help you or not."

I was granted split custody as long as I stayed in Nicolet County, which meant Cal and I would each have the kids for six months, and have visitation rights when they weren't with us.

Dr. Schackmann had asked Cal if Uncle Walt had been capable of child seduction. Cal had said, "Yes."

***

At our next session, I asked Dr. Bradford, "What other awful things do I have to discover? It's like being scheduled for surgery without anesthetic. But how can I ever figure things out when part of my mind blocks the other from finding out?"

"You must accept that your uncle and husband were Jekyll and Hyde characters," he said. "They were sadistic and manipulative while maintaining a respectable front."

Part of me resented hearing they weren't what I'd once believed, still wanted them to be, and what others still thought them. I'd never lost the fear of falling into a black void, even after Dr. Schackmann had said reality wasn't much different than how I saw it, and what people feared was often worse than the reality.

I shook my head as Dr. Bradford waited patiently before I said, "How do you deal with an uncle and husband like that? How do you accept it? I remember my friend, Caroline, telling me, 'They're out to crack you,' but I didn't believe her. Susan, another friend, also said it. How do I accept that? If I do, I'm left with a terrible reality, a world too awful to live in. And what could I tell my kids about them? I'm always on edge about what else I'll find out, afraid it'll be the final straw that pushes me under."

"You can't do everything at once," Dr. Bradford said. "Just take it step by step."

"I don't know if I can accept what happened. It would leave me with nothing and it'd be like trying to walk without bones."

"Don't worry about that. You've lasted this long, so you know you're strong. Write out your feelings. Take all the time you need. The more you release them, the more you'll lose your need to rescue."

I jotted down what he said: write what you feel, you are strong. But I didn't tell him that I'd written the letters he suggested but it hadn't seemed to help much; how I'd tried and tried to cry, telling myself that I wouldn't fall into ever expanding unfathomable blackness if I did—but instead all I managed was to stare at the flowers on the box of facial tissues I'd put in my lap for tears. Perhaps I shouldn't have tried to figure out the reason I'd be crying. The more I did the more I saw reasons for things in the pasts of Uncle Walt, Cal, Aunt Hester, and the bystanders to explain why they acted the way they did. I did write some letters in pencil so the words wouldn't be as noticeable, but I felt guilty I immediately tore them up, afraid they'd be proof of disloyalty.

"Do you have any brothers or sisters," Dr. Bradford asked.

"A brother," I said. "I hadn't seen him since Uncle Walt's death." After Dr. Bradford brought him up I realized even more how different we were and the gap between us was growing wider as if we were two planets following different orbits.

After that appointment, I went to the rest room feeling like a diver returning from a deep dive. I shook my face after splashing it with cold water, took deep breaths, swung my arms, and swiveled my head, meanwhile making faces to relax my jaw as I tried to recognize myself in the mirror. My brother had his center in the Church but so far I couldn't detect mine.

My writing professor said fiction was a journey of self-exploration. I hoped writing would get easier and that I'd develop what she called "your own voice." But how could I ever use "life experiences" when I didn't know what really happened?

Cal And Dr. Schackmann

After months of putting myself to sleep with whiskey and smothered crying when the kids were small, Cal had surprised me by saying, "I called Schackmann. Rachel had to rearrange my schedule so I can take time off to find why you're so out of it."

We'd be driving to see Dr. Schackmann in a few hours, and my stomach was upset. I was in the beauty parlor, and the well-thumbed *Good Housekeeping* I was pretending to read slipped to the floor when I heard the train whistle. I saw myself as a bird following the train as it wound its way through the landscape, leaving only smoke as evidence that it'd passed. The fresh air was my natural environment; I knew the currents to glide with the least movement through dips in temperature and scents, through breathtaking nuances in color and form. The clouds would always thin just before I reached them, and the only time I dipped or wobbled was if I worried about falling and being smashed below. When I no longer heard the train's whistle, it seemed that only part of me remained, and for a moment, looking around, I didn't recall where I was. When I did, it appeared depressingly drab and ordinary.

When we got to Dr. Schackmann's office, I introduced Cal, who sat on the couch with me. I hardly breathed, and the tension shimmered like heat off pavement in the hottest day of July. Cal had his mouth open; Dr. Schackmann's silent appraisal of him brought to mind a *National Geographic* gliding eagle lining up a trout in a shallow stream. The only movement in the room was the blinds settling back after being brushed by Dr. Schackmann's chair. I knew he wanted Cal to begin, and wondered if I was more afraid or more curious as I waited.

Finally, Cal draped his arm over the back of the couch and said, "Lily's even more irrational and harder to live with since she's begun therapy."

The knuckles of my hand clutching my purse were white.

"You want her to be more rational?" the psychiatrist replied.

"Yes. I'm tired of playing games."

"Games?"

"Word games. She doesn't talk, she plays word games."

"I haven't found that so," Dr. Schackmann said.

Cal got out his red and white pack of Winstons, and snapped his Zippo. "You don't live with her," he remarked shortly.

"No."

After exhaling, Cal said, "You don't have the pressure of surgery day in, day out, the responsibility of people's lives. Those who aren't surgeons don't know what that means."

"I often deal with suicides and breakdowns," Dr. Schackmann said.

"But if someone dies, you aren't blamed."

"People don't see it that way."

Cal laughed. When he adjusted the pillow behind him, his lip curled.

Dr. Schackmann flushed. "Cal, you made this appointment because you want Lily to stop being irrational."

"That's right. I'm fed up with not wanting to come home."

Dr. Schackmann turned to me, and the anger in his eyes faded.

"Things aren't the same between us," I said, fighting back the lump in my throat. "And I can't reach him."

"Cal?"

"I have to build up my practice," Cal said, "and when I get home I can't deal with more demands."

"Lily?"

"Having him come home every night to eat and fall asleep in front of the television," I said, "doesn't make for much of a life."

"There's weekends," Dr. Schackmann said.

Cal's arm jerked as if it had been snagged. "I work every day but take Saturday afternoons and Sundays off; emergencies don't wait to happen at convenient times. When I can, I go out on my boat fishing."

"With Lily?"

"She doesn't like going."

"Was it different before?"

"Our lives are different now," Cal replied, tugging at his tie.

"Different?"

Cal looked at Dr. Schackmann and at me and threw up his hands. "Both of you don't know the pressure I'm under. When I have time off, I need to relax."

Dr. Schackmann nodded. "Everyone needs to relax."

Cal said, "It's relaxing to fall asleep watching television."

I twisted the handles of my purse, recalling the snoring that competed with the television, and asked, "What about me?"

"Talking with you isn't relaxing," Cal said.

"But I need some support."

"What support?"

"When I said I won an essay contest you said the check would hardly feed us for a day."

After he laughed, he let his cigarette ash fall to the carpet. "Well, I was right." Cal added, "She drags me to these art films."

"Tell me about one."

"The only one I remember is about a boy who runs around all day serving his master and he keeps trying to get to a village he sees far away. The master chains a goat to his leg after he tries to escape. When the master finally takes the goat off his leg, the boy is so happy he runs around even quicker serving him, and makes dozens of these silly paper dolls. The boy sits and talks to the dolls about the village far away." Cal concluded with a confident laugh to show he understood the film, "He should have coped instead of going off the deep end like that."

Doctor sat a few moments with an expression I'd never seen, then rose with a shiver as if he was cold, took the top off a marker and drew three red circles on the dry erase board behind his desk. He wrote Ego, Id, and Super Ego inside them while I looked at his hair curling over his ears, enjoying a feeling of proprietorship. He had gone through this with me, and now he was showing Cal the same concepts in order to resolve our difficulties.

Cal crossed his arms tighter on his chest, and every time Dr. Schackmann's marker squeaked, he smirked. The session ended with Cal's diagnosis that "You need one person to run any situation. Every boat has a captain. That's just the way it is, and if it weren't, nothing would get done and I can't see how talking can change things no matter how long we sit here."

"It takes time and effort, but any relationship can be improved," Dr. Schackmann concluded.

As soon as Cal was behind the wheel, he said, "Schackmann's like a missionary telling me I'm a heathen, but I won't be manipulated. Is he married?"

"I don't know." I hadn't asked, and I'd told myself that in a doctor-patient relationship it didn't make any difference. But I knew, of course, that he'd never mentioned a wife, and that he didn't wear a ring.

"It's the first time I've seen a doctor wear leather pants," Cal commented. "Is that some European thing like his mustache?"

With his first cut made, he paused long enough to make me anticipate and worry about the next.

"He sure charges enough to buy proper clothes and a shaver." Cal lit a Winston and tossed his lighter on the Buick dashboard. "I'm a stable person, and I can't see why you feel you're rejected," he went on, in the lecturing tone I knew so well. "People have to figure things out for themselves, so why can't you just get on with things? If you think things are bad with you, think about what pioneer women had to go through."

Pioneer women usually didn't last very long, I thought as I so often had the other times he'd said that. When he expressed this stiff upper lip ideal, I could understand it, though—surgeons needed it in their occupations. Catholic school also had emphasized it, so he must be right.

"If you want to see people with problems, just follow me on rounds. You wouldn't last this long," he said, snapping his fingers, then motioning that he wanted his amber tinted sunglasses, which turned his eyes the color of creek bottoms. "Don't you think I've often wished I was just a jazz musician with no worries? How happy would you be living on nothing?" He laughed. "I can tell you that you'd be even more dissatisfied than you are now."

I felt panic rising after I handed him the glasses, because we were approaching a large yellow truck with the words "Smith Canaries" printed on it. A few days before, Mark and Jenny had found a small yellow bird on the road and put it in a box with food. It was trembling with fright, couldn't fly, and soon died. The kids were sad, but I wasn't, because how could it live if it couldn't fly? Mark buried it under a tree, and Jenny put a flower over it.

Now, the thought of hundreds of birds locked inside the yellow truck on their way to cages made my heart race. All I could see at that moment was the truck, and all my attention went to holding myself together. No matter how hard I told myself I wouldn't shatter like glass hitting cement, I might as well have willed rain to fall upwards. But once we got closer, I saw that it said 'Carriers'—not 'Canaries.' The looming black abyss disappeared. Everything was safe again; it was fine, everything was going to be fine—there were no terrified birds struggling to get free at all. I could breathe again. The iron band around me relaxed.

Cal glanced at his watch and said, "I hope things aren't in a mess at the office when I get back."

Seeing Cal and Dr. Schackmann together reminded me of two dogs with the hair raised on their backs, circling each other. Cal's suit clung to his body, and his sneer contrasted sharply with Dr. Schackmann's taller, angular body and open look. And when had Cal's face gotten that oily film? In college he'd earned money one summer as a model because he had the build of an average man, but next to Dr. Schackmann, he appeared less than average.

More and more when I saw a cat or a dog alone by the road, panic would roll over me in waves. My heart would pound, I'd become hot and dizzy, and my stomach would fall with a sickening plop. Time would stop while I clenched my teeth to prevent more gashes in my mouth. I was terrified of duplicating a PBS television documentary of the Big Bang explosion. During those episodes, the only way I could tell if things were real was to remember how things were before we moved. I wrote 'Not Before' on a piece of paper I kept in my purse, but with each new compulsion, I'd rationalize that it was different and so it didn't apply. It wasn't until years later I read that when a mind experiences too much trauma it is altered.

That evening after we saw Dr. Schackmann, Cal said, "You must realize that building my practice takes all my energy, and accept that as reality." He was mixing his martini before dinner on the glass-topped mahogany sideboard. As he spoke, I studied the sideboard's inlaid rosewood and ebony squares, again thinking he was a good surgeon, widely respected, and it must have been my fault that I wasn't a good wife.

Cal must have read what I was thinking because he said, "My relationship with Rachel and the other girls in the office is much better than with you. I married you to have a wife, home, and children. You're best suited in those roles, and if you're not satisfied, you should accept whatever I can give."

I got a coaster and placed it on the sideboard. He frowned and turned it so the pheasant on the coaster squarely faced him. "You don't even know why you're so dissatisfied," he said, and laughed. "How can you not even know that?"

He was right. It seemed I didn't even have enough sense to know even that, and his voice reflected his annoyance at my not living up to my responsibilities. I couldn't read much from his eyes. They were behind a curtain that had been securely drawn since we'd moved to the house in the Winnebago Creek subdivision in Nicolet City. What was wrong with me? Aunt Hester kept repeating in her soft, litany-like church voice that Cal was a good provider. And he was. I'd never seen him drunk; he always had a dozen red roses delivered for my birthday and our anniversary; he gave me electrical appliances for Christmas; the kids loved him.

Cal's cigarette smoke rose like the exhaust of a car winding up a mountain road. The two horizontal lines across his forehead formed the wings of two flying birds, the one just above his eyes longer, making his ears appear to tilt forward.

My thoughts drifted with the wavering smoke rising from the cigarette in Cal's well-manicured fingers. Fingers that always smelled of antiseptic. I wondered what it would be like honeymooning with Dr. Schackmann in the Smoky Mountains, the two of us sitting close together in his gray Mercedes. In fact, I didn't know what kind of car he had, but gray seemed the right color, Mercedes the right make. He'd have his arm around me and have a hard time driving because I'd look so radiant and smell like honeysuckle, which he liked. His eyes would have lost all their usual arrogance, and he'd be seeing only me and be happy.

Cal's fist struck the table, startling me. "Life's a well-run machine," he said. "You have a routine, and you don't think about what troubles you." His voice rose, "I was raised to be a winner."

What was wrong with me? Good wives didn't anger their husbands.

Cal's self-assurance about where he was going had been one of his most attractive qualities when we'd been dating. I fell in love with him in the spring of 1963, when "Two Faces Have I" was a popular song. Cal's lectures made me feel he cared, and it was after one particularly long one about his well-planned future that I decided to marry him. He wasn't the type who said, I love you, and I admired that because love wasn't a word to be used lightly. I loved him and had assumed he felt the same way. My children would have financial security.

During the '60s it was only the aberrant, out-of-it women who pursued careers because "they hadn't been able to catch a man." Those who didn't marry were destined to be the ugly old hag illustrated on the card nobody wanted in the game of Old Maid. Marrying someone like Cal was what I was expected to do. As Uncle Walt said, "A general surgeon, but, sure as hell, still a surgeon." And when my girlfriends began falling away, I saw it as a sign of envy.

What had Dr. Schackmann meant when he said, "You feel the way you do because you're being deprived of what you need?" It didn't make sense even after he added, "If Cal saw his snowmobile rusting outside in the rain, he'd do something about it, wouldn't he?"

***

Dr. Jenkins closed the door, rolled the stool from under the counter, studied my chart, and asked, "How are you?"

"Fine, thank you," I said, thinking it a silly question—and a sillier answer. He took a pen from his pocket, made a few notations, turned to me and began reeling off numbers and terms that meant nothing until he said the word surgery.

"Surgery?"

And when he said, "A hysterectomy," things blurred.

"I've done hundreds of them," he said. "It's a standard, common procedure, as your husband well knows." Focusing on me for the first time, he added, "But first I want to try something new that just came out," and he turned aside to write a prescription.

After handing it to me, he put his hand on my arm and said, "It's going to be fine. If you need a hysterectomy, it will just mean a few days in the hospital, and then you'd be back home again." He rubbed the back of his neck, stretched his arms in front of him, and added, "In these cases, aggressive action is necessary, so it's best to be prepared about what may happen."

When I saw the back of his white coat going out the door, I pictured my insides spilling out in a bright red river on a white operating table; this time it would be different from having my appendix or tonsils out.

While making dinner, my mind kept returning to Barb, a woman I'd worked with who'd had a hysterectomy. She wound her hair around her fingers and talked like a little girl whenever men were around; women rolled their eyes when her name was mentioned.

I wondered why I was upset, since I didn't really want any more children. Then I realized what the ability to become pregnant meant, how much of my identity was connected with it beginning with the attention men gave me when I'd turned that certain age; with some men, at any rate. With Uncle Walt, it seemed it'd always been there, however unspoken, like Aunt Hester's jealousy.

The next time I saw Dr. Jenkins he said, "If you don't get a hysterectomy, you'll have to get off the pill." But I knew I'd get something, because I'd gone through the fear of pregnancy after being date-raped: the awful waiting, then swallowing the small, bitter, white pills from an out-of-town doctor to make my period start. At least after you were married, I thought, there was no stigma when the husband did the raping.

When the kids sat down for dinner, I looked at them with extra appreciation, hunger, and love. Mark's blond hair parted naturally on the same side as mine; Jenny had my nose and green eyes. They were the part of me that would continue, and I was proud of them. They must have sensed the tension, because after dinner they asked to go out to play as soon as they'd carried their plates, glasses, and silverware to the kitchen, rinsed and separated them the way Cal required.

I told Cal about my high number of abnormal cells; he narrowed his eyes, shook his head as if shaking off sand, keeping his arms flat on

Carol Smallwood

the captain's chair. His resemblance to the Sphinx disappeared when he snapped on his cigarette lighter, his expression one of recalling a trying surgical procedure.

When I kept looking at him through the film of blue-gray smoke, he looked down to locate his ashtray with an odd expression that I'd been noticing lately. As if guessing that I'd seen it, he exhaled and said, "A hysterectomy would help level out your moods." He picked up his table knife and studied it as it balanced evenly on his index finger, and in the professional air he must have used many times that day, he went on, "It would help end your romantic dreams, make you satisfied with your role of wife and mother. When your hormones are stabilized, it'll make my life a hell of a lot easier, instead of seeing you wandering around like a ghost in a B movie." He lined up his silverware with precision and said, "Marriage to a professional is different than if you married someone with just a high school diploma, you know."

I nodded apologetically. He was surely knew what he was talking about, and, as his wife, I'd let him down. Maybe my dissatisfaction could be removed, and then they'd sew me back up? It would look like a ball of mesh the size of a grapefruit, and if Dr. Jenkins found the dissatisfaction too pervasive, he'd just close me back up with catgut or maybe the synthetics Cal said were beginning to be developed because of the risk of infection.

When I began to wash dishes, I felt myself meld with the sink. I once was desirable, but if I had the operation, I'd be like the women who people talked about as if their life was over. Cal grabbed a towel, surprising me by wiping dishes while he watched the evening news, and I smiled my gratitude. I could go through anything if he cared.

On his way to turn on the television, he noticed a paperback on the history of sex I'd left open to the page about troublesome wives being committed to madhouses. I also learned that crying uncontrollably, not being able to move, and other symptoms called hysteria, were once attributed by male doctors to the uterus; that Freud recanted his belief that the basis of hysteria was "perverted acts against children" because it was so socially unacceptable. His lips narrowed like Aunt Hester's hearing one of Uncle Walt's dirty jokes and said, "Put that book away before anybody sees it."

In the evening, I watched Jenny and Mark playing while Cal snoozed in front of the television, and told myself that if I had the hysterectomy, at least I'd no longer experience monthly cramps. Sometimes they were so severe all I could do was stretch out on my stomach, sweating, muffling moans, while warm blood spurted. When each cramp began, I'd hope it might be the last and that I wouldn't have to drag myself to the bathroom to throw up; while they lasted, I merely existed as a host for pain. Staring through narrowed eyes, I'd will myself elsewhere, gathering a quilt between my fingers, curling in a ball to ease the spasms, trying to think of all the other pioneer women who'd gone through this "without letting it get them down," as Cal advised.

But it did no good to think at such times.

It must be what a tree concluded in a storm: it had no choice but to give itself up to being buffeted and tossed, because if it didn't, it'd break. The dark clots of blood resembling wobbly pieces of raw liver carried by bright blood from my very middle like lava from the earth scared me; they came from that part of me that swung moods and controlled more of me than I'd like. I always felt that no matter how much I learned, that part of me, of primitive   essence, wasn't impressed at all.

Midol helped dull the pain sometimes. Aunt Hester had said that women, as descendants of Eve, were doomed to suffer, and to offer it up for my sins. When I was at puberty, my cousin, Mary Elizabeth had given me a pamphlet by the makers of Kotex when I hinted that I wanted to know what was happening. But she wouldn't talk about it. A family doctor had said the cramps wouldn't be so bad after having a baby.

When the cramps did ease, I'd feel weak and only able to eat soup or toast, grateful it would be a month before I'd again be as powerless as a body of water against the tides.

But if I had a hysterectomy, would I grow a mustache? Lose my figure? I wished I knew more about it, but all I could remember was what Uncle Walt had said about Aunt Hester: "She went around like a bat out of hell, making me damn glad to be away at hunting camp."

I decided it probably was one of those things that couldn't be explained unless you experienced it—like falling in love, giving birth, or getting old.

A week or so later, after dropping Jenny off at nursery school, I got another test at Dr. Jenkins's office and then went shopping at C&C. Some days when I pushed a cart between aisles, I'd pretend that my subjects were lined up to see me. When no one was looking, I'd make a slight waving gesture to both the right and left, my head inclined like Queen Elizabeth's. The tile floor spread before me like alabaster marble, the recessed lighting became chandeliers, the forced air vents were ladies-in-waiting with fans, and the piped-in music was my own ensemble.

My exquisite crown was heavy and I walked slowly with queenly elegance. When my shadow fell on bottles of extra pure virgin olive oil, their labels blanched; when I passed purple grapes, they turned green with envy. In the spring I wore a tiara of seed pearls, and in the fall, blazing rubies. On some days my train was ermine, and on others, crackling taffeta. I wore diamond rings the size of robin's eggs on both hands, and emerald buttons the size of lima beans; samples extended to me in paper cups were not local cider but French champagne in long-stem crystal, and were handed out not by a gum-chewing Babs in a nylon uniform, but by titled ladies in flowing velvet. I imagined what they, my subjects, were saying about my beauty and clothes, how they bragged about me to those outside my kingdom. Tears filled my eyes when I imagined my funeral procession stretching as far as the eye could see, the road crowded with grief-stricken subjects tossing pink rose petals.

When I turned a corner, I saw a big display of carefully stacked boxes of fortune cookies. Removing just one bottom box would probably bring the whole thing crashing down, and I was picturing the mess when an attractive man in shorts appeared. I followed him until my view was obstructed by a low-hanging banner showing chickens wearing straw hats and hiking boots, and turkeys in top hats and tails. After a hysterectomy, did they package your remains in a paper sack like the gizzard, heart, liver, and neck, inside a roasting chicken? I tried not to think about it, but saw the words HALF A WOMAN on my forehead, along with the familiar banner, Damaged Goods.

***

"You're good-looking, Lily."

I thought I hadn't heard right, then saw that Dr. Schackmann's eyes were caressing me the way some men's eyes did. He seemed amused by my confusion, and I looked away, distracting myself with the specks of dust dancing in a beam of sunlight that struck the arm of the couch.

He added softly, "I enjoy working with you more than my other patients."

What had I done? Aunt Hester had reinforced what my missal said about helping men enter Heaven. "My dear," she told me, "you join in their sin if you inflame men's desires."

Dr. Schackmann was looking at me as if he knew every thought I'd ever had. He asked me then what my perfume was called, and when he leaned back, his swivel chair squeaked as he continued in his German accent, "It brings back good memories of my mother. When I was a small child in World War II, it didn't matter how awful it got as long as someone loved me." He paused until I looked at him, and then shifted his position, his unlaced leather vest parting to reveal more of his chest under his partially buttoned shirt. I saw his gold chain, and tried not to stare at the untied leather laces of the vest rising and falling, faster than usual. I imagined myself in an exotic garden, where he was offering me a large sun-dappled apple, the kind I'd seen in fruit baskets. He was smiling under the shade of a swaying palm. In a Hawaiian shirt, his curly hair gently tousled by a breeze carrying a hint of honeysuckle: the only sound in Eden was the occasional thud of a falling apple.

"It was such a relief when I read Freud's explanation '...obsessional neurosis is a caricature of a religion,'" I said and flushed, certain that he'd guessed what I'd just been thinking. When he leaned back and crossed his arms, I held up my purse a little longer than necessary, trying not to admit that I was hoping he'd appreciate how nice my Peach Delight nail polish looked. "I keep it here," I went on, "and when things get too crazy I read it. It's reason in black and white."

He leisurely stretched his long legs and crossed them at the ankles, his eyes not on my nails, and when he said, "You'd never have imagined such a thing unless you'd experienced it would you, Lily?" I had a hard time concentrating, because of how he'd caressed my name. "I've thought about your definition of love as wanting to find out what you really wanted to know through another person. It's the most beautiful I've ever heard" he said, as I admired the crook in his nose he must have gotten in a fight rescuing someone.

Yes, I thought, this is how it should be, this is it; surely it's how it should be. I wanted to freeze the moment: the way one of his socks drooped, how his hair curled over his ears, the squeak of his swivel chair, how the 1973 Rexall Drug calendar dipped a bit to the right. Something squeaked. He was bending in his chair, tying one of his boots, and when he finished, he waited in silence.

As if reciting a catechism lesson, I finally said, "Cal said I should accept the limitations of love, that romance doesn't exist in real life."

Dr. Schackmann's look became clinical, and he said, "Your marriage is a repeat of your childhood, because Cal and Uncle Walt say they've given you a good life."

After that session, I looked in the restroom mirror and moved my chin up and down, my face from side to side, trying to see why he'd called me good-looking. But all I saw was a married woman in her thirties with two young children.

On the way home, I passed the huge boulders forming the entrance to Boulder Park, carried there during the last Wisconsin Glacial Age, the Tioga, which had only ended about 10,000 years ago. The horizontal boulders resembled hibernating animals tolerating pines and hardwoods as upstarts, while squirrels and chipmunks used them as springboards to overhanging branches. Jenny had named the largest boulder Bigfoot; Mark played King of the Mountain on the smaller ones.

I remembered being fascinated reading about the Bering land bridge that allowed the migration of humans to North America from Siberia. I pictured my ancestors making the trek peering at the moon, sun, and stars, while managing pregnancy, birth, and infants. They must've been a smelly bunch in animal skins always looking out for prey. On their journey, did they cook their meat after gutting it with chipped stone or had they eaten it raw? Had the women experienced the luxury of love, or had they been spared--the scales so exquisitely balanced between happiness and sorrow.

***

At a session two weeks later, Dr. Schackmann asked in his caressing tone, "Why doesn't Cal play with Lily?"

I didn't answer. I knew if I did, I'd cry. I saw him looking at my wedding ring, and managed to say, "I think love's only one percent physical."

"It's not even that," he replied, and I felt even more of myself dissolving into him. "I've had difficulties in the past in extending myself in love," he said, and added, "With your background, it would be dangerous."

"I think I've loved on my terms and only around the edges before," I admitted.

"I'm available to you any time," he said. "You're innocent, and I'm trying to get you across the road like a snail, without being smashed and yet without walling you in a shell."

On my way home, I realized I was in love with him.

A Hearthstone Party

The Hearthstone Party was held in a township hall a few miles from Nicolet City. I'd received an invitation in the shape of a teacup covered with the names of door prizes from two women I'd gone to high school with.

After three Bingo games, played with Indian corn markers in Blue Bonnet and Parkay Oleo tubs, a peanut butter pail with folded slips of paper was passed around. The paper I picked had the penciled word VANITY and, for it, I received a Pepto-Bismol pink plastic grinning Buddha, sprouting spines to hold jewelry, and duly smiled when the women around me said, "Oh, isn't that pretty," "My, aren't you lucky," "I can just see that on my dresser." After more Bingo, the peanut butter pail was passed again and I traded it for cookie cutters.

I pictured the mice scurrying in the walls behind me were dressed in pastels like the Beatrix Potter books I read to the kids. The mice were getting ready to sit down to dinner at a mushroom cap table spread with woven grass. The boy mouse wore blue overalls held by string suspenders and the girl mouse had pink thread apron strings. The smiling mother mouse, in a lace trimmed apron, placed acorn shells of corn on the table ... but my reverie was interrupted by a little girl who bumped the corn markers from my hand while running to reach the piano before some friends. I studied the patterns on the remaining orange, black, yellow, brown, maroon corn; each kernel was different and felt good between my fingers.

After another set of games, the three sponsors picked up the markers and cards. Catalogs, order forms, and pencil stubs were distributed and it was announced, "The lady having the highest order will win her sponsor a Hearthstone Inner Circle Prize!" The three sponsors standing in a row, shifting their feet and wringing their hands with smiles of embarrassment, made me hum Gilbert and Sullivan's, "Three Little Maids from School."

In my catalog I saw a man and woman in a gondola with the words "Escape to paradise, become a living legend. Make him follow you anywhere when you wear Legend of Romance." The woman, in a red evening gown, was gracefully trailing her hand in the moonlit water; the hovering man in a tuxedo extended red roses.

I relived Dr. Schackmann words when he said, "I'm available to you any time."

The woman in the gondola looked so happy--the scent of roses and lapping of waves made me cry. Relieved no one had noticed, I turned to the cleaning supplies and ordered laundry detergent.

When I left after coffee, moths were milling around the outside light; the newly mowed dew grass and Queen Anne's Lace stuck to my sandals. It was quiet enough to hear fireflies, a silence only broken by a passing car, which, after it passed, made the silence more intense, the night more inky, the stars brighter and closer, until I felt one with the spinning earth under my thin sandals. Standing very still, peering at the sky not obscured by trees, I willed answers to questions I didn't even know how to form till recalling what happened to Prometheus for taking fire from the gods: he was kept tied while an eagle ate his liver every day only to have it grow back and be eaten again the next day.

Lately I was realizing how deep darkness really was, the narrowness of the path a lamp makes at night. I felt the presence of all the other women who'd just wanted to be one with the earth under their feet—knowing it was too much to understand the stars, wise enough to know it, instead of milling around light in the darkness like moths.

When I got home, Cal was asleep with the television on and the kids were in bed. I made some tea and watched the end of a program showing Vietnamese Buddhist monks torching themselves. Earlier I'd heard names like Thuan Yen, Phnom Penh expertly pronounced by newscasters like Chet Huntley and David Brinkley on the 6:30 nightly news (I never could decide which I liked best—the classic blond good looks of one or the distinctive delivery of the other). They made the war familiar but at the same time foreign as the Buddhist monks torching themselves. The news had concluded our soldiers weren't winning because the jungle made the enemy impossible to see.

When I turned the television off, Cal opened his eyes and told me to turn it back on. I sat wearing wet sandals and sipped my saffron amber tea.

The Picnic

I'd thought of suicide not long after the Hearthstone Party when Cal was asleep. I'd get the professional samples of sleeping pills in the bathroom and take them with the whiskey, gin, or vodka kept by the cans of Planter's nuts in the kitchen. I reasoned that Cal would be up in the morning before the kids, so he'd find me and keep the door shut so they wouldn't see.

I'd gone with Mark and Jenny to the Father's Day picnic that day at Little Chicago Lake Park, which simmered under the hazy sun. Adults were barely moving, and there weren't even seagulls in the hot humid air. It was so hazy that you couldn't tell where the horizon ended and the lake began. Cal wasn't with us.

Uncle Walt had selected a picnic table under a large Maple by the main path to the dock, and we were sitting with Aunt Heidi and Uncle Bob. "God, it's hotter'n hell," Uncle Walt said, his eyes zeroing in at two approaching girls as if they were flushed-out rabbits. "Bathing suits now don't leave much to the imagination, do they? This damn heat sure hasn't shriveled their peaches." In a thick voice he added, "They'd be good rolls in the hay."

Aunt Heidi held the pie she was passing in midair and asked, "What'd you say?"

"Uh, they'd be good in roles for plays," Uncle Bob said. Uncle Walt grinned, rummaged around the cooler, and asked Aunt Hester, "Hey, where'd you hide the thigamajig?" When she'd uncapped his beer, he said to Uncle Bob, "Hey, check out that young thing." He growled and slapped his knee. "Christamighty! Look at her bounce—half in, half out, comin' and goin'—hell, her chassis might as well be buck naked."

"Look at Mark and Jenny," Aunt Hester interrupted. "They're having such a good time. When I saw Carla Deerfield at church, she said Mark knows all his numbers and Jenny all her colors." Her glass eye looked more artificial in the sun, and her light eyelashes gave her a look of a Cyclops.

"You were as tan Jenny is in the summer," Uncle Walt told me, jangling the change in his pocket.

Aunt Hester was cleaning as if she were at home. She carefully brushed crumbs and cigar ash on the picnic table into the shape of a triangle before disposing of them. "Your uncle likes a spotless home," she once explained, "and the only way that's possible is to use the strongest antiseptics in scalding water. You know his mother's favorite saying, 'Clean houses make clean minds.'"

I remembered Dr. Schackmann's triangle he put on the board when I told him Cal kept telling me I should do more housework: 1. Please me. 2. Try harder. 3. Frustration. But I only understood it when Mark brought home from school a book two grades beyond his level and Cal demanded, "Aren't you out of that book yet?"

Aunt Heidi said, "Remember going swimming? Those were the days, weren't they, Walt?" She cleared her throat and wiped away a few tears before continuing, "We'd walk the railroad from home and pick wild strawberries—I'd be the one checking for trains by feeling if the rails were vibrating. Your father, Lily, was interested in plants way back then and would fall behind to study them."

"God, he'd bury his nose in every damn weed he saw," said Uncle Walt.

She continued talking, but I was picturing the ship that Odysseus sailed on his adventures while my eyes were on Mark and Jenny playing on the sandy beach. A loud slam made me jump.

It was Uncle Walt, the engineer, testing the picnic table. He bent down, inspected the sides, and when he straightened up, adjusted his suspenders with a snap. "It's too damn bad Cal couldn't come today," he said to me. "He puts in long hours providing for you and the kids, and you sure as hell should be glad to have a husband who's not some damn piss-willy playboy."

Watching tiny fluttering butterflies brought a shiver down my spine for some reason. I excused myself from the picnic table by saying, "I have to go check on the kids." Like so many other times, certain things stirred memories from some murky depth, bringing engulfing fear of falling into space.

Once down at the beach, the longing to stuff Uncle Walt in the cooler the way Alice stuffed the Dormouse in the teapot subsided as I helped the kids dig holes and build sandcastles. How wonderful it would be to once again put twigs in rivulets after a heavy rain, and join them going down the Amazon to join the ocean.

As an adult now, I knew everything had evolved after the Big Bang and that water was constantly evaporating into the sky only to fall back to earth either to be absorbed in the soil or join a stream or river and join a larger body of water. As I looked at the lake, the inability to determine where the water stopped and the sky began filled me with such uncertainty that I drew an imaginary horizon. It would be comforting to once again live in a world without science, where trees and rocks were as real as people, to not know rain carried pollutants thousands of miles away. The lapping waves, the warm sand giving way underfoot, the lulling breeze were hypnotic.

I walked back to the table slowly with the kids, trying not to notice the husbands hovering over the fires. When we got back, J.D. walked up, put his arm around Uncle Walt, and rumpled his reddish hair, saying, "What's new, you sly old devil? Hot enough for you? Joyce and I were scouting around for tables when I spotted you."

Before Uncle Walt could remove the cigar from his mouth, J.D. asked me, "How's the happy wife?"

I said, "How's Joyce?"

Looking around, he said, "Ah, my dear, the wagons have circled."

"What do you mean," I asked, though I had a good idea because Cal had told him about Dr. Schackmann. He'd told me that J.D. referred to Dr. Schackmann as the Lone Ranger and had said he'd better keep a "tight grip on his silver bullets."

J.D. merely grinned in response to my question, then said, "My dear, I see you're enjoying the solid front of family respectability." Eying my shirt buttons, he said, "How's it feel to be in the bosom of your family?" He raised his eyebrows. "Are you sure Cal's at the hospital? I heard he—" He stopped, as another couple had joined them.

Just last evening J.D. and Joyce had come over to play Scrabble. As soon as he'd entered he grinned and said as he handed me a bottle of wine, "Here, my dear—the nectar of Dionysus." He winked, knowing Cal wouldn't know what he meant. When he'd hooked his thumbs over his checked vest and asked Cal in a mock serious tone, "Who do you think will win the city council seat?" Joyce only looked at her husband with adoring eyes.

After the Scrabble tiles had been set up, J.D.'s air of errant schoolboy surfaced again when he asked Cal, "So, how's that receptionist of yours? You paying her overtime in cherry Kool Aid? Her hair gets redder every time I see her." When Cal ignored him, J.D. turned to me and said, "I like your new hairstyle, Lily."

J.D. was the only one we knew who was not impressed with Cal being a surgeon. Cal was acquiring a growing dislike of him after J.D. had laughed at how precisely he'd lined up his Scrabble tiles the last time we played, but put up with him because of J.D.'s friendship with Uncle Walt.

Cal's first word with his tiles was kitten. Then car, blood, smash, and others he knew would make me think of when he slowed the car and pointed them out on the road. With each word, his lips curled. If I hadn't known better, I'd have thought that putting me in my place meant more to him than winning. J.D. spelled cad, creep, and grinned.

J.D. had walked over to where Uncle Walt was inspecting the construction of another picnic table. Uncle Walt began grinning and strutting with one hand on his hip, so he was probably telling about the woman in her bathing suit calling for her dog: "Here Tizz, here Tizz."

I also recalled J.D. spelling the word "thorn" with his Scrabble tiles and asking me, "Have you come across the phrase, 'a lily among thorns'"? When I shook my head, he said, "No, you Catholics aren't Bible readers, are you?"

To forget Cal's caustic comments after J.D. and Joyce left, I watched the most colorful sailboats and wondered what happened to the Chinese robe embroidered with exotic flowers and birds Nicolet wore to impress the Winnebagoes. Or the Iroquois prisoner he was on his way to save from being tortured to death by the Hurons. A sudden gust of wind had overturned Nicolet's canoe—most likely it was just like the birch bark canoes in Pineville's museum. He must've known how thin a layer separated him from the water, so why hadn't he learned to swim? Why hadn't anyone in his canoe or in another canoe saved him? Yet, perhaps he'd been alone. After crossing the Atlantic and exploring countless rivers and lakes, drowning on his way to Trois-Rivieres must've been the last thing he'd anticipated.

When I got home and read a letter that said the job I'd wanted had gone to someone else, I felt even more drawn to an affair with Dr. Schackmann.

That night, when I considered killing myself, I settled upon the bathtub as the most considerate place. I'd wear my powder blue robe, lay the powder blue towels in the tub so the porcelain wouldn't be cold, and rip open several professional samples of sleeping pills. I'd spray the bathroom with the Avon room freshener always left on a scarf I'd embroidered on top of the toilet tank. It was a new pink can of Tea Roses, so I'd have plenty. I'd leave no note.

In bed, I recalled the tabloid headline at the C&C: THOUSANDS APPEAL TO THE VIRGIN OF GUADELOUPE TO WIN LOTTERY, as I stared at the ceiling, arching my neck as if easing the pills down my throat. The bedroom didn't have bars like *in The Yellow Wallpaper*, only one window so high you couldn't see the road. Our bed did have the feel of being nailed down as the one in the well-known story did because the bed wouldn't fit in any other spot. I listened to bugs hit the window while the refrigerator turned off and on. My hair had been done the day before, and it'd look good if I put an extra towel under my neck. The men hauling me out would comment, "Such nice-looking blond hair that smells like roses." But the more I pictured myself dead in a graceful pose, the angrier I got at them, even if I didn't know exactly who "them" was.

Slipping out of bed, I felt my way down the hall in the blackness, searching for a light or any movement that would give me clues as to where I was, some reassurance of safety. The walls, which closed in on me during the day, were old friends in the dark as I felt my way. When I reached the living room, the windows seemed like the unblinking eyes of prison guards, and the moon a discarded watermelon rind from the picnic. I turned on a light, and a moth fluttered in a spider web outside the window. By the time I got the broom it was gone. That afternoon, before I could put it outside, a buzzing fly had died on the window sill—it gave one final frantic buzz spinning around on its back and that was it.

It was muggy outside, and I walked down the sidewalk, ignoring the stones under my slippers, picturing myself dead near the roots of a tree. I heard Cal say, "Didn't I say I've seen this coming?" his nostrils flaring as if detecting something bad.

Realizing Mark or Jenny would be afraid if they saw me standing there in my robe in the middle of the night with the broom, I gave the walk a few sweeps, came back inside, and returned it to its spot between the stove and the refrigerator.

It was quiet in each of the kid's rooms, and Cal's snoring stopped after a strangled snort in our room, which smelled of Brylcreem, Winstons, and antiseptic.

Rain began hitting the window; when I was found I'd be clean and the falling rain would keep me company. I could see my favorite old white pine, smell the soil, feel the roots of the tree arching from its bed of dry needles. To die beneath its spreading branches of its soft needles would be good. White pines originally had covered much of Wisconsin and some can live almost 500 years but most had been cut down during the lumbering era.

Under the old pine, the largest of any tree around, I could listen to the conversations of birds, see how long it took a new species of snail to evolve, see if it would be my teeth or bones that lasted the longest. I'd no longer hear the cries of homeless cats or deserted dogs. The tree roots, arching above the ground, would provide a pillow for my head as the train whistle faded. It'd be like when I was a child, listening in the early morning fog, trying to guess what sort of thing made that sound, that whistle piercing miles of fields and woods.

In the spring, I'd offer myself freely to the falling rain in a way I never could in marriage; listen to the age-old thunder of ice cracking on the lake heralding the end of winter; in the summer I'd no longer have to climb my grandfather's apple trees hoping to see what my grandfather called a train; in the fall I'd be host to falling leaves; and winter would round me "with a sleep." No longer invisible I'd be part of the soil of the earth.

To support new life would make more sense than having my blood drained and stuffed in a coffin in Sunday clothes. Aunt Hester would see that I wore Clorox-clean underwear. She'd lift her eyes, murmuring, "Jesus, Mary, Joseph!" and Uncle Walt would say again, "I got a wife who'll bleach the hell out of the robes of the God Almighty."

Who knew what changes I might see? Hadn't I come from an earth still forming? The lake, where I first went swimming, was formed by Nipissing Lake cutting into the even older Lake Algonquin bed formed by melting glaciers.

Rain began hitting the window harder, and, pressing my face against the glass, I realized I was crying when my face felt cold. I'd be okay, things would pass. Couldn't I feel the earth spinning like a game of roulette? To rest under the giant white pine, the tallest tree around, while night turned into day, winter to spring, would be good. To have the time to detect thousands of nuances of sound, to have the luxury of time to learn the languages of moss and leaves, to see how long it took stone to turn into soil, to give the moon more imaginative names than the Greeks, and even glimpse its other side.

The wind had risen, and the snapping branches tapping on the roof sounded like visitors knocking. Above me, particles were flying, flung perhaps from faraway fantastic places I'd surely see someday. Mark had asked me to explain the wind once when he was four, and it wasn't until then I realized how little I knew about the wind. How do you explain how wind makes you feel? But I know now that a child can understand the language of wind better than any adult.

The listening house wrapped around me, whispering, "There are things you'll never know, never could guess. But don't worry, isn't it better that way? You don't realize how new the earth is, and that you walk on a thin layer above the molten rock of an infant planet still forming."

The next day, when I looked at the glass-covered dining room table and saw trees standing upside down in the lake of sky, I became dizzy. Then everything around welcomed me, rejoicing that I'd chosen to live. Like a child, I was one with the unseen, part of the universe. An incredible tapestry of color, texture, design, and harmony made it clear that, "we are such stuff as dreams are made on."

That overwhelming experience was too intense to last more than a few seconds. When it ended I felt banished but knew I'd never think of suicide again or be so alone.

After a few sessions had passed, when I told Dr. Schackmann about my thoughts of suicide, he had me promise not to take my life, and to make what he called a 'contract' with him giving a date I chose.

On my drive back home I daydreamed. I saw Cal's obituary in the Nicolet County News:

LOCAL SURGEON FOUND DEAD

Calvin P. Hyde, M.D., 34 of Nicolet City, was found dead on August 30 in the Nicolet County White Pine Reserve.

Dr. Hyde turned up missing a week ago. Neighborhood children found him after the recent windstorm.

Dr. Hyde leaves two children. His wife said memorials may go to the Nicolet County White Pine Reserve.

Friends can call at the Poppins Funeral Home, Monday at 7:00 p.m.

That night I dreamed that Cal and I were walking on high scaffolding. I was behind him, but he turned into Uncle Walt, and when he fell to his death, I felt guilty for feeling no regret.

The dream occurred after I'd taken the kids to see *Mary Poppins*, wondering if anyone could've guessed I'd just considered something so unacceptable as ending things. I was glad it was night so people couldn't see me very well and tried to relax my mouth. While waiting in line to buy tickets, I looked at men with their arms around women, women reflecting their love, children's happy faces basking in both reflections. I'd peered down a deep, cold, hypnotic pit for the first time, and its impersonal finality, its ridiculously easy access, made me realize the paper-thin separation between life and death. To delay going home, I made a game for the kids spotting details in the large posters in the lobby of *The Paper Moon* and *The Paper Chase*. I watched people come in for the second show, and for days kept singing, "Just a spoonful of sugar makes the medicine go down," seeing Mary Poppins rise and descend with her umbrella, toes pointing in opposite directions.

Mrs. Simons

Mrs. Simons lived by herself on the lake near me in Nicolet City in a house that had been winterized after she and her husband had moved there upon retirement. She'd been an elementary teacher in Milwaukee, and she kept all her large print *Reader's Digests* neatly stacked by month, with her name printed in large block letters on the covers. She still had that schoolteacher bearing that left me feeling self-conscious that I hadn't brushed my hair well enough or wasn't standing straight whenever I was with her.

One afternoon, I brought Mrs. Simons to the optometrist and guided her to a vacant chair in the waiting room. The receptionist's extra sweet smile made me suspect that the doctor was running late.

I found another chair and browsed through a large print *Reader's Digest* until I came to an article on mulching and recalled piling leaves onto Jenny's old sled and dragging it to a hole I'd dug. After several treks, and when the hole couldn't hold anymore, I shoveled the dirt back, trampled it down, and dug another.

The neighbor's dog had come running over, grabbed the rope on the sled, and then run around my house a few times before diving in the hole. He sniffed loudly, dug furiously, then leaped out sneezing. When I brushed the red bandanna around his neck, he expected me to play with him, so I put the sled rope in his mouth and said, "Pull." That didn't work, so I said "Fetch," putting sticks in his mouth, walking to the hole and dropping sticks in a few times. But he just sat scattering leaves with his tail.

Some leaves were still partially green, others were red, yellow, orange, and some had black spots. A neat yard was such a hopeless task; a good wind could cover it in seconds. I'd seen leaves come rushing down the road like a dam had burst; how many landed in your yard depended on how the wind blew. The day before, I'd leaned against a moss-covered tree by the road and watched the wind curl the leaves against the house like a surfer's wave.

Sometimes I uncovered unburied leaves from previous years matted in blackened clumps. They were a stark contrast to the neon ones, which I associated with Dr. Schackmann. The time when I had gone in for my appointment--it was in October and saw he was wearing a wedding ring. After that session, I stopped the car by the side of the road because I couldn't see through my tears. The neon leaves mocking me as a crow jabbed a dead animal in the ditch.

In the optometrist's office, the receptionist was smiling sweetly at arriving patients who had nowhere to sit. When a certain young woman arrived, a drab woman pointed at her and said to an older lady with dyed hair, "That's the one who was living with Ted Winkleman." Other women were talking about making dill pickles, no-salt diets, and children who never came to visit. The only male in the waiting room, an elderly man sitting by the door, smiled and asked everyone who entered, "Got the time?"

PART TWO

"When one illusion vanishes, another shall appear, and, still leading me forward towards an horizon that retreats as I advance, the happy prospect of futurity shall vanish only with my existence."
— Maria Edgeworth, *Letters of Julia and Caroline*, 1795

Ithaca

Ithaca was a college town with many hills. I wasn't allowed to bring Mark and Jenny, but wanted to finish my masters degree in geology to support myself and the kids after filing for a divorce. It was a subject I'd liked before, and I'd heard there were jobs available all over in government survey positions, as well as in colleges. I planned on moving with the kids when the divorce was final and after I'd finished my degree. It took all the determination I'd had to keep driving when Mark and Jenny ran after my car when I left, pleading for me to stay or at least take them with me. The anguishing imagery of that was something I'd never erase.

Classes were enjoyable and I so liked being there. It was the opportunity I wanted, and I did well despite the strong fear of failure and heavy work load. The success, the feeling of acceptance, made me more confident, and the students I became friends with gave me much needed encouragement.

When I first saw Mitchell, my academic supervisor, it seemed I'd known him from a different life. He moved with an easy grace. The way he tilted his head forward when he spoke, and everything about him, was very scrubbed and fresh. He liked people and was shrewd about assessing them. His smile said that he was no stranger to trials by fire: he had emerged more in touch with his humanity and with his innate elegance intact. I wondered if Uncle Walt would approve of him.

I met Mitchell to see *Aida*, and can remember so clearly the woman who sat behind us describing how rain showers started very suddenly in Bermuda, the excitement in a student's voice as he talked about the discovery of a new galaxy.

It had been so much fun to get dressed up and, as we sat waiting for the curtain to rise, it seemed I was a bird that had been blown off course and finally had made it home. During intermission we talked on the balcony while the kind of people I'd wanted to know drifted up and down the wide staircase. But the perfect evening ended for me in the final act when the characters were buried alive.

"I know I'm being so silly," I whispered, "but I have to go. I'll wait in the lobby for you."

"We'll get some fresh air," he said.

We stood on the steps outside until the paralyzing terror I felt of being suffocated faded. When we went back for our coats, the attendant said, "Did you and your wife enjoy the performance?" I was pleased that he saw us as a couple. When we left, I remember looking back and feeling very sad seeing the immense closed red and gold curtain, passing my hand slowly over the back of a plush seat so I'd never forget that places like it existed. I pushed back tears wishing Mark and Jenny could share this world I so wanted for us.

When Mitchell walked me to my car, his blazer blew against me, making me feel a part of him. He tilted his head, smiled, and said, "You look like the flower you're named after when you wear green. Wear it often." When I slowed my steps, he stopped, put his hand on my arm and said, "How can I not want you? You were meant to be loved. Why couldn't we have met earlier?"

I bowed my head. My tears transformed flowers skirting the sidewalk into stained glass. The trees became a vaulted ceiling, and for a moment I couldn't reply. With stumbling syllables I finally said, "At least we met," knowing that the surest way to keep love was to never attain it.

***

After returning to Ithaca after Christmas break, I drove to my apartment from campus one day and, with difficulty, managed to put my key in the expanding and contracting door. I didn't remember driving. Dr. Schackmann had prescribed new pills after I'd told him that Delmane often didn't put me to sleep.

During Christmas vacation Cal had shouted, "So, you think you've got some mission in geology, don't you, don't you, don't you!" shaking me again and again. "You'll never get out. I told you I'll have your ass in a sling and I'll get you, you witch—just wait and see, just you wait and see. You'll never succeed, never, never!" His eyes were so full of rage as he shoved me out the door when I left I was afraid for the kids and myself. Thankfully some boxes broke my fall.

At work, Mitchell came to my desk and asked me to join him for coffee. When we were in the lounge, he said, "You can't give up now, when you're almost finished and have done so well. I've noticed a lot of positive change in you in the short time you've been here."

He looked very worried so I must've looked awful. The notes I'd taken in class the day before scared me because they couldn't be recognized as writing. I'd just made myself keep at it so I wouldn't lose consciousness and fall off the chair.

"Lily, you must take care of yourself," Mitchell said. "Do you understand?"

He left abruptly, his hands balled into fists, after I'd promised to get some sleep. I was still cold most of the time, and I hadn't had such fear of falling into a black pit since the deposition Cal arranged about my relationship with Uncle Walt. If I quit I'd be giving up on a better life for myself, Jenny and Mark. But I felt powerless, as if the script that Cal said everyone had to follow was drawing me in, no matter what I did. My clothes told me I'd lost more weight which I could ill afford.

When I could, I listened with earphones to Chopin's Piano Concerto No. 1 in E Minor, op. 11 I'd discovered in the music library—the piano notes beyond what I'd ever heard before, weaving an elegant world of incredible grace and beauty: girls with cascading hair running down staircases to waiting lovers, and when meeting not knowing if they were themselves or their lovers—apple blossoms fell that caught every current to delay descent in moonlight. I'd leave, exhausted, in tears and yet full of hope thinking of a life with Mitchell. Whenever I heard Chopin afterwards, it brought renewed gratitude for meeting Mitchell, to know that people like him existed.

Mitchell suggested a lawyer but the lawyer wasn't encouraging because of the backing Uncle Walt gave Cal to keep the kids in Nicolet City. When I saw the lawyer Dr. Schackmann suggested it was obvious he was just protecting himself.

How could I marry Mitchell when a tenure job kept him at Ithaca? Wouldn't I come to resent giving up split custody to be with him? And what job could he ever find in Nicolet City?

When I saw a woman counselor on campus and told her about Dr. Schackmann, she said, "Doctors like that take advantage of women. It happens too often and there's no excuse for it. You're in a very vulnerable state, and he was only thinking about himself."

The depth of her anger surprised me, and I could only think that she didn't know what Dr. Schackmann and I had or she never would have said it.

"Lily, you're much better off without him," she said. "You're lucky you got out of it when you did."

Having to leave the room of my own in Ithaca was difficult. I wanted to remain for the daffodils, to hear bees among the lilacs. Even mosquitoes in Ithaca would've been special. Spring would have come earlier than in Nicolet City, and maybe if Mitchell had seen how well I looked in a tan who knows? Before I closed the door for the last time, I and walked slowly across the room to adjust the curtains that no one had ever seen besides me. On the way back, the floor felt as unsteady as it must have for Nicolet in his canoe when it overturned and he was drowned. I grasped the green couch knowing the support it gave was something I'd always have.

Mitchell's letter was the first one I received after leaving Ithaca. When I studied his handwriting and passed my fingers over the ink, blood from the ridges of my split fingernails, which had scraped the mailbox, smeared the envelope. After I washed my hands, and when I couldn't cry anymore, I read the letter. He wrote about what was going on, said he missed seeing me around, and told me who'd taken my place at the graduate job I'd held. He said that Professor Macul often talked about me.

Macul's wife had observed, "You're probably driving them up the wall, surviving under their very noses." But my smile faded when she said, "If a woman doesn't have her family, what does she have?"

***

Tulips as tightly closed as Aunt Hester's lips would soon be appearing on both sides of Uncle Walt's drive. She planted them so precisely that as a child I used to connect them like dot-to-dot puzzles. I saw her life as a series of neatly written signs like "Cleanliness Is Next to Godliness" and "Prayer Is the Answer." But Uncle Walt had said that Aunt Hester had worn her dresses short when she was younger, and that it was her legs that'd first caught his eye.

I could see Aunt Hester saying "Jesus, Mary, Joseph!" Her eye, the one not made of glass, should have been filled with devotion, with anticipated glory of the hereafter, but instead it had venom or, at best, pained forbearance. In the Catholic Girl's Missal she gave me as child, it was said we should think well of everyone, so I'd attributed it to the narrow shoes with high heels she said she wore as penance.

When she put her black rosaries down on the white dresser scarf, they always formed something new: writhing snakes, letters of the alphabet, nooses; the rosaries with large crosses resembled anchors. Her worn black prayer books, edged in red or gilt, had ribbon book markers and holy cards of saints with hands folded in prayer or dripping blood from upraised palms; some cards were prayers, ejaculations, or indulgences. When I started studying astronomy in the fifth grade, I thought of the rings of Saturn when I saw a halo above the head of a saint.

My aunt's numerous blond wigs made miniature straw stacks on her dresser. A picture of the Sacred Heart on the right side of the dresser showed God pointing to a large heart outside His body—or was He extending it in His hand? On the left was St. Anthony, in Franciscan robe and sandals, whom she always evoked after losing something. There was a font of holy water under a bust of the Virgin Mary.

When she asked me if Jenny and Mark had been baptized and I told her they hadn't, she intoned like a Cassandra, "They'll go to hell."

Aunt Hester gave me a Catholic Girl's Missal when she returned from a Sacramentine retreat at Our Lady of Sorrows. She always returned from retreats with St. Anthony scapular, Infant of Prague or the Virgin Mary statues; holy cards of the Lily of the Mohawk, Catherine Tekakwitha, were the most numerous. The thick gilt-edged book soon automatically opened to "Living in a Vale of Tears," which was about the lives of martyred virgins, how to help fathers and husbands as heads of households, and how to live without impure thoughts. The duties and suffering of women as wives were heavily veiled in mystery, but I greedily gleaned as much as I could from between the lines. I soon knew the section having the shortest indulgences giving the longest release from Purgatory. And I knew where the lists of venial and mortal sins were, and tried to figure out exactly when a venial sin became a mortal one, which meant you could go to Hell if you died before it wasn't confessed. What about eating meat when you weren't sure if it was Friday night or Saturday morning if there was no electricity to tell the time?

To show that I could get a job to support myself and the kids. I got the closest one to Nicolet City I could to since my lawyer said the judge preferred the area. When I didn't have the six months custody, visitation would also be easier, but it was soon decided that I had to live in Nicolet County to have split custody.

I knew I was almost home when I saw the marker commemorating where Nicolet had stopped on his quest to find the Northwest Passage. In the fog, I just managed to see it. Had he felt the uncertainty I was experiencing, a fear of falling over the edge? Nicolet had been within a few days of reaching the Mississippi, which he thought was the route to China, when he turned back.

When I got home, the fresh lake air greeted me. A bird appeared, descending in the fog above the crackling trees making me think of Icarus falling from the sky after his wings had melted as in the mythology book I'd gotten Mark. The utility lines drooped with ice like ropes stretched too often in a high-wire act, and the unlit streetlights waited like scaffolds. I couldn't see the lake in the layered mist, but I heard the loud snap of ice separating; the foghorn and seagulls sounded close enough to touch.

Gusts of wind blowing gray ashes from a neighbor's drive increased the feeling that I was part body and part ghost. When a limb from a white birch snapped and joined others littering the ice crusted snow in the yard, I recalled the philosophy question about a tree falling in a forest: if no one heard it, did it make a sound? Then more tree limbs snapped, sounding like gunshots while the smoke slipped sideways from a neighbor's chimney.

A babysitter was staying with Mark and Jenny, because school had been closed. Seeing the kids so happy to see me reinforced my decision about doing what I could to be near them. I'd decided they were more important to me than anything else—if I didn't put them in first place I'd always be torn by guilt and the anguish of missing them.

My quest had ended where it had begun.

The house wrapped around me as if I'd never left. My feet automatically adapted to the spot on the hall floor that dipped, and, without looking, I knew the exact distance between the windows, which window gave the most light, and at what angle the glare on the clock was the least. The shingles needed replacement and the walls looked higher with fewer things on the shelves, the television and stereo gone.

The heavy birch doors provided a feeling of solidity until I discovered that one of them stuck. The feeling of not being able to get out filled me with panic. I calmed myself by reasoning that if I couldn't get out, I could always telephone for help, or crawl out the window above the kitchen sink.

Despite my happiness of being with the kids, I recalled the conversation between the Cheshire Cat and Alice: "How do you know I'm mad? said Alice. You must be," said the Cheshire Cat, "or you wouldn't have come here."

The scent of "a little dab'll do ya" Brylcreem clung to the empty, hollow bedroom I'd once shared with Cal. Two mirrors remained, and when I looked in one I was endlessly repeated in the one behind it until I got so small I disappeared. The last time I'd looked so long in a mirror was the night before I was married. The mirror had been an old one, producing a wavy reflection as I'd stared, holding bits of frayed ribbon. Now, instead of saying goodbye to Lily Alger, I was seeing the dissolution of Lily Hyde.

Dark vertical stripes in the yellow wallpaper resembled bars and seemed to mock, "So you thought you were going to get away? Cal said he'd get your ass in a sling and you'd never leave with the kids. Well, he's gotten his way, hasn't he?"

The wallpaper had acquired the shade not unlike that described in *The Yellow Wallpaper* written in the nineteenth century about a wife who peels off the wallpaper to free the woman she thinks is trapped behind it. I shivered when I remembered that her husband was also a doctor, and had, instead of calling her Dolly like Cal and Uncle Walt had called me, called the woman, "little girl."

I found Mark's crayon picture of a woman with red lines falling from a heart split in two. She was in a cage. Nearby was a smiling man with dollar signs for eyes. There was a dog dish by the woman, and above the cage there was a woman with dashes spilling from her face onto the cage.

I'd shown the picture to Cal and told him what Mark had said: "The woman's bleeding because her heart's been broken. She was given dog food in a cage. The woman above is her mother crying in Heaven."

Cal had replied, "If a woman acts like a dog, she belongs in a cage. Dogs eat dog food."

After giving the kids laminated fallen leaves I'd found on campus sidewalks, the first thing I unpacked of my own was the bronze bow I'd taken with me to Ithaca. I hung it near the door that faced Ithaca, where I'd been happy. It was the direction in which the train left Nicolet City in the afternoon, its whistle growing fainter and fainter, like the memory of *Aida*, Mitchell, the red and gold curtains, and the wide winding staircase.

The Church

A petition was circulating to have Father Teiresias removed. When Mark, at the time only nine years old, said the new priest was probably closer to God than those tossing him out, I was amazed at his insight. The petition started when Father Teiresias invited a Protestant to speak at mass, and the older parishioners walked out in icy indignation.

It was a reflection of the modernization that'd wiped clean the ceiling murals of St. John's, along with most of the candles and vases. The altar still reached the vaulted ceiling but its many niches were no longer crammed under graceful spires with little statues. The railings, most of the pedestals, candles, large statues, and the pictures were gone. It was no surprise that St. John's now had a hollow, empty sound. I missed hearing words like Kyrie Eleison because they were more imaginative than Lord Have Mercy; Sanctus so much more interesting than Holy. People were now supposed to seek God more directly, and thus were not thought to need all the trappings. Even the two rows of fluted pillars connecting the arched ribs to the vaulted ceiling had been either removed or partially cut like amputated limbs. I suppose it was done to provide more of an unobstructed view of the altar, but I worried what supported the roof now. St. John's was destined to be closed and sold because of the shortage of priests.

I remembered going to Confession, now called the Sacrament of Reconciliation, when I reached what the Church considered the age of reason. The sins I confessed on my knees in the dim confessional were the only ones I knew: disobedience, for having forgotten to shut the basement door every night, like Uncle Walt said; and impure thoughts, because I wondered about boys. The priest would tell me to say three Our Father's, three Hail Mary's, and an Apostle's Creed.

There were several churches in Nicolet City, and stores used to be closed on Sundays. When people went to church, they wore Sunday clothes.

As soon as Uncle Walt was behind the wheel on the way home, smoking a cigar, the propriety that'd kept him silent during the service would fall away with something like, "Doesn't Henry's wife think she's something? She acts like her dump's cleaner than you other piss-willy women and didn't even answer my comment about her dress. They probably don't have enough money to wipe her stuck-up ass with toilet paper."

Aunt Hester said, "That's *hardly* the language of a member of the Holy Name Society." But the way she said it, I knew she realized how useless the admonishment was.

"Why don't priests wear gloves giving communion?" Uncle Walt continued as Aunt Hester sat clutching *Our Sunday Visitor* and *The Wisconsin Catholic*. "You can bet your sweet ass they pass a hell of a lot of germs putting their hands in everybody's mouths." He gave his suspenders a snap and said in thick voice, "God, who knows what priests get up to with their housekeepers?"

Years later, after my return to Nicolet City, I climbed the stairs at St. John's half expecting to hear the swooping wings of the angel of retribution because I'd married out of the Church and hadn't attended mass since college. I'd done a lot of questioning but valued the discipline necessary for survival that the church had instilled. One Sunday, when married couples were asked to stand up to renew their vows, Mark said, "It made me feel illiterate."

Jenny corrected him, "You mean illegitimate."

It wasn't until I stopped going to church altogether that I understood the impact it had. Instead of a psychiatrist, you went to confession, and when things got bad, you could dwell on the hereafter; each day of your Catholic calendar had some significance, usually the self-sacrifice of saints. But when I'd returned going to St. John's, it soon become merely a routine, and I missed the artifacts, the Latin, that lent a sense of mystery, wonder, tradition, and imagination.

The last time I'd gone to mass, in the unadorned, modernized church, the man sitting in the row in front of me was picking his nose, while his kids read *Archie* and *Jughead* comics. The woman on my right was copying a *Family Circle* recipe, and the couple to the left pawing each other. The phrase "God wept" came to mind and I thought they wouldn't have acted that way had the old elegance, mystery, and ceremony of the unknown still been present.

***

When I made an appointment to see Father Teiresias at the rectory and told him I liked the Phoenix on his sweatshirt, he replied, "You're the first to recognize it. When I explained it to the only parishioner who asked about it, the man looked at me like I was either a pagan or an insurance salesman." It wasn't until after the appointment that I connected his name with Oedipus.

Father Teiresias made me feel at ease. He waved me to a seat across from his desk. When he smiled and said, "Please call me Ted," I realized I'd never seen a priest in a sweatshirt before and something about him made me miss Mitchell more sharply than I ever had before.

I wanted more than anything to leave Nicolet City with the kids, and I told the priest that the uncle who raised me had backed my husband in keeping the children there, though he'd known about Cal's abusive behavior.

Father Teiresias didn't appear surprised but looked at me like a seer looking into the future. "Don't panic or look too far ahead," he advised. "If you don't get another job, there's welfare."

"My greatest fear is having the kids taken away. My ex-husband said he would, if I couldn't support them. I went to the bank to see how much my house was worth if I had to sell it, but what I owe him is secured by it."

"If they were taken away," the priest said, "you'd value them all the more."

"Oh! How could I ever deal with that? I'd be out on a limb by myself just like my ex-husband predicted."

"If you had to, you would." He shook his head and predicted, "Both of you having six month custody isn't natural and won't last."

"My hope is that if Cal remarries, his wife won't want them."

"The woman usually gets the kids and support money," he said, and slowly added, "But I've heard of those with influence getting their way in small towns." After a moment, he took up a chain of paper clips, added some, and said, "It's taken a long time to get in this situation, and it'll take time getting out."

"My uncle got upset when I said I'd answered an ad for a window cleaning job. I told him it was better than working as a barmaid."

"What did he say to that?"

I looked down, recalling his string of swear words, and admitted, "He wasn't pleased."

When I looked back up, he seemed to know what I'd omitted, so I continued, "If I were to go to confession, I don't know what I'd confess," then added with a smile, "But if I feel like that, I'm guilty of Presumption and Pride, am I not?"

He returned my smile and said, "Trust God, but do as much as you can. You could have your marriage annulled so you could marry in the Church, but you'd better wait in case you decide to marry a Protestant." When I didn't reply he pushed up the sleeves of his sweatshirt and confided, "You know, I've found that people here have a defeatist attitude and don't have much ambition."

"I've long tried to understand that."

"If your ex-husband gets married, it'll open new doors for you and it will be like he died. Perhaps his new wife won't like playing nursemaid as you hope, but the chances of changing things legally are small and you'd best accept it and face the future."

Accepting things wasn't what I wanted to hear, so I changed the subject, saying, "It must be hard listening to so many people's troubles."

"I have it easier because I don't live them," he said, "and when people leave my office they take their troubles with them." I wasn't sure if he was being ironic or not when he added, "I'm really very lucky."

Father Teiresias straightened the large calendar from Stan's Gas on his desk, put his elbows on it and leaned forward. "I hope you don't have trouble with God being a He," he said. "With your background, that would be hard to take. Do you think you'll remarry?"

His lips were expressive and sharply defined. He had no business having sensitive lips like Mitchell's; a priest shouldn't have such thick wavy hair, or look like he'd just come from playing tennis.

"I don't know," I said and stared at a stack of thick red paperback books behind him, with the title, *Vatican Council II: The Conciliar and Post Conciliar Documents.* My brother Vincent had given me one, as well as a devotional book he said was similar to what nuns used.

As if reading my mind Father Teiresias confided, "You know, I've found that women here don't want to be liberated."

"Sometimes I really envy their peace of mind," I said, and wondered again why he had to be my age and good looking as I stared again at the stack of red paperbacks, restraining myself from verbalizing about women being like sheep. Given the Good Shepherd parable, I didn't think he'd appreciate it.

"I'm considering becoming a waitress," I said, "since there aren't openings here for what college prepared me for."

"Don't do that," he said. "The way men treat waitresses may finish you off. Hold out for a professional opening."

After telling me about some church activities I could attend, he glanced at his watch and said, "Just don't be a Phoenix that stays in the fire too long, or you won't be able to rise in the updraft. Feel free to make another appointment."

I didn't know if I believed in God, but it felt safer to retain my Catholic school teaching that a priest was God's representative on earth. I didn't make another appointment so I never got to share Elie Wiesel's experience in the Holocaust: "Never shall I forget those moments which murdered my God and my soul and turned my dreams to dust."

Not knowing what else to do, I wrote a letter:

Dear God:

Dear God doesn't sound a proper salutation; there's no recipient address because I'm not sure where Heaven is.

I'll just begin by saying as a creator you could've made human nature less bloodthirsty—even less indifferent so we wouldn't boil what we eat while it's still alive. And the arrogance to rule everything. How can man be made in your image when we're destroying the planet? And keep having wars with rape the common side dish?

As a maker of countless galaxies you could've come up with a better combination than the closely related land mines of love and sex. And why a virgin birth? And you could've planned things better so whole species don't keep dying out.

I do not see much evidence that you are Love when, in order to live, we must eat living things. The world's full of the dying from lack of food and water, not to mention earthquakes, tsunamis, hurricanes, and epidemics. War lords prosper.

At least when you're in Heaven it's easier to guess about such commandments such as "I am the Lord thy God." In that famous icon of your finger stretching to meet Adam's, they do not meet. Michelangelo's ceiling fresco portrays Eve so small as if a different species, an onlooker in shadow.

It is said many unbelievers pray to you when they are about to die. Aging, by the way, the indignity of falling apart, isn't a gracious precursor to you. The Greeks had goddesses too and didn't pile on guilt and fear. Still, would we pray if we weren't afraid of the afterlife of "weeping and gnashing of teeth" mentioned seven times in the Bible?

My conclusion is that deities are of human origin and I am not sure if my prayers come from conditioning in the first grade when the nun said if we were bad the cracks in the floor would widen and we'd fall into Hell, or from some deeper need.

Since men acquired power in patriarchal tribes (and things change slowly), you are a male god. Why did so many women become saints for refusing men? Have the rules for canonization changed?

Women need new paths. To find our way out of the old labyrinths requires more than one lifetime.

Sincerely,
Lily Alger Hyde

***

I dreaded thinking about Mark and Jenny moving back to Cal's in September and having them only on weekends. When the kids left, I cried and cried until I became afraid I'd never pull myself together to begin a new job the next day.

Maize, my cat, followed me around the empty house as I repeated the words of St. Francis, "Only by dying to ourselves do we live. Make me a channel of your peace. Where there is hatred, let me bring your love."

Father Wisniewski had said, "When you pray, 'Give us this day our daily bread,' it doesn't say for a year; prayer's a continuous effort."

I desperately wanted God to be real, and be able to experience what Oral Roberts had said, "God meets us wherever we are."

Dr. Schackmann said, "People are attracted to those who have inner security," and I hoped God was using me to make Cal a believer so he'd change and we'd be a family again.

After Mrs. Stoke wrote, "Your relationship with Cal can only be repaired through God," I hummed the hymn with the words of St. Francis, "Master, grant that I may never seek so much to be consoled as to console, to be understood as to understand."

I recalled Mrs. Stoke's dimly lit church during early weekday mass, where a few elderly women knelt far apart, their rosaries rattling against wooden pews the only sound breaking the silence before mass. The candles in red votive holders gave off the familiar scent of beeswax. But the peace ended when the priest broke the rituals of the mass by saying in his short sermon, "Accept things the way they are because it's God's will."

I'd felt like standing up and protesting loudly in the nearly empty church, "Accept things? How can you accept things? Don't you see what goes on around you?"

***

One evening I came upon a report about the Catholic Church by a group called the Victims of Priest Abuse. A spokesperson said that no less than the credibility of Holy Mother the Church was at stake; a second grader had been raped by a priest in school and was told never to tell or she'd burn in Hell.

I flipped channels to a CNN program, "The Arrogance of Power, the Marginalization of Women." It said clericalism must be uprooted or else the abuse would continue, and bishops didn't trust the laity composing ninety-nine percent of the Church.

The first victim was breaking silence to relieve the pain. After thirty-five years, he said, he realized that he shouldn't have directed his anger at himself, that the seduction of children is a result of taking advantage of the affection a child needs. But an abused child feels worthless. The victim became an alcoholic and was still in counseling. Uncovering the abuse is like peeling an onion, he said, and destructive coping skills are often developed.

The second speaker was abused in his home when he was six. The priest was a respected relative, so he thought it was his fault. He had had years of counseling and medication, struggling to keep his fourth marriage going.

A bishop had abused the third speaker. He'd wanted to become a priest, and he did, but felt at fault for what happened. To free himself he told what happened but the Church blamed him for telling, so he left the religious life after a breakdown. His perpetrator became a cardinal.

An illuminated picture of the Virgin Mary with the baby Jesus was in the background as people spoke. That and the bright clothes of the women helpers, provided color in the crowd of clergymen.

The last victim said she was molested by a priest. It left her feeling a fraud, and not wanting to leave her house. She believed that programs should be in all Catholic schools so kids could protect themselves, and that the church must not turn away from the horror.

The next speaker said that one-third of the women around the world are abused before they're eighteen; that victims seek love, and perpetrators know this; that secrecy is the cornerstone of abuse. A child remains silent because they think (in most cases rightly so) no one will help, and children need the fantasy of believing someone would help if it were known. The shock of the trauma is so overwhelming that the victim retreats into dissociation to preserve sanity, and though that might seem to afford protection, it leads to a trapped existence. Traumatized people lose their ability to integrate what's happened. Post-traumatic stress disorder is so hard to stop because it is self-perpetuating. To fight it, the victim must mourn, go through soul-fragmenting pain, face what they've lost, and accept that the past can never be restored.

The term "soul-fragmenting pain" echoed at the conference, referring to the effects of abuse. And the pain of the victims, the horror of having them say aloud what I hadn't completely admitted yet, kept slamming at me. The victims all looked like regular people, which surprised me as I thought it set you apart as surely as if your forehead had been branded SPOILED GOODS or SLAP ME.

That night, I again had the vivid dream of waiting for an airplane to crash. The plane leaned at various angles and changed directions. I tried to see where it would crash so I'd know which way to run, but it kept shifting. In other versions of the dream, no one would look when I pointed to the plane about to slam into the earth.

The day Cal got married I knelt by the side of my bed, knowing the kids would have a stepmother the next time I saw them. I wondered what Aunt Hester and Uncle Walt had felt at the wedding. Did the kids think of me?

A few days later, when I went to pick up Mark and Jenny at Uncle Walt's, Aunt Hester showed me Cal and Rachel's honeymoon postcards while Uncle Walt watched *The Lawrence Welk Show*.

Dirk Bailey

When the kids were in high school, my obsessions about strays again drove me back into counseling. I saw in the *Nicolet County News* that a psychologist, Nicolet City's first, had opened a practice. I made an appointment.

Dirk didn't have Dr. Schackmann's accent, and in fact looked as American as the Fourth of July. He was average in looks. His office seemed made for Penn's "Treaty with the Indians" and the "Midnight Ride of Paul Revere " on the gray and pink faux marble wallpaper. Dirk looked younger than I was, which made me feel safer. When he shook my hand, I noticed his wedding band.

He looked at the questionnaire I'd filled out and told me that in cases where there'd been child incest, United Way would cover most of the charges for counseling. I was relieved to hear that, even if it made me feel as if I was on welfare. To change the subject, I said, "How do you like Nicolet City?"

"Everyone's been very friendly," he said, and motioned to his desk where there was a photograph of his family. "My wife and daughters, though, miss the stores in Minneapolis."

"When I moved, I did, too."

He nodded and smiled. "We feel we're old members in the Prince of Peace Methodist Church already." I'd heard that he was already a well-liked Sunday school teacher. "I grew up in a small town in Minnesota, so it's like coming home."

After I'd told him about some of the sports opportunities for children, I plunged in, saying, "I want to get rid of my obsessions about strays."

"I see you sought help twelve years ago," he said, peering at my paperwork.

I looked down at my white knuckles, then made myself look at him. "The psychiatrist made advances," I said.

He regarded me for a second, then said, "It's good that you told me right off. You never have to worry about that with me." His eyes didn't falter as he spoke, and he sounded sincerely angry when he added, "That psychiatrist was only thinking of his own needs, not yours."

***

While waiting to get my car fixed, I recalled telling Dr. Schackmann years before, "I'm tired of trying to change things, because it just makes you alien to your environment," and when he hadn't responded, I'd added, "Cal says there's friction between you."

He'd folded his arms on his chest and said, "I wasn't aware of any."

Through the window of his office, I saw cars streaming back and forth beyond a spruce tree whose top was leaning from an ice storm. I hoped it would right itself rather than break.

On the drive home, I wondered what I'd do if I left Cal.

Uncle Walt had sent me to college, emphasizing the importance of finding a professional husband, and when I married Cal, I felt that I was repaying my uncle.

When I'd told Dr. Schackmann I was considering ending my sessions with him, he had said if I did, we wouldn't get around to discussing our relationship. I wondered if he knew what he was doing, but also wondered if loving him was my shortcut to finding out what kind of man he was.

I did my telephoning for the bake sale and selected my best-canned relishes for the county fair; Cal continued to fall asleep in front of the television before I finished the dinner dishes. And there were parent-teacher conferences for Mark and Jenny, and Uncle Walt's birthday dinner, picnics, so many things to think about and plan for. But I couldn't stop my mind from drifting back to those last sessions with Dr. Schackmann.

In the next session, he had avoided anything personal and smoked for the first time, inhaling with short jerky puffs after using several matches to light his cigarette.

I remember saying, "Everything is six one way and half a dozen the other."

"If you can't figure out things," he'd said, "it's best to go back to when things were simpler and let time decide things."

"If I were to get a divorce, I don't know if I wouldn't go and get myself in another mess."

"It's best to work on yourself and feel secure before you decide," he'd said. With that special look I'd recall often in between sessions, he added, "You know I'm available to you day or night."

In the next session, which had taken place in his new office, he'd worn a suit for the first time, and asked me what I thought of the place.

"It's very nice," I'd said, looking around the stucco room for familiar objects from his old office.

He was located an hour and a half from Nicolet City in a town where storefronts and municipal building had been recently renovated on a classical Greece theme. Greek plays were performed at the fairgrounds during the summer, restaurants offered traditional Greek food, and musicians in colorful costumes gave street performances.

"Cal got angry," I had told Dr. Schackmann, "because I was out picking apples with the kids and I wasn't there when he got home. He shoved me around when I got back."

"Did he hurt you?"

"He didn't leave any marks," I'd said, not thinking that the bruises on my upper arms counted because they were covered by my sleeves.

"Do you think you were right in going?"

"It was right, but not right in the relationship of marriage." I had hesitated and added, "Cal doesn't want me to get a job."

"It isn't wise to come to any crisis now," Dr. Schackmann had advised.

While canning corn relish, I thought again of what he'd said about the law of compensation: when you lose something you gain something. And I smiled at the comforting sound of canning lids sealing. But the next day I worried about worms dying in a can that Cal had left on his boat, "Belly Achers," after he went fishing.

It seemed the only way to comfort myself was to imagine being with Dr. Schackmann. When I went anywhere, I looked at men to see if their nose, mouth, or walk in any way resembled his. I kept telling myself, hang on, hang on, hang on, and remembered the tree in the woods near my grandfather's barb-wire fence—dead except for one branch. For the past two years, I'd gone to the woods to stare at it as the kids made a game out of not stepping on any sticks while chasing each other. When it had lost its last branch one spring, I was glad no one saw it die—it was too private, too sad after hanging on so long.

That winter, I went for frequent walks with Mark and Jenny, muffled in my jacket. The wind often made it too cold to walk along the lake shore, strewn with blocks of ice as from the Ice Age. It was on one of these walks when I concluded that winter was the most honest of the seasons. It didn't hide things like green summer leaves did; a red strip on a freighter in the distant channel was the only thing interfering with what I saw as being a black and white painting. As I looked for patches of moss on trees, Mark found depressions in the snow and told Jenny they were Bigfoot's. Jenny pretended to be scared, smiled at me and took my hand.

When we returned to the road, a sunbeam shone on the top of a large bent pine, creating the image of a question mark. I walked back and forth looking at it until a hawk began circling. Mark scrambled up and down a snow bank heaped up by the county plow. Jenny tried to keep up.

We walked to the tree-lined winding stream among the overhanging branches until I heard water running under the ice. Hearing the water without being able to see it brought a feeling of peace and relief. A plan must exist, I thought. Things did make sense, and had a pattern. There was a way out even if I couldn't see it. I'd be fine, I'd be fine.

I followed the gurgling water to the lake. As I stood smiling in the biting wind, with tears freezing on my face, a memory of my last session with Dr. Schackmann resurfaced.

It was when I had told Dr. Schackmann that I'd decided to stop coming.

His chair had squeaked, and I knew how much I'd miss that sound.

"I'll always wonder what's on the other side of things," I had told him, "but it's equally bad not to enjoy what's under my nose. Things are better with Cal because I want them to be, and if I left him, I'd still be searching—my feelings for you happened because I needed them to."

I recalled the long silence, in which it seemed he was trying to convey something without words. He'd finally said, "You can come back."

I could still taste the blood from biting the inside of my cheek when I had said, "There's a job coming up I may be able to get. I've enjoyed the sessions, and I'll have to find something to replace them with."

His face had flushed, he'd said, "Maybe studying Hinduism would interest you and give you some direction. I've told you about how meditation helped me." He'd reached for a book with the picture of a bald man on the cover, sitting cross-legged, his thumbs and index fingers forming a circle. But meditating by staring at a point between my eyes never held much appeal for me. "And take lots of walks," he'd said, "because they may teach you more than books."

On the drive home, I tried to forget how he'd laughed when I'd said, "Things are better with Cal because I need them to be."

***

I felt relieved and grateful that Dirk didn't appear to think any less of me after I told him about Dr. Schackmann. After several more sessions, my trust in him increased. I confided, "When I was at Aunt Hester and Uncle Walt's for dinner, she said her cousin's girls were afraid of Uncle Walt's hugs and kisses. She said she told them it was the way he showed them he liked them."

Dirk's left eyebrow raised. "And you don't feel that way?"

"No."

"Trust your instincts," he said.

I looked out the window but couldn't see the street below through the fog, only the false square fronts of brick buildings erected in the late 1800's. They presented a solid front, hugging the curve in Nicolet River like a set of false teeth, except for the gaps where some had been torn down. I'd seen pictures of white pine logs jamming the river with men standing on them as they headed to the lumber mills.

As a child, I liked going into the city's only department store, where pulleys shuttled money in metal containers to pale clerks perched on the second floor like angels. There were tables of feathered hats, drawers full of buttons, bolts of all kinds of cloth in the dim light. The hardwood aisles dipped in the middle from wear. The descendants of that department store ruled the city's society, and a historic marker in front of their Victorian home was on the Nicolet City Historical Society Annual Tour of Homes.

Nicolet City was known for its largest sand pile in the state. The huge mound overlooking the Nicolet River was a legacy of lumbering days when the river had to be regularly dredged and was said to be frozen at its core even in summer and to conceal skeletons of horses that'd fallen through. It guarded Nicolet City like a pyramid of the Nile, and its only enemy was high wind. Children didn't bother it because of buried hobo tales from the 1930's.

The sound of a psychiatrist's throat being cleared snapped me out of my muse and back into my chair in Dirk's office. He was located in a Victorian house built when white pine made Nicolet City boom. The house, surrounded by tall elms and maples, had a large porch with white wicker rockers. The carved oak door opening to a hall and staircase gave way to an interior with massive marble fireplaces, urns full of dried flowers, and narrow windows with borders of stained glass. The waiting room had carved acanthus leaf molding joined by a border of roses circling the high plaster ceiling.

At the next session, I told Dirk about giving Uncle Walter an article I'd written. "He was watching a baseball game," I said, "and he told me he'd look at it if I opened the magazine to the right page. But when the game was over, he just said it took a hell of a lot of money to raise kids and it was nice that I had a hobby and waved his cigar to show me where to leave it."

Aunt Hester had been dusting her Hummel figurine, Apple Tree Boy, the one with the bird that had eyes like her glass one. Her hands had blue veins like the veined marble in their bathroom. The few times I could recall that she ever touched me, her hands were just as cold as the marble.

I didn't tell Dirk that Uncle Walt had watched most of the game while sitting on the toilet with the door open, or that I knew he'd be coming out when I heard the faucet turned on. As a child, I thought Uncle Walt didn't close the door because he liked people and didn't want to miss what was going on, and that the unused squares of toilet paper replaced on the roll and the unflushed toilet showed thriftiness.

Aunt Hester left the tightly closed bathroom smelling of bleach, with squashed insects in the basket; Uncle Walt left it smelly with National Rifle Association mail. Aunt Hester went through so many bottles of toilet cleaner that, as a child, I kept expecting to catch the pine tree man or the lemon lady featured on labels on the toilet tank.

Dirk chuckled. "Why didn't you get mad at him?"

"Mad at him?"

"When he so cavalierly dismissed your article."

I shrugged. It was just the way it'd always had been with Uncle Walt. I didn't tell him about Uncle Walt walking around inside and outside the house in his white boxer shorts, and his amusement at my discomfort.

"You need to seek people who're supportive," Dirk said. "You're obviously very capable, and your obsessions about abandoned animals are a way of coping."

Dirk drew a sketch on the board depicting a prisoner of war camp surrounded by brick walls. "When help came," he said, "the prisoners discovered one of the walls was made of paper."

What he was trying to make me see wasn't clear at all so I told Dirk, "The first thing I recall had to memorize in grade school was to 'Love and serve God in this world and in the next.' Then I learned about honoring your mother and father, which was doubly binding if you'd been adopted. Being obedient was the same as being a well-brought-up Catholic girl." I'd been corralled as surely as a customer I recently followed at Burger King, who approached the labyrinth of railings leading to the counter like a sheep entering a corral.

When I left Dirk to get the kids at the gym, I smiled at several birds perched on utility wires like beads on an abacus.

***

I was thirsty one morning and couldn't stop thinking about a cat across the road being thirsty because I wasn't sure the owner was around. Then I realized that I was projecting what I felt on the cat.

The realization had made me so shaky, the next day I fell at work. I put out my right hand to break the fall while the sidewalk rose to meet me in slow motion. When I got home, my hand was severely swollen and black and blue so I went to the hospital emergency room. When they told me it was broken, I remembered that the mother/wife of Oedipus had warned him not to pursue the truth.

At the next session, I said, "Don't bring up any new things. I'm feeling fragile right now," and I told Dirk about falling to explain the cast I had on.

He looked at me closely, folded his arms and said, "If it gets too bad, you can go back to the obsessions."

I stared at his shoes, trying to absorb his presence and warmth. He was real; he existed. I could see him breathe, and I yearned to absorb his warmth to blot out the terror and feel safe.

After a long pause, he said, "Your hand will heal. You've made a big breakthrough."

I wanted to move my foot closer to his, to feel the warmth of human comfort. I made myself look up, and said, "Is what I project on strays what I feel?" I knew the answer before I asked, because it had the feel of other truths that'd slammed into place.

"Yes, it is," he said.

I stared at the arm of his long-sleeve plaid shirt and counted how many different shades of blue and brown were in it, tracing squares with my index finger on the arm of the chair. My finger moved imperceptibly when I dipped in and out of the squares. I forced myself not to stay in one of those warm havens too long because I'd never want to leave. I strained to hear his pulse, seeing his shirt rise and fall, and compared where his T-shirt sleeves ended under his shirt on both arms. I forbid myself to imagine his naked arm. Doing so made me dizzy. He smelled of clothes that had been dried outside, but I knew I could've made them smell even fresher. Dr. Schackmann hadn't worn T-shirts under his shirts, and he'd left several shirt buttons undone, revealing his gold chain.

Such thoughts had to be ended before Dirk guessed them, so I said, "It's awful finding out. I don't know if I can really understand and not be pulled under."

I absorbed more of his presence by keeping his arm in view as I studied the nicked wainscoting behind him. The hot water register gurgled, chugged, and hissed as I studied the shades of gray and pink in the faux wallpaper; a beeping horn below came from some world far away. I knew I had to remember as much as I could of the room, of him, to stave off the terror when I left.

In a thankfully normal voice, I heard myself say, "Having the kids around to look after and doing routine things like washing the dishes helps. I'm trying to understand, but don't know if I want to or if I ever can."

"You're doing very well," he said. "I want you to tell yourself that."

When I looked at him again, he was looking at me so intently that I averted my eyes to the stained glass white dove with a black branch in its beak at the top of the window, hoping he hadn't seen me flush. Then I made myself look out the window.

I couldn't see the river because of the buildings and trees across the street, but I imagined it winding its journey through town to join Lake Michigan, one of the Great Lakes called the Inland Seas. Main Street hugged the river as if it didn't trust it out of its sight. It was uncertain where the Nicolet River started; it was somewhere miles south, where water drained into streams formed during recession of the last Ice Age. Trees bending over the river with their roots and stumps near the banks, added to the secret atmosphere of the deep water dark even at noon. A few miles to the south, the Nicolet widened where it was joined by the Cloutier.

Cal and I had looked at a house on the banks of this convergence when we left Detroit after the race riots. I was glad that Cal thought the house needed too much work, because the strong currents constantly eating at the steep banks made it not seem a safe place to raise children.

It was an overcast day, and I was thankful for that, imagining I could hide in it, that it hid my stunned expression in a way a sunny room wouldn't. When Dirk said, "I can help you get a new coat to protect you, instead of the obsessions," I looked down at his brown shoes. They were plain shoes; he didn't wear wing tips or double tie his laces like Cal had, nor did he wear suede shoe boots like Dr. Schackmann. His shoes were the kind in Sears and J.C. Penney catalogues.

Please God, I prayed, don't let him be a fraud.

I knew that to be put back in a hole another time would be terrible. I never wanted to love again like I'd loved Dr. Schackmann. It's true what they say about loving deeply—nothing is the same again.

At the end of the session, I looked around the room to remember it: the stained glass white dove; the wicker basket with the frayed handle holding cattails, heather, and baby's breath; the Sam's Small Engines calendar with its picture of Sam leaning over a green Lawn-Boy; the faux marble gray and pink wallpaper furling like ostrich feathers in a Victorian fan; the places where the wooden floor dipped; the exact tan of Dirk's socks.

I breathed deeply, to take in some of the air he'd breathed. When I left, my finger tips free of the cast clung to the smooth security of the worn oak railing. I didn't hear the heavy, carved door close or the dead, dry leaves under my feet.

Thomas Hirsch

One snowy afternoon I saw Thomas Hirsch looking for my house, standing in the road with his coat blowing in the wind. He wore what Uncle Walt called "a damn Russian Cossack hat," with the jutting earflaps giving him the profile of a pitcher with handles. I'd called the newspaper after reading his appeal for memorabilia on the local opera house. I put on my coat and ran out to meet him.

Thomas rarely took the time to button the cuffs of his shirts, so he was affectionately called "Cuffs." His wife had taught adult education art for years and was a respected portrait painter. When I took his coat and hat, I saw a pair of Mark's underwear, he'd put on a chair when I went outside, and whisked them into my pocket. I heard him snickering in his room.

Under his shirt Thomas wore a T-shirt that said WORLD'S GREATEST GRANDFATHER. His large round eyes, and his brows shaped like inverted V's, gave him a startled look. I knew he was hard of hearing. Some people said he just pretended to be, so they'd speak openly around him and he could gather tidbits for the newspaper, at which he was a reporter. They said he could hear very well clear across a room when something was newsworthy, but if someone under his nose wanted free publicity, he'd lean forward, shake his head, and tap his hearing aid.

I, too, was becoming acquainted with selective hearing. Odysseus put wax in his sailors' ears so they wouldn't be tempted by the Sirens; I kept earplugs in to not hear people talk about lost animals.

After Thomas smoothed back his hair and dried his glasses, I showed him my grandfather's plate. He was delighted, took a few pictures, and then said, "Have you been doing any more writing since your book on Wisconsin geology?" He smiled encouragingly and commented, "You're such a remarkable lady!" but I didn't believe him.

He always seemed sincerely interested in my geology books, so I showed him some of the boxes of source material I'd gathered and he shook his head and said, "I'm amazed at all that hard work you do. It takes you hours upon hours just to collect the material. How do you do it when you work too?"

"Because of budgetary problems at Centerville," I told him, "I'm only working part-time now, and I like to keep busy."

Even as I said it, I realized I felt guilty for talking about my work, as if I was flaunting my independence. In fact, my writing was a secret source of security for me. Whatever else was happening, however frightened or terror-stricken I felt, I knew it was something I could do. But now, asked to talk about it, it seemed that if I acknowledged the success I'd had, I'd be saying that my adoptive father and ex-husband hadn't measured up, that I didn't properly regard men as the head of a household, just as Christ was the head of the Church. I could still hear Aunt Hester's hushed church voice telling me about the Catholic girl's role in helping men get to Heaven. And how could I be competent when I wasn't able to protect myself growing up or been able to keep my family together?

According to the Church, Cal, Uncle Walt and Aunt Hester, and most others, the blame was mine. Cutting up my old clothes and those of the children's and sewing them together to make quilts was one way of going back to my proper role as a woman. Maybe the Church had been right in saying that sex and marriage was for the procreation of children. But where did love come in, or was it one of nature's tricks?

When I gave Thomas the inch mat of compressed mosses, liverworts, and fossils I'd found when burying leaves, a specimen similar to one I studied in college, his gratitude was sincere and made me glad I was able to share my interest in the past with him. I'd held the specimen many times, trying to will it to give me clues about how life began. Knowing that glaciers shaped the landscape around me always filled me with awe. It seemed that the gouging and relentless movement of immense sheets of ice, miles thick, had happened only yesterday, that Lake Michigan lapping close by still had ice under the water with fantastic secrets. Knowing how the ground I walked upon was formed made it feel more stable and helped make things predictable, less likely to split open into a black pit and swallow me. And yet, knowing the Ice Age could have been caused by a change in the orbit of the earth around the sun wasn't very reassuring. Nor was knowing that all species die. I wasn't ready to admit that the life force that compelled me not to give up was intertwined with the drive to love and to understand, like a ball of twine without an end or beginning. A tight ball that, no matter how hard I tried, wouldn't unravel. Perhaps Caroline was right when she advised, "Don't look to this world or in yourself, lift your eyes to Heaven."

Wisconsin was shaped by the past, a past determined long before man. To help ground me, I got out my childhood atlas and once again was reassured that Wisconsin was surrounded by Lake Superior on the north and Lake Michigan on the east; its western boundary was Minnesota, Iowa; the southern was Illinois. By the way the roads converged, you could tell Milwaukee and Madison were the main cities. The Great Lakes were dwarfed by Hudson Bay on a map of Canada. Milwaukee was the only city noted in Wisconsin; straight red veins (railroads) radiated from it.

On my globe, Wisconsin is an orange spot surrounded by green Minnesota, yellow Iowa, pink Illinois; the Upper Peninsula of Michigan is sandwiched between the blue of Lakes Michigan and Superior. The globe squeaked when I turned it to French West Africa. The name Anglo-Egyptian reminded me of a hyphenated name of a modern bride.

The globe was made in Chicago but had no date; an eagle with outspread wings clutched branches over the LEGEND showing three dots for Ruins, a long blue line for Steamship Routes, blue dashes for Glaciers, and symbols for other man made and natural features. The Population Classification for Cities was indicated by the size of the dots, and the capitals by stars. The LEGEND was between the North Pacific Ocean and the South Pacific Ocean, the Marquesas Islands (Fr.) on the left, and the expanse of blue water on the right.

Under the stand I'd written: "Lily Alger, Grade 6, Age 11, 3/11/51, Sunday." There were traces of rose decals I'd applied long ago below Alaska to make the expanse of the North Pacific Ocean less empty. The globe still was a pleasure to hold, to look at. It still felt solid, provided security. To think of all those who had done so much to fill in the uncharted land and dare to go beyond the Ultima Thule, the unknown, was a delight. Places far away like Drake Passage, the Weddell Sea, Port Darwin were there. But it was a little sad too, that there were no more uncharted areas although who knew what the vast oceans hid? Seeing pictures of the earth from space partly obscured by clouds without the neat pastel divisions into countries had been an unforgettable revelation.

The North Pole had a sunrise, sunset, high noon, midnight moveable circle so you could tell time all around the world once you pointed the current time where you were. I found that the sun was setting in Ireland, and rising over the Territory of Hawaii.

The amount of water covering the earth was so overwhelming I wondered why fish hadn't evolved and ruled everything. As the globe revolved, I could've been looking at the very spot where my ancestors evolved. The continental drift had once sounded too fantastic, but when I saw how the coast of eastern South America and the western coast of Africa fit together like an old married couple, it was unreasonable not to accept it.

***

When I told Dirk about my visits to Mrs. Simons, he laughed and said, "You don't go to the desert to get a drink of water. Half the people I see shouldn't be coming to see me—it's their families that should be—and you're one of them."

I also told him about Thomas Hirsch, and said, "Do you think I should've given Thomas information about my situation? I mean, my job being part-time, and trying to make ends meet?"

"Go right ahead," he said. "Why shouldn't you let it be known you're doing so much because your bastard of an uncle won't help?"

I was so taken aback that it took a moment before I said, "But it'd show him up."

He folded his arms on his chest. "You've more than paid your dues, Lily." I was surprised that being a Christian he'd say that.

Dirk's office had become a sunny oasis I didn't want to leave. I prayed that he would indeed turn out to be the good man he seemed, to make up for Uncle Walt, Cal, and Dr. Schackmann. Between sessions, Dirk was on my mind more, but I was determined not to repeat the dependency I'd fallen into with Dr. Schackmann.

Losing Dirk

It was spring. As I sat with Dirk in his office he looked at me intently for a long time. I imagined he could hear my thoughts willing him to help me out of the terror I felt seeing an animal that could be a stray. Please, I exhorted him silently as if reciting a prayer: I want to live. Help me to live.

Time stopped. I was only conscious of him looking at me, and of the beam of sunshine on the hardwood floor between us. I suppose I didn't want to recall that other time when he regarded me the same way, when he brought his chair closer to me and moved his pelvis in an odd thrusting motion as he continued to stare. It reminded me of Uncle Walt's excited male dogs that humped visitor's legs. I tried to forget it, telling myself it couldn't be that—he'd never do anything so suggestive. I averted my eyes.

When I'd seen the thrusting movements, I'd almost asked him if there was something wrong with him. But I didn't want to call attention to what I didn't want to see. To say anything, after all he'd done for me, would've sounded ungrateful.

No one else in Nicolet City besides Caroline and Dirk saw Uncle Walt the way I did. And who would believe me if I said I'd seen Dirk do something questionable? He was a valued community member, a Sunday school teacher, someone trained to help others. Wouldn't Caroline stop being my friend if I suggested something like that about him, a fellow Christian?

A few days later, when a beam of sunshine stretched across the floor in my house and almost reached the computer screen, I felt a wave of warmth for Dirk, as though I loved him. How could that be? Feelings of anger, pleasure, surprise, disbelief, and denial rushed over me as if they'd escaped from Pandora's box. I tried to push them back but couldn't. I wondered if it wouldn't be wiser not to go back, but Pascal came to mind: "One must love even if all the evidence denies the emotion."

Everything looked different. I thought that it had to be transparent to everyone that I was in love. I resented the time when I wasn't able to think of Dirk, to see his plaid shirts smelling of fresh air, the way his hair was parted, his smile, the muscles in his thighs and arms. I'd found shoes like his in the J.C. Penney catalogue and would stare at them, as if I could feel the warmth coming from them. I'd admire their solidity, dream about what he was doing and when I'd see him again. It felt like typical teenager behavior. Something I'd never known because of Uncle Walt's constant dominating inquisitions of me about boys.

I'd forgotten how much love and spring went together and to ignore what I felt was like telling the grass not to turn green. I kept hearing the words of the song: "I never heard birds singing before I meet you." I moved my houseplants outside, mowed the lawn, dug up the garden, washed windows, started another quilt, and lost my need to drink a half glass of Gallo wine to help me sleep.

Jenny said Mark skipped school on senior skip day but that was okay--he was with some good kids: lately he'd been like a volcano waiting to erupt. I got him an unabridged dictionary and clothes for graduation. He received awards for leadership, sports, and was voted 'Most Handsome Boy' in the senior class.

After going to an open house for one of Mark's friends, I felt I should see Uncle Walt and Aunt Hester. When I did, my uncle handed me a copy of a story about a dog named Sex and what his master did with him, saying, "Here, use this in your columns to increase circulation."

He was referring to the columns I was writing for the *Chicago Tribune* about geographic trivia on the Midwest. It was a freelance job that I'd gotten after sending samples of the work I'd done for various magazines and was grateful for the extra money.

To dispel my uncle's words, I remembered the warmth of Dirk's smile. When he smiled at me in that special way, it brought up feelings I thought never possible again.

It was how I'd felt with Boyd. I was nineteen and in my second year at college. He was my first boyfriend, the first to say I looked like a flower. When I returned to the dorm after we had taken one of our walks by the river, I knew something had changed, but it took me several days to realize that the ache I felt was love. I knew nobody could have explained it, no matter how hard they tried--what I'd read or heard about love hadn't even come close. I'd wanted to be with Boyd all the time but knew Uncle Walt's expectations for a husband didn't include a teacher, and I wanted to please him since he and my aunt had raised me.

I thought of getting an earlier appointment with Dirk, but I didn't want to end the blissful reverie that I knew wouldn't last. When I saw him again, he didn't refer to our previous session but began "I heard at a regional meeting that the psychiatrist you saw was known for having affairs with women patients."

Why, of all times, had he told me that now? I stared at the stained glass white dove with anesthetized numbness.

So, other women patients had fallen for Dr. Schackmann, and, unlike me, some had loved him with more than their souls. I thought I'd been so special, and when Dr. Schackmann had told me, "You're deeply in love with me," it made me love him even more. "There won't be anything physical or seductive between us," he'd said, "because I don't think it's ethical. A physician's role is to heal and never hurt."

But it was his advances that prevented my lawyer from having him as my witness to support me when I wanted to move away with the kids. I'd been keeping a diary which Cal had been reading. It had never occurred to me that he would do that because it was something I'd never do to him. I found the diary and mustered up enough courage to read an entry:

Dr. Schackmann said that I was the one that had to believe I was OK. That when he was in therapy, nothing could convince him—his intelligence, his looks, how he got along with others—he had to accept the fact himself. I said being next to another color influenced colors but he said I wasn't a color.

Thank goodness I had enough sense to tell him how I stood with his advances—that it wouldn't get me anyplace. He said it took guts. I told him he said if I changed, my relationship with Cal would, but it hadn't. Doctor said he was treating me as if I was an OK person. So if I am OK how can I regard myself that way when Cal doesn't? Don't I want him to? That it would mean dealing with Cal as an adult and I am afraid of that—because I'd find out he wasn't what I wanted? He had me read what I wrote on the pro and con reality of good:

Purity is remaining in tune with what is good. Good is beauty. Beauty is soul. Soul is recognition of an individual's connection with what is not understandable but what exists. It cannot be proven but the essence of a God or an all embracing plan or cosmos comes out and cannot be disclaimed by the mind. It may be just in man's mind because that is all he has, or it might be the need is so great. Like a child's need to always finish an uncompleted circle.

In the physical sense it is being in tune with another who values what you do or gives you a better understanding of the best in you. Impurity or perversion is destruction to your soul, which is your first priority if you are to have any peace. Not peace, but a continual growing of what is best in you. That is what should be. But how much of it is reality? Experience has shown me that reality has little respect for purity. Purity, or what is good, seems to be recognized but only because it cannot be ignored and is dealt with cynically.

What I feel for you is without evil. It is of beauty and an affirmation of good. It is a way of recognizing my soul and defining it. It is obtaining an awareness of good. But I continue to rebel because the beauty is my fantasy. Yet I must accept the reality and believe. So I am back to where I started. Play the system. Don't get out of it. Do not involve yourself in it, but use it because it is reality. Beauty can be sought in the accepted place in society, in art, in acceptable creativity. But to actually live it?

My adult tells me to learn from loving you and to go on and make a better life for myself. Perhaps I still have not recognized what I am and believe in myself enough, to become independent of you. I feel it is only through you I can learn what I need, but only hope I will accept it positively when we say goodbye. It is like discovering the other part of your being and then being alone again.

You said I was trying to find a home and it was like homesickness in defining my soul or what I really am and want. You said you had once given up on idealism but found that beauty or goodness could be lived, more easily though, in some environments than in others. I only hope that I am not being lead down the garden path with my old securities gone and nothing to replace them.

***

My last diary entry was the day before I was married. As the sun set, I remember tying the notebooks with ribbon and packing them away, trying to forget the impression that nothing would ever be the same to pre-marriage jitters. When I trimmed the checked frayed ribbon, the scissors sounded very harsh and final. I remember looking in the mirror afterwards, holding bits of ribbon in my palm, saying goodbye to an apprehensive Lily Alger as the light faded. The mirror was old and made me appear as uneven as the frayed ends of the ribbon in my palm, held upward like an offering to the gods. I packed the diaries away because it seemed my individual life was ending; that to continue them as a wife would be somehow disloyal—it'd be as if I'd not lost my previous life, had not merged as was expected when I became Mrs. Calvin Hyde. I missed my mother very much that night and longed for her to tell me what to expect and if she'd been frightened too.

It was Dirk himself who had pointed out that I had unrealistically high expectations, putting myself down as I elevated others to compensate for Uncle Walt. And I did this with men, he said, because I defined myself by them. A man in one of my classes in Ithaca, that I'd become friends with, once told me that I didn't know how to appreciate good men. He said I saw men's roles as dominating women. It wasn't until years later that I understood what he meant.

Keeping the perfume nearby, Estée Lauder's Azurée, that I'd worn to my sessions with Dirk, helped me. With Dr. Schackmann it'd been Avon's Honeysuckle.

I had two lives: one the everyday, the other with thoughts of Dirk. One evening when the moon was full, I drank in its beauty, jealous that it saw Dirk and I didn't. It seemed so close—as if it'd moved out of its orbit just to prove it was real and give me a link to Dirk. I saw patterns on it so clearly and I somehow knew it'd never be like that again: I felt secure and happy, knowing Dirk existed, and I lived in a caring world without the worry of strays. At the same time, even though I knew this golden haze might be fool's gold like with Dr. Schackmann, I clung to it because I'd be more of a fool not to. The following night it appeared further away, smaller, not luminous white but a bit tinged with yellow, and I could no longer see patterns.

When I next saw Dirk I said, "I'm grateful for the security I feel with you."

He folded his arms on his chest, putting up a shield, it seemed, and said, "I'm moving to Winnebago Bay. A good situation has opened up for me, and I have to take advantage of it."

My smile was automatic and said, "I'm pleased for you," before I realized how much I'd come to depend upon him.

I got up and paced back and forth while he continued to sit with his arms folded. I wanted him to say, "I just wanted to know what you felt about me. I'm not really leaving," and when he didn't, I wanted to shake him until he did.

Afterwards, I remembered that Dr. Schackmann had also told me to walk around when I'd seen him with a wedding ring after taking "some time off"—a ring that looked like a the one from a Cracker Jack box that I'd worn as a tie to him even if it turned my finger green.

In Dirk's office, after he told me he was moving his practice, I sat back down and asked him if I could have an ashtray. When he said he didn't have one, I took a traveling ashtray from my purse and lit a cigarette because it was better than having him see me cry.

He said, "My last day for appointments is August 15th. How many appointments do you want before I leave?"

I stared at the stained-glass white dove and felt like making this the last one, but knew it wouldn't give me time to adjust.

"It would help if you write what you're thinking," he said, "and bring it to me the next time." When I didn't reply, he asked, "Will you do that?"

When I got home, my desire to move right away was so strong that I considered doing it, even if it meant leaving Jenny. I didn't know how I'd feel the next day, or the next week or month and it didn't seem important.

***

The next day I forced myself to visit Mrs. Simons. She showed me how to fold a napkin into a bishop's hat. She gave me some iced tea and we sat on her deck overlooking the lake as she talked about when she was young,. I watched a couple of swans, and when I saw one turn upside down, I realized I'd been seeing things wrong. Dirk had given me a sense of worth. I'd stopped drinking half a glass of wine every night to help me sleep, I'd lost weight, I knew that what I felt for strays was a projection of what I felt, and that when I loved the obsessions went away.

In the future, I believed, Dirk would think of me with pleasure. But I wished my time with him would have been longer. It had also been spring when I first fell in love at nineteen and my time was running out.

I had a vivid dream that I was with a boy from out of town, sightseeing in an old city that often appeared in my dreams: a medieval, ornate city full of ginger-colored, crumbling buildings so large they covered blocks that had no doors. One of us found a cat that was dead, and I was relieved that it was. We were in an alley, and I was overpowered and injected with many needles by evil people. I turned into a white dove and was put with thousands of variegated pigeons in a large courtyard. At night we were experimented on. The only time I had any hope of being rescued was when I was out in the courtyard. I stood in the same place in the front row, where people passed, and rolled my wings in an intricate pattern so someone would recognize I was different and be rescued. Finally, the boy from out of town walked by and recognized me, but though he tried to get me out, he couldn't.

Every time I heard the words of Mr. Mister's popular song, "Broken Wings," "Take these broken wings and learn to fly again and learn to live so free," the dream resurfaced.

To help time go by, I washed all of Jenny's clothes, and, after I'd hung them outside, they looked like day after day of her life in review. I avoided looking at neighbor's yard because I knew there was a squirrel trap there. The squirrels were let go elsewhere, but I didn't want to think about them trapped.

After I told Dirk my vivid dream about the dove and pigeons, he said, "It has a feeling of hopelessness." He leaned forward. "You know I'm the boy from out of town."

He told me that, given my experience with Dr. Schackmann, he didn't think I should have individual sessions with a male therapist in the future. I gave him what he'd asked me to write, and hoped that, after our next, final session I'd be able to carry on without him. I knew I could've continued to see him in Winnebago Bay which was not that far away, but it didn't seem right.

Dirk said, "My wife and daughters are away visiting relatives the rest of the week." He looked at me in an odd self-conscious way, and then gazed at me intently, like Uncle Walt about to tell a dirty joke.

I felt ashamed of that comparison and smiled politely.

"So I'm alone," he added, "and I've been eating my meals out of cans."

He seemed to be expecting something, and I didn't know what to say. Was he hinting for a home cooked meal? Shouldn't I do that, I asked myself, after all he'd done for me?

But I didn't say anything. The next day, when I thought again about the session, it seemed to me that he was making himself available. But the week passed, and I worked on my book, tried on new eye shadow, conditioned my hair, and found myself wishing that at our last session Dirk would say he wasn't leaving.

I also bought a summer dress, new nylons, a slip, shoes, and made a hair appointment.

There were times I felt such a great need for Dirk that everything else seemed unimportant. Had I been a fool not to have responded when he said he was alone? The last words I wrote in my journal, which I'd given him, were: "Going to my last session will be like going to the guillotine. Funny about guillotines—they were invented by a doctor so death would be more humane."

***

As soon as I saw Dirk, I felt his eyes sweep over my new clothes. "I like your new hair style," he said.

My uncle had told me I had nice legs, and I knew they looked their best in nylons which I'd never worn before with Dirk. A part of me didn't want to make it easy for him to leave. He returned what I'd written, with the envelope taped shut. "You should seek out organizations to join and get involved in the community," he told me, then read from a list. He'd smiled at some of the names, because he knew I'd helped start them. Then he said, "You shouldn't end relationships because you're afraid of being left. That's what happened before, and you're doing the same thing now."

When the session was over, he handed me his new business card.

"Best of luck in your new job," I said with a smile, and offered my hand.

He didn't take it. and, for the first time, he let me open the door myself.

The next day, while working on a quilt, I realized that he'd acted as if he'd been rebuffed—he must have wanted me! I recalled when we began the sessions that Dirk had said he believed that actions change things, that I shouldn't be just an observer. Did he think an affair would help me?

I basked in the thought of him wanting me and found the business card he'd handed me: THE GOOD SHEPHERD COUNSELING CENTER.

Over the next few days, I cleaned the house thoroughly while thinking of having him over. And though I'd already lost weight, I wanted to be still thinner forgetting that I'd done the same thing with Cal and Dr. Schackmann; I still believed that if I just lost a few more pounds, I'd be loved and ended up hovering one hundred pounds.

I remembered Dirk's smile while he was reading the list of community organizations in the service directory. Then him telling me, "Two years is a long time to wait before moving." I remembered the time he began talking about how important faith was in women's lives, and when I'd paraphrased Voltaire: "Yes, if God didn't exist, men would've had to invent Him, wouldn't they?" how his expression was like when he told me his wife was out of town.

On the nights I couldn't sleep from wanting Dirk I cleaned the house till it shone with sterility. And kept going by losing weight and believing I'd see him again someday.

Jenny told me I looked younger, and Mark whistled with raised eyebrows when I wore my new summer dress to church.

Rebecca

I saw Rebecca in Pineville for almost a year, but I never knew much about her. I'd sought a counselor after Dirk left because I wanted to know if I was out of touch with my "no marriage/no sex" belief. She didn't tell me much about herself, which perhaps went along with her being a good listener, totally wrapped up in her clients. She showed her identification with social causes by wearing an assortment of buttons with slogans.

Pineville had been planned to become the major hub of the Manitowoc & Nicolet, Marinette & Iron Mountain, Green Bay & Escanaba Railroads, so the streets were laid out like spokes in a wheel on glacial outwash plains. But it never flourished the way developers anticipated. Pinnacle's name was changed to Pineville, and the county seat was moved to another town. Rebecca's office faced the center of town's memorial to the lumbering era, a huge Paul Bunyan and Babe the Blue Ox, which were always kept carefully painted in bright colors. The spruce tree near Babe, was strung with Christmas lights in December, circled by tulips in May.

To escape the feeling of being trapped in the windowless room, I'd look at the two orange matted pictures of sunflowers on the wall, which for some reason were identical. The glass reflections provided me a necessary illusion of space. I smiled when I recalled Mark Twain's quote: "Don't part with your illusions. When they are gone you may still exist but you have ceased to live," wondering at what point in his life he had come to that conclusion.

I told Rebecca, "When Cal talks to me now on the phone, it's more between equals. He knows that when the kids graduate, there'll be nothing to keep me here."

Rebecca just nodded, so I took some notes from my purse. "I just finished Hymowitz and Weissman's *A History of Women in America.* They wrote, 'When Betty Friedan in 1963 wrote *The Feminine Mystique,* feminism was considered an outdated concept....'" I looked up. "If I read that to women around here, I'd just get stared at. Or do I think that because Cal said women feel sorry for me because I don't know my place?"

***

I dropped Jenny off to see the Fourth of July parade with her friends, but all the "Stars and Stripes Forever" music and flag-waving about freedom made me want to curl my lip like Cal's.

On the way back, the old terror claimed me when I saw a dog chained to a house. It was behind a picket fence just like mine, and the yard had an American flag almost as large as the one Cal had put up.

Rebecca made me feel out of date when she said, "Sex out of marriage is okay if there's caring." It was also her opinion that adultery committed in people's minds wrecked more marriages than casual sex. I wondered how long it would take me to find someone when I moved. Or would I find something to block me? Did I want to feel the deprived victim? Was that a part of my Catholic upbringing that emphasized suffering and denial? Still, I cared about my appearance. I bought an ointment to put on my nails so I'd stop biting them, and a cream for the brown age spots that had begun on the back of my hands.

When I went to my high school reunion, many of my former classmates were thinking of retiring, while I was planning on starting over. Religion came up at the reunion, too. Fred Ritter talked about how the Catholic doctrines he learned at St. John's "were crap," and his wife said that Catholic kids used to say she was going to Hell because she was Methodist. They talked about how Father Teiresias had recently shocked parishioners by saying he didn't believe in novenas and asking, "Who knows who the Virgin Mary was?" When he was late once in administrating Last Rites, he angered still more people with, "Why are you so upset? You think I'm some witch doctor with magic charms?" I wondered if he would last as a priest, but he probably would since so few men now were going into the priesthood.

Mark laughed when I told them about the reunion; Jenny asked if I'd met anyone.

***

I shook my head when I read that men have sex for sex, women for love, but Rebecca counseled me to do whatever felt right; if it felt bad, she said, I'd know. With her, it wasn't a question of good or bad with Dirk when I brought him up. It was more to the point to consider what I would have gained if I had an affair with him. She said that in their profession, practitioners were trained to deal with those who might fall in love with them, that transference was a part of a successful therapeutic process. It was normal and usually good, but the client must eventually lead him or herself out of it. And now that I wasn't Dirk's client, Rebecca said that the constraints of that relationship no longer applied. This, however, didn't agree with what I'd read. And though he'd moved not far away, it didn't seem right to continue sessions.

She asked me to close my eyes and imagine myself as a child I'd have to leave behind. I didn't feel safe closing them, though, and from the corner of my eye I saw her rubbing a piece of paper together with her right thumb and index finger, as was her habit. She said I was an attractive, beautiful person, and to mother myself; that this was what I was doing with strays.

***

At one of our sessions, Rebecca said, "Ask Jenny how she felt about Uncle Walt's attentions."

I'd nodded, but knew I wouldn't because I didn't want her to think about it—or perhaps because I didn't want to.

I hesitated and then said, "I try so hard to remember what happened with Uncle Walt, but, at the same time, I'm afraid if I did, it'd be too much."

"You know you have to leave your uncle," she said.

Dirk and Dr. Schackmann had told me the same thing.

"As a child, what warmth you received was from your uncle, and so you probably feel guilty seeing him in a bad way."

I knew she was right. And I felt guilty, too, about the divorce and told her, "I destroyed a family for the kids."

"Think back," she said. "What would've happened if you'd stayed married?"

I sighed. "I'd be a walking nothing, wandering around like a ghost in a B movie like Cal said I did. It affected me and no matter how hard I tried, I don't know if I gave the kids all they needed."

Rebecca held her coffee mug in both hands like she was warming them and said, "You shouldn't feel guilty if you couldn't give as much as you wanted to your kids when they were young. You weren't getting any support."

"I shouldn't have told Cal about Uncle Walt."

"Why did you?"

"I wanted to move after the psychiatrist said that when I was growing up Uncle Walt was a lover figure to me instead of a father figure."

During our sessions, I found that the subject shifted between Cal and Uncle Walt as if they were interchangeable. How I recalled seeing Cal's outline one night when he came to bed. "He reminded me of my uncle," I said, "and afterward, I just couldn't lose that dread; it must've been what Oedipus experienced, discovering that he'd wed his mother." I stared at the cover of *Newsweek* on the coffee table: *Rocky IV*, Sylvester Stallone draped in an American flag, before asking, "What do I want from men but don't seem able to get? It must be unrealistic: I need a man for my identity. I want an equal partner in marriage and yet to be taken cared of."

It didn't help much when she said, "Many women are struggling with the changing roles for women" because it reminded me of Cal's advice about remembering what pioneer women went through. Rebecca was about to retire. What need did she have for figuring out what I had to? All the more reason for me to get love before my time ran out. Then she said, "Are you going to be able to handle the holidays?"

"I'll be relieved when they're over."

"You must take care of yourself, Lily." She took a sip of coffee from her mug and said, "There are parts in your life you'll never recover."

What parts? I wanted to say. I felt like I was standing on the edge of a wide chasm that stretched as far as I could see. But I didn't ask — what good would it do to know? It made as much sense as when Dr. Schackmann told me to enjoy the sensuality locked inside me.

Dreams

When I told Rebecca about all the jobs I'd been applying for, she said, "You sound like you're looking forward to moving."

"Yes, I can't wait! When I watched part of Fergie and Andrew's wedding, I thought I'd look that happy the day I left Nicolet City. Do you think if Jenny had been born in Detroit like Mark that any of this would've happened? Or if she'd been a boy, or even a girl who didn't look like me?"

"You were living with a time bomb waiting to go off," Rebecca said. "You didn't choose abandonment as the topic of your obsessions because it's one of the biggest fears anyone can have. You've lived with fear of being left most of your life."

She had to be right I concluded as I stared at Rebecca's mug with Wisconsin's state motto, "Forward". Could it be that Cal and Aunt Hester had abandoned me when they ignored Uncle Walt's behavior? But how could that be when everyone saw them as exemplary people and me the misguided one? Could it be that the worst thing was not my uncle's actions, but rather the fact that no one helped me? That the weight of silence is more harmful than what could have happened? Could I blame society's practice of hearing no evil, seeing no evil, speaking no evil? The patriarchal mindset of religion? Or was it human nature?

I said, "Maybe it was a mistake telling Cal about Uncle Walt. But I wanted to leave Nicolet City, to have what our marriage had been before." After a pause I continued more slowly, "Perhaps, after learning about Uncle Walt, it was too late for both of us."

Rebecca just nodded like she did when she wanted me to continue, but I had to change the subject that seemed too fatalistic and hopeless. "Yesterday, when I was getting a new alarm clock, I heard a dog barking and couldn't wait to get out of the store to stop worrying if it was abandoned. When I saw that it belonged to one of the customers, I felt great relief that people cared."

Rebecca asked, "How are your projects coming."

"I sent more chapters to a publisher who requested them. I think I'll get a contract."

That night, I had a hard time falling asleep and recalled my philosophy professor's approval after he'd seen my well-worn, *A History of Western Philosophy*. He admired Bertrand Russell; I admired the professor and became his top pupil. But lately I'd been wondering if Russell had merely provided a justification for not believing in anything—that drifting, formless feeling of a bed of marshmallows.

Russell wrote in "On Being Modern-minded"that "Our age is the most parochial since Homer."

When I returned to bed after pacing the hall, I thought about how we see, and concluded that the strangest thing of all was not to see how strange things were.

My dreams were vivid, so real that often I didn't want to remember them, even though I wanted to know what they said about the past. I kept paper and pen on the nightstand beside the bed, and when I awoke from a dream, I'd make myself write it down without thinking about them. Most, however, evaporated before I could. The next time I saw Rebecca, I brought her my latest ones.

My cousins came to visit Uncle Walt's. I hadn't seen them since I was small and I offered them my hand, but they only halfway extended one finger and looked at me strangely. I felt they'd been told something was wrong with me by Uncle Walt and didn't want anything to do with me. I brought chairs for them but they stood away from me. I had open wounds on my back and stomach that looked like they'd been made by bird beaks.

Rebecca gave one of her nods so I read her another.

I was watching an appliance demonstration and I could see fire between the appliances but no one else could see it. I stuck a yardstick between appliances and it came out burning, but no one believed me. Soon, many buildings were on fire. It was the place where I'd purchased an alarm clock the week before. I was with Jenny, trying to get back to our car, but I couldn't find it. People were on stretchers, waiting to get moved, afraid as they watched the fire come nearer. There were kids in a nearby restaurant practicing for the junior play, and Jenny's friend Marie was speaking her part when smoke came from the top of a building across the road. The building next to them also began to burn. Then there was a car pile-up. People who were occupied with the fire got hit, and other cars and motorcycles crashed into them. I wanted to get away before the cars exploded. We walked into town and went back to try and find our car. I told Jenny I was impressed with the play and how Marie did but she said Marie only said one line."

When I'd finished, Rebecca leaned forward, and I could sense she intended to walk me through the meaning of it. She said, "What did you think this one meant?"

"I saw the fire." I said.

"Meaning danger."

"Yes, but no believed it, after I pulled out a burning yardstick to show them. The store was where a prosperous tannery once was that turned out leather. "

"How your life was once."

"Could be. I'd purchased an alarm clock there. The feeling of disaster was strong, and yet the play continued and I watched it closely no matter what was happening and glossed over Marie's part in it."

Rebecca's eyebrows rose ever so slightly. "You were ignoring reality."

"I think the fire was like the dream of the falling Gothic towers that I told you. My past was being destroyed but no one could see it, even after showing them that the yardstick—which was my life—was on fire."

She did the 'continue' nod.

"I watched a TV program, 'After the Sexual Revolution,' on the progress and status of women," I said. "It left me wondering because women are more alone, poorer, and still do most of the housework. My chances of marriage at my age are about one in a hundred. It almost makes you support the traditional beliefs that women should be in the home, subject to men, because women function differently. Still, some women are striking out on their own. It said that other countries have day care centers sponsored by the government. Americans don't see that the majority of women are working and the traditional family largely isn't there anymore."

After Rebecca commented about the changing roles of women, and before I departed the session, I left her three written dreams she requested to keep for my file:

I was taking care of some plants in the Catholic Church basement, which looked just like Uncle Walt's basement. I was watering and then placing the few green vines where sunshine fell on shelves with jars of dusty nails and tools. I had moved a few plants to the left side of a jigsaw to catch the sun that came through the narrow basement windows just above the ground. Looking at all the piles, I wondered how Uncle Walt had ever collected so much stuff. I saw an old teacher I didn't like in high school, and he told another teacher that I should be a future award winner. I figured he must have read about my research but when I looked at him again, he'd changed into someone I didn't know. I was given keys to other basements and made a U-turn on a lady's lawn.

That night at Uncle Walt's, they talked about the teacher I recognized. The only person who knew me turned into another person, and even though he knew of my work, he still saw me as a student. Both places were underneath the structure everyone saw. In the dream there was very little space left on the shelves because most of it was taken by hoarded items. I thought that the sun, as it fell at a slant was beautiful, and I could see the dust motes in the air. Some rays were narrow and some were wide. The impression of color I had was dusty gray, dull black, and the only cheerful color was the pale yellow sunrays and the green leaves. I knew the light would not last no matter where I placed the plants. The basement was very quiet, timeless—like it'd always been there. The plants were not seen by anyone else. They were in peanut butter jars, like the collections of nails and other things. I was part of the collection of Uncle Walt's things, but I wanted life and beauty. When I did an about-face and was defying society, I didn't care about the lady's lawn and didn't feel any remorse. I was in a hurry to go to the other basement to take care of plants, which actually were me. Church and Uncle Walt were one, each supporting my second-class status.

I was entering some large modern building, saw a gray cat in the vestibule and wanted to see if it belonged to someone. I went inside, saying I could check back later and see if it was still there. The building was very large, and I went upstairs where everyone watched a program. They were divided into groups. I was with a date I didn't like, but I knew two of the other girls. I lost the group I was with when we were going down long stairs. I was then directed into a room where those in charge said they would make me look beautiful. They said I wouldn't feel a thing and had to have it done. Everyone was dressed in white, and I didn't trust anyone. I was drugged and my eyes were drilled out and replaced with two plastic pieces to resemble eyes. Everyone said how perfect I looked. When I looked in the mirror, I saw that my right eye was loose. I could see the edges, and, when I looked closer, it fell out. It was made to look like a doll's eye. I saw a gaping hole where my eye had been—it was red and watery around the rim, like the gorged-out eyes of Oedipus. Everyone there was having the same operation. My teeth were drilled down also, and replaced with perfect white plastic teeth. I wanted to get away before anything else was done to me so I made myself believe nothing was wrong. I went to various rooms but everything was programmed or controlled. I kept wandering around, hoping to find some place or people that were not programmed or drugged and that a man would recognize what I was and know I didn't belong there. Wanting to get back to the dorm I'd started in, I asked directions, and someone pointed to a group of three buildings. To get there I went through a shopping center, but it had no exits in the direction of the dorm. I thought that if I got back to where I'd started, I could get back to the way I was. All the exit signs were on the right side of the shopping center and the dorm was on left.

I felt a sickening impact. My eyes were drilled by society to look like a doll. The gaping hole where my eyes were taken out felt very true, symbolizing my marriage, and on a gut level I felt that I didn't have any other choice than divorce, or I would have become completely artificial. Because I was told it was the way it should be, I felt mistaken, ungrateful.

My cat fell down the side of an elevator when it was looking down. I was in a panic, trying to find out if it was alive and whether to spend what money I had to have the elevator taken apart. I knew I would always be wondering if it were alive, hurt, trying to get out.

The cat was the primitive, instinctual side of me. It fell in a dark, deep, alien place and couldn't get back. To get out, the elevator had to be taken apart—which was my psychoanalysis—at great cost.

I was in a big city trying to find my way back to the dorm. I came across a group of art people, asked directions, and they told me to come with them on a tour. I walked with them, pushing my bicycle, admiring their work, and was singled out by a man who took me to a large theater. It was nearly empty, and we waited for the performance to begin. Then I noticed that the auditorium had been closed by a series of iron gates that were artistically. When I noticed the final one coming *down, I felt panic and noticed that the man beside me now had a pig-like face and holes for ears. Before, I had only noticed that he was nicely dressed in a three-piece suit, looked intelligent, and had quoted Arthur Miller: "I think if art has any kind of a social function, it's to illuminate what's being denied." Then I remembered the cynical references to sex and knew I was going to be raped, and that he'd do it like looking at pictures.*

***

How I wished I had that dream I'd given Dr. Schackmann, because perhaps now I had the strength to look at it. Why hadn't I kept a copy?

I did try to locate Dr. Schackmann, hoping he might have kept the dream that haunted me. I wrote to his old address, but my letter came back, so I sent a letter to the American Psychiatric Association. I got a letter saying that Dr. Schackmann had died in 1982. I mentioned it the next time I saw Rebecca.

"How'd it make you feel," Rebecca asked.

"Sad, and surprised. A sense of irony at the waste of all his knowledge. Gratitude for surviving, and a desire to know if a patient's husband had killed him. It was as if part of my past had died. So many things. I wonder what really happened to him? He was still young."

Rebecca took a sip from her coffee mug. "When was the last time you saw him?"

"At a restaurant, for coffee. He suggested it since I was in the midst of the divorce procedure and my lawyer wanted me to be done with counseling sessions."

I swallowed away the lump in my throat and tried to smile. "I've heard it said that you get jobs through contacts but I want my record, my accomplishments, to get one for me. I've cleaned my desk at work, so I'll be ready when my new job comes."

"Just take one day at a time," she said.

"I look forward to the mail every day, but most likely a job will come by phone."

"What does Jenny think of your plans," asked Rebecca.

"So much is happening with her right now, and I'm glad. Last night Charlie came over, and he seems a nice boy. I shook hands with him and asked them to sit down at the table where I was working on my book. I picked up a page and started in reading off questions as if

I'd prepared them for him to answer about himself and he was pretty surprised."

Rebecca laughed.

"She's looks better when she wears panty hose 'cause they hide the bruises she gets from sports. She's got her first job and there seems to be a bond between us now because of Charlie that's neat; I don't feel the sense of rivalry with Charlie that I felt with Mark's girlfriends."

After seeing Rebecca, I went to Fowler's Car Repair and Sales. While waiting to get my car fixed I also looked for a used car to buy. I didn't know anything about cars and, as a woman, felt out of place there. I'd taken it in after Mark told me, "Ma, one day you're gonna be going down the road just on wheels," but thankfully the man was honest and said it was rusted too much to repaint. I didn't want Mark being ashamed to ride with me.

***

In the next session, I told Rebecca that the University of Illinois-Urbana had called me to arrange an interview, and they would pay for my transportation and lodging.

"I'm not sure if the kids could get in," I said, "but Jenny and Mark said I should take the job if they offered it."

"It has a very good reputation," she said.

I saw several curled papers in the basket, and assumed she also rubbed paper between her right thumb and index finger when she was listening to her other clients.

"If the kids can't get into Urbana," I said, "I hope something else comes up. I've gotten fifty-three job rejects so far, but thirty-five applications are still out."

Someone knocked on the door. Rebecca got up and when she returned, she was very upset. "I'm sorry but I have to leave right away to admit a sexually abused woman to the psychiatric ward in Fort Beloit."

When Rebecca guided me out I couldn't help but feel grateful that I'd never had to be admitted and tried to imagine what the woman looked like and related, "I'm sorry it happened and hope she'll get better. She's so lucky to have your help."

Aunt Hester and Uncle Walt stopped by the next day. I'd told them previously about the interview, and Uncle Walt had said, "Be sure and speak up. Christamighty! Don't be meek." He walked to my windows, rubbed a coin on them, and said, "You better pay attention to your windows and do some damn caulking."

That night I dreamed about a woman who fell from an

airplane. She walked around talking, but nobody could understand her.

***

The next time Mark visited, I was making cookies. We talked about philosophy, his plans, what he was doing. I could never figure out why he brought clothes home to wash. Perhaps it was some kind of need, or primal instinct like the way dogs roll in grass? He said he was finding out about himself and what you were determines what you'd do.

When I'd fallen asleep that evening I dreamed I was at Uncle Walt's and everyone there turned out to be naked, ill-smelling perverts I couldn't escape. Then I was in a canyon with many rectangular stone doors that opened with iron rings but each had a different maze of horrors and you ended up where you started. At one place people started killing each other but they weren't people after they were killed but were flat giant paper dolls carried around like suckers by those killing them. I'd get surges of hope about escaping only to have them change to a more devious entrapment.

To forget about going to find the stray cat I'd seen at Mrs. Stoke's, I shoveled snow, painted, and tried to cry. When I read the material from Survivors of Incest Anonymous, it was all there: the first step is acknowledgment, then you feel anger, but you waver back and forth and must get support elsewhere than from your family, since family members want to keep the family together.

I dreamed I was walking in the woods and got separated from my cat. I became frantic and walked and walked; it seemed I was about seven years old, but as the searcher, I was my current age. It was getting dark, and I called out, trying to retrace my steps. I came to a house and asked a man where I was. He said a place I didn't know.

When I awoke, I remained frozen in bed, my mouth bleeding from biting it, and I concluded that getting out of bed couldn't be any worse than the fear that the dream engendered. Recalling that the cat and the little girl had merged gave me a feeling of hope, because it crystallized what my obsession with stray animals was about. But at the same time, I didn't want to fully acknowledge that the obsessions could be a way of protecting me from the past.

Survivor Meetings

The meeting for incest survivors organized by the regional women's counseling center was to be held in what had once been the living quarters for nuns near Pineville. Rebecca had told me about it and urged me to go.

It took me a while to get the courage to attend, afraid someone might recognize me and label me as damaged goods. The phrase, the presumption of innocence until proven guilty, seemed as ironic as that of the blindfolded figure holding the Scales of Justice.

But I'd been reading about the desire of victims to keep their families together, and the importance of going outside the family for help; not to expect support from family. If I saw real life victims of incestuous relationships, I'd hopefully see that I was wrong and let it rest.

Partitions had been opened to make three rooms into one, and even then the chairs had to be removed so everyone could fit in by sitting on the floor. I'd found a spot near the hall door and leaned against the wall. The women were mostly younger than I was, and wondered why there weren't more my age. Had they given up trying to understand things, or had they successfully come to terms with it? Could all those younger women hopefully reflect a trend not to keep silent any longer?

> The night before I'd dreamed I was with Jenny, and a man at Uncle Walt's had me down so I told Jenny to tie him up. I called the telephone operator but got no one, then tried the state police, sheriff, city police, but couldn't get them. I was frantic. He kept telling me I was a nut. I went to the county building and the sheriff thought I wanted to be jailed. I blamed myself for not knowing the numbers to call. Then I found the numbers but they were written sideways, too small and crowded to see. I interrupted calls screaming it was an emergency but nobody would listen.

Rebecca began the meeting by saying it was first of its kind in the area and that we should all give ourselves credit for coming. But even with the sporadic hand clapping I could feel the women cringing. Rebecca was the type that Uncle Walt would've described as wearing the pants in the family, or, if she wasn't married, as one who'd "never had a man look twice at her."

Rebecca continued, "I've asked my former instructor, now the director of counseling services at Elkland Community College, to start things off for us."

As a woman about my age stepped forward, I stared at a bulletin board. She began, "Incest is commonly defined as sexual contact with someone who's a blood relative or who's related to such a degree that marriage is—"

Hands went up asking her to speak louder.

She squared her shoulders and in a louder voice continued, "...it is a type of sexual abuse that makes the victim appear guiltier than the criminal. But remember, you are *not* to blame. Please, everyone say aloud three times: I am not to blame."

Everyone avoided each other's eyes while repeating the phrase like grade school multiplication tables.

The woman, in a still louder voice, said, "Incest is so hard to deal with because victims feel they have to protect the perpetrator because of their relationship to them. Most never tell. Untold numbers hide this secret, take on the shame, and assume a burden that shouldn't be theirs. This meeting couldn't have taken place if it weren't for those in the women's movement who've spoken out and braved the threats and the ridicule of those around them. All of you have shown this bravery by coming this evening. Let's give each other a round of applause."

Applauding felt theatrical. I felt that I didn't belong there but made a show of joining in.

"Self-help groups are an effective way for women to help one another and see themselves as survivors instead of victims. I've been told that meeting rooms are available, and though there aren't enough counselors to go around, we can get groups started. Along with your name and phone number, please write down the day of the week and the time that would work best for you. There's no cost involved."

Sign-up sheets were passed out as she went on with the meeting.

"One of the effects of incest is to make women feel that they are isolated," she said. "That what's happened to them hasn't happened to anyone else. But you're not alone. Please stand up so others can hear you better, be brief, to give as many other women as possible a chance to speak out. You are among those who understand and will not blame you. I'll start things out."

She hesitated, cleared her throat, and then said, "Each time I tell my story it gets easier. Just remember, the first telling is the hardest, and it helps us all. My father fondled me at an early age, and when I was of school age, he demanded oral sex or he said he'd tell what a bad girl I'd been. He was a school principal, so I believed him. Rather than blaming him, I blamed myself, because a young child needs parents to be good parents, have the world a safe place, and so blaming myself was typical. I didn't know if my mother knew, and I didn't ask her until I was out of the house. When I did, she excused him by saying he'd been poor as a child. There wasn't any information on sexual abuse around." Yes, I believed that; I'd just tried to get a book on incest for the local library but the request wasn't approved.

"In college I was institutionalized for six months. No matter how high my grades were, I didn't feel I was good enough. My father did the same thing to my sisters. My older sister still refuses to admit anything and keeps getting into abusive relationships; my younger sister died from an overdose."

She cleared her throat again, and then said, "Who'd like to be next? Remember, you're among friends."

A pretty girl, about eighteen, with bangs partially covering her eyes, raised her hand and stood up. "Things started when I was about eight," she said. "My father would come home drunk. He wouldn't allow locks on any of our bedroom doors." She took a deep breath and continued, with her head down. "It was easier to believe that he didn't know what he was doing. I never told my mother because I knew she wouldn't help because my father kept threatening to leave."

Several of the women nodded.

Then a woman in her late twenties, dressed as a waitress, spoke. "It was my grandfather," she said. "I don't know when things began, but I was real young. My mother had to work because my father had left us, so we went to live with my grandfather. When she'd find me crying in the bathroom, she'd get angry and tell me she couldn't understand why I was unhappy since I had a home. I quit school as soon as I could to get out."

Listening to the women testify, I could see the pattern that applied to me as well. Aunt Hester, who, for one reason or another wouldn't, or felt she couldn't, acknowledge the behavior of Uncle Walt. Aunt Hester wasn't a blood relative and I always felt her jealousy. She'd come from "a hole in the wall," as Uncle Walt put it, and enjoyed being the wife of a prominent engineer. Her Catholicism valued suffering and classified women as second class; it was the way things were. If she felt any remorse, she probably expended it on an extra recitation of the rosary while contemplating the sorrowful life of Christ. Or attended extra novenas, or said her own prayers nine days in a row from her prayer book to Our Lady of Perpetual Help. Or washed a clean floor, rubbed spots off the wall with hands red and raw from bleach and antiseptic, and, when they bled, offered it as penance.

And yet, I was certain that even if she'd known something, she wouldn't have done anything. Perhaps we both knew it wouldn't have done any good, because when Uncle Walt had obstacles placed in his way, they only spurred him on to get his way. She tried to control him through religion, to make him feel guilty for not going to church as often as she did, but he'd laugh and respond, "Christamighty! You want me to turn into one of those dried-up old bats hugging rosaries to their flat chests, praying for something to fill their brassieres? You go and feel holy for me."

The next speaker spoke in an apologetic voice. "I'm not sure if I belong here," she said. "When I was babysat by a cousin, he'd show himself to me, but we never had actual sex. He was my cousin and wouldn't accept money for babysitting, and my mother had to work two jobs. Now I keep getting into relationships with losers."

A woman in front of me was next. "My brother said he'd help me know things that girls needed to. He was seventeen and I was eight and said if anyone knew what we were doing we'd both get in trouble. Our parents were very strict, and I believed him. I made myself forget as much as I could, but when my daughter turned eight recently, a lot of it began coming back. I know I have to tell her about sex and growing up, but I don't know how to without scaring her."

A thin, tired looking woman stood up next. "My stepfather beat my mother, and I was nine when he forced me to...do things. I thought I was saving her from being beaten. She'd dropped out of school to have me and was afraid she couldn't make it on her own. My mother said her bruises were from falling down the stairs. The Lord has been a great help, and I plead with Him every night for help."

The girl who spoke next was sitting near a table lamp, and half of her face was in shadow. The sweatshirt she was wearing, half black and half red, made her look like a harlequin, a medieval jester; appropriate for someone who'd led different lives. "I ran away from home to get away from my dad and lived on the streets."

"I know a girl," another girl said that looked like a high school freshman. She's afraid her father will go after her younger sister next. A girl I knew got pregnant by her father and nobody would talk to her. How can I help her?"

It was dark by then, and the moon came into view through the far window. The cool, perfect, impersonal moon seemed to belong to ancient Greeks, Doric columns, and amphitheaters. A perfect backdrop as the women's voices blended together like a Greek chorus or a Catholic litany.

"Nervous breakdown"

"I overdosed"

"Not to tell"

"Destroy the family"

"Thought I was bad"

Many of the women who got up to speak could only get a few words out. One had to be led away: it was such an outpouring of pain I felt embarrassed for her. How could someone let their emotions go like that?

Most of the women hunched their shoulders. Their voices lacked confidence and they spoke as if afraid to draw attention to themselves. Even if the majority could've been considered attractive, it seemed there was a mist, a cloud—some incense of indecision, guilt, and fear. But as one after another spoke, a sense of unity, of transcendence, emerged that I'd only felt in church. This, however, was a deep, collective suffering, a sense of commonality both healing and terribly sad. There was a moth on the floor so I got out my earplug container to carry it away so it wouldn't get stepped on.

I envied those women who knew what'd happened to them, and again I wished that I too could remember. What testimony could I give? What could I prove? My uncle's dirty stories, cuddling, having children look for candy in his pockets, walking around in boxer shorts, and all the rest didn't result in pregnancy—even as a child I knew somehow the boundary was penetration. Uncle Walt's actions had been accepted, joked about. So perhaps Aunt Hester hadn't been guilty of covering up anything. The term, emotional incest, used by Dr. Schackmann, was one I'd never heard before and I only knew that something had happened to me because of symptoms. I didn't make them up, and more than anything else I wanted to get rid of them. Wasn't the foundation of the panic I felt when seeing abandoned animals because no one had cared that boundaries had been crossed by my uncle when I was a child? That and then when Cal distanced himself, it triggered things? It wouldn't be until I'd moved to White Water when I read studies that had concluded the harmful effects of overt and covert incest were similar. I so wished that I remembered something physical, something defined by law, something physically defined as incest so I would know and not be suspended in an undefined territory, a no man's land. I related to Wilfred Owen, a poet killed in battle who wrote: "No Man's Land under snow is like the face of the moon, chaotic, crater-ridden, uninhabitable, awful, the abode of madness."

I wrapped my arms around myself to stay the chill and remembered Alice protesting in *Alice in Wonderland*, "But I don't want to go among mad people."

"Oh, you can't help that," said the cat. "We're all mad here."

It was, however, the people not attending the meeting, causing others to need to come, who were mad.

I was the first to leave, slipping out in the moonlight before anyone could see me. The feeling of being trapped eased when I let the moth go, willing it to use its wings to reach the moon, trying not to realize what I wanted was as unattainable. And that as a woman, my tie to the earth was stronger, even with my growing desire to travel the galaxies.

The moon that morning had been low in the sky like some errant girl returning home; now, on its appointed course, it was more distant and remote. The fresh air welcomed me as if returning from a long dank subterranean journey, my hope that nothing had happened in the past fading in the open air. When some branches came between me and the crescent moon, giving it a look of grinning piano keys, I heard a nocturne played out of tune.

When I reached my car I put a hand on it for security and looked at the moon in picturing all the happy couples walking hand in hand, convinced they'd always be in love, conscious of every mood of the other although they couldn't clearly see in moonlight. They were unaware they were walking on a planet with a molten core—a bubbling, boiling, crimson, massive lake of lava that proved its existence with eruptions of volcanoes and earthquakes. They had no thought of being on a planet that'd have no light if it wasn't for the sun, or that they were orbiting in a vast blackness—an infinitesimal part of an untold number of galaxies in an ever expanding universe.

***

Years later, when Dr. Bradford told me about another meeting of incest victims to be held at the student counseling services in White Water, I wasn't as apprehensive. Mark and Jenny were married then, Uncle Walt and Cal were dead, and no one knew me.

The participants were women of another generation, and again I envied those who remembered what'd happened to them. The incidents they related were pretty much the same, although they also added incidents that the women in that first meeting I attended wouldn't have thought of as incest: fathers who questioned them minutely and constantly about what they did on dates, or followed them on dates as if they were in competition with their dates; giving their daughters negligees; fathers undressing in the room or entering their bedrooms when they were dressing; brushing against their daughters; engaging in dirty talk, and cuddling "Daddy's little girl" on their laps long after childhood; telling a daughter how cold their mother was and how the daughter could keep the family together; threatening to kill the family pet if not allowed to show "affection."

Maybe times were changing; maybe things were being recognized for what they were. Whatever the reasons, there was an awareness now of how father figures convey their sexual preoccupations with their daughter's sexuality—the effects I was still uncovering like a many layered onion. As soon as I'd conclude there couldn't be anything more to uncover, another layer would come off in the light of dreams, counseling, reading, and reflections that'd make me feel I couldn't breathe and was about to fall into a murky pit. Each time, each revelation would catch me off guard, as in the recurring dream of trying to scream and not being able.

I noticed at the meeting the emphasis placed on trusting gut feelings. In response to the examples the women brought up, the counselor noted that the definition of abuse was changing, becoming more inclusive. "An adult's sexual traumatizing of a child," she stated, "is the betrayal of a minor by an adult who is in a position of authority and who exploits his own sexuality to dominate the child physically, spiritually, or psychologically. Incest is still held by many as being an unmentionable topic to be shoved under the rug." She looked like a professor, and maybe she was. "Surveys have found that childhood sexual abuse is a very strong predictor of the likelihood of PTSD, post-traumatic stress disorder."

Likelihood, I reassured myself, doesn't mean for sure. She went on to say, "Rape has been established to be the trauma most likely to produce PTSD." Again, the word 'likely' provided reassurance that rape might not apply in my case. "Research has shown that trauma is the most severe when it is by a guardian of a child's safety and well-being. The abused tend to take on aspects of the person who had abused them, since they'd had so much control and influence over them as a child. Victims usually didn't abuse children themselves, but often adopted one or more characteristics of the one wielding so much power over them."

I told myself it would be a cold day in hell before I'd be anything like my uncle, then realized with a racing heart that I'd just used one of his expressions.

The counselor sounded even more like a professor when she said, "Post-traumatic stress disorder wasn't even in the diagnostic manual of the American Psychiatric Association until 1980. Even now, the disorder is often not diagnosed. Incest is a crime in which the victim is stigmatized as unstable, destined for victimization again if she tells, while the perpetrator almost always goes free. Some victims of abuse develop multiple personalities." When she concluded, "Trauma destroys the synthesizing capacity of the brain, the normal connection of memory, emotion, and knowledge,"

These women were more vocal about what they wouldn't tolerate than what I'd experienced in the past. I was glad that this new generation didn't need to see their reflections in men. I thought of the popular detergent ad in my generation: looking at the dishes you washed to see your face reflected, proof that you were a good housewife, an acceptable woman part of society.

When I glanced at a flyer that had been handed out from a woman's group using the phrase, battered women. I pictured poor women in slums or prostitutes and then read what battered included: being degraded, being controlled by threats, experiencing physical force by a partner. Part of me denied the definition because it made me remember so many incidents that'd been accepted as the way it was. I stared at the flyer until too many flooded back--telling myself it looked good on paper but how much of it was being getting real action? I'd seen derogatory comments about women written in chalk on the campus sidewalks. The campus newspaper had a recent article reporting that one out of three, or four out of ten women have experienced some form of sexual abuse.

"Nervous breakdown," someone said.

"I overdosed."

"Not to tell"

"Destroy the family"

"Thought I was bad"

The voices still blended like a Greek chorus or a Catholic litany.

Mark And Jenny

When I got Mrs. Stoke's spiritual bouquet card for Easter and she asked why I hadn't written, I felt guilty. But how could I tell her it was because of the cat I saw at her place? And of course I couldn't tell her about my long nights wanting love. After all, what did she know of passion, except the passion of Christ presided over by priests during the Stations of the Cross during Lent? When she said her rosary, the worn pearl beads rattled like white bones; the possibility of her relating to hunger for a man was as remote as me speaking in tongues.

But I smiled when remembering the times my mother's girlhood friend and I would leave at the last moment for daily mass and her husband would tell her, "Now, don't drive so fast that you surprise St. Peter at the pearly gates." Once out the drive, she'd accelerate so fast that church bulletins, St. Anthony's Messengers, rosaries, and St. Christopher medals pelted me from the dash. Sometimes her trunk would fly open. The first time it did, I told her, "Things are flying out," but the next time I didn't, because I knew she wouldn't stop and risk being late.

When Mark came home, he showed me an essay he'd written for a college class. It began: "I grew up in Nicolet City, one of Wisconsin's small northeastern communities, slowly realizing that the people there discouraged change or being different."

We had some good conversations in the kitchen, where he helped me prepare dinner. He asked me about the job applications I'd been sending out, and said he could take classes and work wherever I managed to get a job. It was what we both wanted: a chance. Though Mark was interested in political science and law, he'd gone to Elkland Community College for a secretary associate degree because Cal said it was all he could afford but I'd come to wonder it wasn't the age old competition a father feels with his son.

I sent a job feeler to the Ohio State, and when they replied that I was the type they were looking for, I was so ecstatic I literally jumped up and down. I called Ohio State, and they were sending information on free tuition for the kids. But Jenny didn't want to uproot and go to high school in Ohio. After I told her to take chemistry, she said she was taking vocational education classes, so I feared that Cal was sending her down the same path he'd chosen for Mark.

When I told Caroline about it, she encouraged me to consider Ohio State, and said that Jenny could visit during vacations. I debated with myself, but in the end decided I just couldn't leave her behind.

Similarly, I'd resigned myself to Mark doing what Cal wanted since if he went to a place like Ohio State, he would feel that he was going against his dad. Caroline said, "It sounds like the kids aren't really Cal's main concern, his practice is."

Mark and I talked about his hopes and expectations over the Easter break, and he related that when he was in the third grade, he'd told kids on the playground that there was no God; the school's principal had called Cal and it made me feel like a bad parent. It was gratifying seeing his face light up when he articulated his relation to the world, which he was in the process of defining.

Mark said, "My generation has no goals, no struggles, no motivation," and he spoke with envy about my college days in the Sixties, when it seemed to him that so much was happening and "people had ideals." He talked about the movie *Platoon* and about Charlie Sheen saying, "Hell was the impossibility of reason." Mark had been born the year Lyndon Johnson ordered the blanket bombing of North Vietnam, and the war in which fifty thousand mostly young men had died—not including those lost afterward to post-traumatic stress disorder, drugs, and suicide. "Hell was the impossibility of reason" was a quote I often remembered afterwards. I tried to find who said it—I thought maybe it was Dante, but it was original to the movie.

***

In my last session with Rebecca I said, "I can feel Jenny's resentment toward me, even if she doesn't say anything." "I know that she must picture me as the one to blame for the divorce and the disruption of her life, and she hears Cal say that I can't do anything right."

"Have you spoken about this to Jenny?"

I gathered my purse closer to me. "How can I?" I said. "Jenny loves Cal, and I know more than most how much a child needs a good image of a parent."

"But by not speaking up for yourself," Rebecca said, bringing me back, "you agree to let your daughter see you the way her father does."

"Jenny needs to be able to look up to him," I said, noticing that Rebecca's nails were not well kept.

She said, "Well, at least you know that you're the healthy one, no matter how Cal might put it."

It was hard to believe what she said about me being the healthy one since I was the one talking to a counselor. I was about to say so but instead said, "Jenny knows that she can't question Cal, that his say is what goes since he has the money. But when Cal isn't around, she's more demonstrative, so I think that on some level she's merely adapting to her situation. I can't blame her for that."

"And what does she think about her stepmother?"

"I guess I really don't know. I never asked, out of the fear, I suppose, of undermining the security I feel Jenny needs. But she's told me I'll always be her only mother."

Rebecca said, "I saw Jenny's picture in the paper, by the way. She's very pretty."

I smiled and nodded. Jenny had played a solo in the pop concert at school. I had attended, naturally, and Cal and Rachel had sat in front of me. "When the concert ended with the audience joining in to sing 'We Are the World,' I smiled at the thought that in little more than a year Jenny would be graduating."

"Yes, keep that in mind."

I said, "*Newsweek* had an excellent feature story on feminism. It said that with liberation comes anxiety, dread, and no-win choices. It gave a bleak picture for women over forty. It said that, as a result of no-fault divorce, within one year the living standards of women and children dropped by seventy-three percent, while men's increased forty-two percent."

"Has your uncle ever offered help," she asked.

I shook my head and stared at one of the sunflower pictures noticing one of the mats was crooked before I replied, "It makes you think of the slaves after the Civil War—conditions were worse than before the war. Well, I suppose if I was honest with myself, I would boycott him, but wouldn't that make more tension for the kids?"

Rebecca didn't respond, which was her way of encouraging me to continue.

"Aunt Hester calls before going to dinner at Cal's, or when the kids are at her place," I said. "I feel a great deal of anger and jealousy from her. She must've known Uncle Walt's relationship with me when I was small. Dr. Schackmann said she knew but didn't want to disrupt things." I swallowed back the lump in my throat. "I wish I had a copy of that dream I gave Dr. Schackmann when I left for Ithaca. He told me that what happened with Uncle Walt was all in there. It was too much to look at after I'd written it, but I might be able to handle it now that I'm getting the hell out of here."

I hoped she wasn't offended by my saying hell, but it felt too good not to. After an apologetic smile and a deep sigh, I admitted, "I don't think that if I knew what I know now I would've filed for divorce."

"Why do you say that, Lily?"

"Well, how better off am I?" It sounded as if I were complaining, so I quickly added, "Still, it'll be different when I leave."

"Yes, it will."

"I creamed Jenny's bedroom doorknob and hid her shoes for April Fool's Day," I said, trying to lighten things, but then recalled Mark's glum look before he went back to Elkland. When he gave me a part of the chocolate rabbit I gave him for Easter, it brought tears to my eyes that I hid.

Before the session ended I asked, "Should I ask Uncle Walt what happened again? He vehemently denied it before."

"It's worth a try," Rebecca said, taking off her glasses and rubbing the bridge of her nose.

Still, not having it confirmed enabled me to believe that nothing happened and keep some security. When I read the passage in Camus's essay, "The Myth of Sisyphus," 'In a universe suddenly divested of illusions and lights, man feels an alien, a stranger,' I knew what he meant.

"I see you're using the tea cozy I gave you," Caroline said, handing me Thomas Hirsch's latest newspaper article on my book based on research for the Wisconsin Geological Society.

"Yes, I like using it," I told her. It was navy paisley, trimmed with yellow yarn bows and red rickrack. "Thanks again for making it for me."

"You're welcome!" Caroline had been looking at me closely, and now abruptly said, "Why, you're really blossoming, Lily!" Her look was so penetrating, I looked away when she added, "You're a pretty woman, Lily."

Had she guessed about Dirk? I wondered. "Most of my tan's gone now," I said, extending my arm. "I hate to think of school starting, of getting up in the dark, driving fifty miles every day, working in the tense atmosphere."

"Just keep looking forward," Caroline said. "Providence has helped you come a long way, and you must give yourself credit."

I poured more Red Rose tea and offered her some of the oatmeal cookies I'd baked for Mark. "I wanted to drive and see Mark but he's coming with Rod next weekend."

"How's he doing?"

"He's doing the best he can, but I can tell he doesn't like secretarial school."

She shook her head, her pageboy hair swaying, and said, "I can't believe Cal would send him to Elkland. You'd think he wouldn't because of what people would think of him."

"I hated to see Mark go, and Jenny misses him. He looked so young and innocent when he left. He took the dishes I gave him, pans, rugs, and the like, but as he said, 'It's something to get through.' He doesn't know what he wants to do, and taking a secretarial course at least will give him a trade. Uncle Walt had told me after church one Sunday that he expected to see lot of presents from Mark after he finished community college. He asked, 'What's his address. I want to send him a picture in the paper of one of his girlfriends.'"

"It's possible that Cal wasn't able to afford anything else for Mark."

"If Providence helped us send Sarah to a four-year college on Frank's salary," Caroline said, "Cal can send Mark."

But I knew that I felt guilty about Mark going there, and indirectly told Caroline as much, by relating a recent dream I'd had: "I was wearing a jacket in Nicolet City school colors that read 'Mother' on the back, and I could only wear it when sacrificing myself for my kids. If I was doing something for myself, I had to take it off and everyone would know I wasn't being a good mother."

When she replied, "It has a lot of truth in it," I remembered a female insect that lost its wings after mating and so could never leave. And that female fishflies deposit eggs on the water and then die. I sought comfort in the warmth of my tea, wanting to tell her of being afraid of seeing strays wherever I went. Of the worm on the sidewalk in town I wanted to pick it up but didn't because Jenny was with me. Later I had to resist returning to where I'd seen it, telling myself that if it were still alive, it could crawl away or a bird might have gotten it.

And I wanted to confide with Caroline about what had happened with Dirk. That the obsessions about strays had gone away when I saw him and wondered if continuing to see him wasn't worth blurring the ethical lines between counselor and patient. That I wondered if the sense of discipline that'd been instilled in me as a child going to Catholic school helped or hindered me. It wasn't that I'd feared offending God, so what was stopping me? But I was conscious of not letting myself do anything that I'd be ashamed of if the kids found out. I just couldn't see myself as some dressing on the side at a restaurant.

What was it about feeling that sex was more than sex? I didn't even believe in God, but couldn't let myself go into what Dr. Schackmann called "mental gymnastics". I'd come across the term 'soul murder' in reference to incest victims but didn't want to think about it. It was too awful—besides, what could I do about it now?

"That's a good picture," Caroline said, pointing to one taken at Cal's graduation.

I'd stood with Cal and Uncle Walter in such a way that they'd look taller. I'd done it as much for me as them because it made me feel secure and wanted. Cal had a sense of assurance, as though he knew where he was going and had a plan for his future. Cal's intern friends engaged in premarital sex, and Cal's disapproval was attractive to me.

It was ironic to see Uncle Walt in the same photograph, because I knew I'd sensed something of him in Cal back then, before I began exploring my past. He'd wanted me to marry a professional, a doctor, like Cal, and I knew that by marrying Cal I'd be paying him back for adopting and educating me.

Caroline turned toward my bulletin board and said, "I see you have a campus map of Ohio State."

"Doesn't it look great?"

"Good for you. I'm sure all your work will get you there, with God's help."

"My deadline for my next study is December," I said, "and proofs of another are coming shortly. Whatever else has been happening with me, at least I'm keeping busy."

"It's not just that," Caroline said. "You're creative."

I smiled, but didn't know what she meant, any more than when Dirk had said, "Obsessions are a creative way for you to handle things, because it would've been too much otherwise."

"Do you think Sarah would be interested in proofreading?"

"I'm sure she'd love the extra money."

"All she'd have to do is look for mistakes on proofs based on what I read to her from my manuscript. I know she's working, but perhaps she could find the time. The last reader didn't blink an eye when I read aloud that the Jurassic Period was followed by the Elvis."

Caroline laughed. "I'll have her call you."

"The reader before the Elvis one chain-smoked and I came to judge time pretty well by the ash piles on the table."

"Don't worry; I'm sure Sarah will want to do it." Caroline glanced out the window at the clothes hanging on the line. Turning back to me, she said, "How's Jenny doing?"

"She left the car lights on the first time she drove by herself, and I had to have the darn battery charged. But getting her driver's license has made her feel more independent."

"That's a big milestone in life."

I told her about Mark's birthday card to me that read: "You're at that exciting age—between the young and the restless and the old and the senseless."

"You're still losing weight!" she said. "Dirk must have really helped you."

"I can wear clothes I couldn't before," I said, smiling, recalling the speculative looks I'd been getting at work. "I hope I still can wear them next year, when I move!"

"I'll be happy for you," Caroline said, "but I'll miss you."

"And I'll miss you. You've been a good friend and the only one that stuck by me."

"God is your best friend, you know."

I smiled politely. Caroline began talking about her new minister and then asked, "Did you see Dirk's picture in the paper? I heard he's booked weeks ahead and ministers are referring people to him."

I bobbed my head in acknowledgment and admired her ceramic pin and figured it was one she made in a ceramics class. How could I tell her how often I thought about him? He'd never said good-bye, and I missed the feeling of being alive with him.

***

Caroline came with some Easter eggs, and I gave her some cookies Jenny and I had made for Mark. I finally told her I had a strong urge to have a baby. "It's a craving like when I was first married," I said, straightening the cream and sugar on the table. "Isn't that the silliest thing?"

"No, not really."

I shook my head. "Things indeed are not arranged right time wise for women." I didn't say that there were still nights when nothing mattered except being with Dirk, and I was realizing I'd never really been with a man the way I should've been—and getting older wasn't something I'd foreseen.

"Times are sure changing," Caroline said. "On the way over I about tripped on couples at the beach doing what God only intended in marriage." Her eyes narrowed and she said, "They didn't care at all who saw them."

I wondered what such freedom must be like. Marriage to me had been like the experience of Tantalus, the king in classical mythology who, as punishment, was tormented by always being thirsty and hungry in Hades while standing up to his chin in water but having the water always recede when he tried to drink. When he tried to get the fruit over his head, the wind would blow it out of reach.

I'd read about millions of women in third world countries who underwent genital mutilation as part of a centuries-old rite to ensure docility. Afterwards they no longer felt sexual pleasure. When one of them died from the procedure little emotion was shown because the practice of mutilation wasn't even acknowledged. Yet, despite risks to one's health, wasn't it more humane if one was psychologically blocked from pleasure—what was the name of that Hemingway soldier who couldn't perform sexually after being in World War I?

Cal had told me, "Going to bed with you is just hard work. You're never satisfied no matter what I do, so can you blame me for doing it less and less?"

I'd said, "When we lived in Detroit you didn't feel like that."

"Well, things are different now."

I'd asked, "What do you mean?"

"I've got more on my mind and don't have the energy to keep going on like that. Why can't you let yourself go? Would being satisfied kill you?"

Always practical, Caroline said, "How've you been dealing with wanting one?" It took me a moment to remember she was referring to me wanting to have a baby.

"Well, I walk up and down aisles of C&C and it does help the jitters from PMS. Up and down, up and down, wearing myself down until I start getting strange looks from the stock boys." It wasn't really answering her question; I didn't want to tell her that the thought of actually having to care for babies wasn't appealing, so I told her, "To save money I've stopped trash pickups, so I buy things in boxes or bags instead of cans, because they can be burned." I didn't tell her I bought meat that was frozen, without bones or skin, so it didn't look so natural. I avoided fish under clear wrap because all I could see was open mouths gasping for air.

Caroline wrinkled her forehead and said, "I suspect there's a lot going on with you now," with a look that invited me to confide in her.

"Rebecca said I was piecing a puzzle together. I think I know things weren't right when I was a child but I'm afraid I'll come unglued if I really find out. When I fell and broke my hand it was because I was so shaky from realizing that the source of the obsessions were my feelings."

I stopped and took a moment to push back the terror. Jung had written that breakthroughs scare us because they were when unconscious and conscious experiences fuse. Rebecca had told me, "At least you haven't been institutionalized," but the thought of that happening to me was too awful to relate, and I knew it would sound melodramatic—and, perhaps, if I didn't say it aloud, it wouldn't be real.

Nervously dipping my tea bag up and down in my mug, I wondered if my uncle's cuddling up in bed with me, his glazed stares, the dirty stories, were abuse. Dr. Schackmann had called it emotional incest and that my "lawyer-like mind" kept me from acknowledging it. I'd been taught about venial and mortal sins and often tried to tell the exact point one switched into the other, so Catholic school probably had something to do with it. My lawyer-like mind also questioned how valid anything coming from Dr. Schackmann was because of his lack of ethics, even though common sense told me not to throw, as they say, the baby out with the bath water.

Caroline broke the silence, saying, "Men love from their waists down, women from their waists up. It must've been different in the Garden of Eden." In the same matter-of-fact voice, she continued,

"Father Wisniewski said the last thing of his to die would be his maleness."

How could Caroline, who saw things with such clarity, still believe in God?

She pointed to the book on the sideboard and said, "What are you reading?"

I retrieved the book, Rollo May's *The Courage to Create*, opened it to a bookmarked page and read, "A child thrown out in the street knows it is rejected and can orient itself to it. A middle-class child, lied to rather than thrown out in the street, is worse off.'"

"You like that sort of thing, don't you," Caroline commented.

I smiled and offered her more coffee, and, after I refilled her cup, told her that I'd sent Mark three pages of quotations and told him to pick out the five he liked the best and to explain them, as payment for the telephone bill I got after he left.

"You should've had him pay it," Caroline said.

"I suppose. But he needed to talk with his friends." I shook my head and added, "He looked so unhappy."

"He'll survive."

"Jenny got recognition for her high grade average. Her tests indicate that she would do well in college, and yet she lacks drive."

Caroline said, "Could it be she's seen what happened to you?"

It took me a few moments to admit, "It could very well be. Maybe she sees more than I think. She was pretty disgusted when she heard the boys' basketball coach tell his team 'you run like a bunch of girls.'"

"How are things working out with Cal?"

"Cal called this morning and asked for Jenny," I said. "He told me he would pick her up at ten, but he didn't come until after twelve; if I was the one who'd been late, I'd have never heard the end of it. She misses him when she doesn't see him for a while, but I know that when she's with Cal, she hears about how awful I am. As Mark put it in one of his college stories, 'the unforgivableness of my mother.'"

"Cal will have a lot to answer for someday," Caroline said.

"When I went to pick Jenny up, Cal said Mark had no sense of responsibility or any incentive. I suggested that he could transfer to the school where his friend Jimmy was going, and Cal told me I could send him there at eight thousand dollars a year. It's awful seeing Mark crushed and unable to do anything about it."

"God will help him."

Religion was a realm in which Caroline and I didn't see eye-to-eye, though when those differences threatened to surface, I didn't press things because I'd have given a great deal to have her faith, her certainty that good triumphs. Now, in response to her remark, anger welled up in me. God will help him? Without realizing it, I was tapping a teaspoon sharply against the glass-covered table saying some of Uncle Walt's swear words to myself.

Caroline raised her eyebrows, but didn't seem to connect my agitation to what she'd said. She began telling me about a Sunday school lesson she was preparing about the choice of roads a person could take. I drifted off remembering a dream:

> *I was walking alone down a country road with ridges down the middle. The road was very long and empty, and I didn't know if I was going the right way. Spotting a group of people gathered at a parking lot, I hurried to join them, thinking it was smarter to be with others, that riding was easier than walking, but I resented giving up my independence. I was afraid I wouldn't reach them in time, but also afraid they'd make fun of me and refuse to let me ride with them.*

Caroline was still talking. I took a quick glance out the window, afraid the dog across the way wasn't being cared for. I'd given it a dish of milk; it had food and water, so I decided it must be okay. While Caroline talked about parables I kept repeating to myself, I must get out when Jenny graduates. Perhaps Caroline was right. Maybe religion was the answer, but I still thought it was people who made religion, and if a great disaster happened and we began life all over again, it'd be the same.

After she'd finished her parable meanderings, we talked about her daughter Sarah, who was in college, and the adult education class I was teaching. We quieted for a moment, and Caroline said, "I read in the paper about your uncle's award."

"Yes, I attended the dinner," I said. On the way there, the radio announcer had said that April was Child Abuse Month. "It was sponsored by the Northeastern Wisconsin Sportsmen," I said, "and the invocation was given by a minister who said he was too poor as a child to have a gun, but that sports were a great way to give our youth the sportsmanship they needed. The highlight of the program was when the master of ceremonies had cream pie tossed in his face by a fellow Republican."

I'd sat next to Uncle Walt near the speaker's podium; Aunt Hester had given me a ticket. When the names of family attending were read, a part of me longed to see my uncle in the way he was being extolled, but it made me think about the madwoman of Chaillot as I stared at Uncle Walt's white rose boutonniere.

"Oh, before I forget," I said, "here's a copy of the research Sarah helped proof. Please give it to her."

"Oh, how wonderful!" Caroline said, getting up to give me a hug.

I wrote about geology because it helped to make the ground I walked on more secure, reassuring me that floors wouldn't, as the nuns had warned, open and swallow me into the fires of Hell. Geology made sense.

***

Caroline's son and my daughter, Jenny had been in nursery school together, and we'd become good friends. When the kids were with Cal, I went to see her and confided that, "Now that I am divorced, I need to keep calm for the kids' sakes, so they feel secure with me." And added in a voice I tried to keep steady, "But it's like waiting for death for Cal to marry."

"Pottery is fired in kilns," Caroline said, "and God put you in His kiln not to break you but to transform you and make you His. We want the pain to stop, of course, but you'll come out of it a better person. Just endure it and don't be afraid. because He never gives us more than we can handle."

I didn't reply because, while part of me thought it was nonsense, another part believed that it was the only thing that made sense. And still another part concluded that I didn't have any choice.

When Caroline talked about the working of the devil, my St. John's grade school image of a red tail, black goatee, black horns, and black pitchfork resurfaced. Evil had been something I hadn't thought much about, but now grinning demons seemed so real in dreams that a few nights I awoke frozen with fear.

"Did you listen to President Carter's speech about people wanting honest answers" Caroline asked. It's so fantastic having a man of faith as the President! He said we had to face the truth and have faith in each other, not judge others by what they own, and, 'Say something good about America.'"

I could barely hear her speaking because I was still remembering how I'd gone into Cal's home and saw the book *Hanging Loose in an Uptight World* on the counter. And on the bulletin board there was a newspaper clipping, "Teaching Children Firm Rules Without Using Abstractions."

Cal often told me, "Don't waste time explaining things to the kids. Just tell them what to do." When I handed him my monthly check for my college loan, which was part of the divorce settlement, I couldn't shake the old feeling of being prepped for surgery.

PART THREE

"We all live by myth, reader: if only by the myth of happiness around the corner."
-Fay Weldon

Cal Dies

When Cal died, my first thought was that the kids would have a chance for student aid. It felt wrong to feel that way, but I had to be practical.

Sometimes it seemed that the marrying Cal and fused him to Uncle Walt in my mind. At the ceremony, when the priest asked, "Who gives this woman in marriage?" wasn't I passed on to my husband by my uncle? One night, when I saw a man coming into my bedroom it terrified me—I wasn't sure if it was Uncle Walt or Cal, as they had similar builds.

I was listening to the evening news when Aunt Hester called, saying Cal had died. Jenny and I went to the hospital and she put her head on my lap and cried; Mark arrived later that night.

Later, when they were with Rachel, I cried in my room until I felt there couldn't be anything left of me. When I dragged myself into their rooms to feel closer to them, I saw the rabbit furs. Mark was six and Jenny was four when Cal put them up in their rooms one evening while I was making dinner. Afterward, when we were eating, he had looked amused when I'd asked him what he'd been hammering.

"Something you'll really like," he'd said.

I had gone up to the rooms after dinner and seen the rabbit skins he'd nailed to their walls—a brown one on Mark's, a white one on Jenny's. With Cal's characteristic precision, they were exactly in middle of the wall, as if he'd pre-measured the spots. The large nails pierced the fur and skin as if they were of the same surgical steel as his instruments.

He'd nailed them up just after we'd visited Uncle Walt and Aunt Hester, when Uncle Walt had talked about the rabbit I'd had as a child. Cal had taken up rabbit hunting with Uncle Walt.

The skins went up after he had stopped going to the counseling sessions with me when I was seeing Dr. Schackmann, saying "Schackmann thinks he knows it all, and I'd rather spend my time watching cartoons." Cal had started to read to me from his college textbook on abnormal psychology that he kept next to his Visible Head, a life-size plastic head from his head and neck anatomy class. It was clear plastic so you could see the variously colored parts which could be pulled apart and fit back together again. I'm only doing this to point out how screwed up you are," he'd said.

He had gone on to read to me about such things as sublimation, schizophrenia, and multiple personalities. He had paced as he read, stopping every once in a while to point his finger at me and ask, "You see what I'm putting up with?" or, "Now can you see why people think something's wrong with you?" He would usually end with, "What kind of a mother takes whiskey to sleep?"

Those sessions would include medical terms which reinforced that he knew what he was talking about. He'd then turn the book toward me, point, and say, "Doesn't this sound like what I said you were? You fit the criteria for a castrating psycho."

It was then, too, that when we were in the car he'd point out dead animals on the road as if he was holding me responsible for the distance between us. Did he really believe it when he told me that I must've liked what Uncle Walt did to me when I was a child?

Was it then that my sense of abandonment I wouldn't realize or accept turned into obsessions with strays? Because of the rabbit skins he'd nailed to the walls and the dead animals on the road he'd point out? No, my first obsession was earlier, when I saw that the family that fed ducks in a pond by their house near us had left for the winter - soon after Jenny was born. I began buying cracked corn for them and worrying about them after the pond froze. It wasn't until I was in White Water that I read about post-traumatic stress disorder and then had it confirmed by Dr. Bradford: the mind finds ways to repress what's too painful to accept, and that later in life certain things can trigger the fear—a taste, a sound, an event, an association. Cal was dead, but I was still living with fear.

***

The day after Cal died, when I walked by the garden, the grass was such a brilliant green in the drizzling rain that it hurt my eyes. After being renewed by seeing how much my potatoes had grown, I went in to make notes for my Will, wondering what had made Cal's heart fail when only in his forties. When Mark came, I hid the notes to my Will, washed and ironed his clothes, and had to smile at a Gary Larson shirt with a cartoon of a bee in the middle of a swarm saying, "Buzzing, buzzing. All I hear is buzzing, buzzing."

When we were eating the potato soup I'd made, he said, "Uncle Bob said the last time he talked with Dad he was prickly as a porcupine."

Yes, I could see Cal's sneer, like the grin of the Cheshire Cat, which remained long after the rest of it disappeared.

Mark helped himself to more soup and bread, and then asked, "Did you hear Grandpa talking about how he wanted to get back to that new car of his?"

"Yes. People are funny." What could I say? I wasn't going to relay Uncle Walt's observation: "He's so anxious to get back; you'd think he was some damn kid getting his first hot rod."

"How you doing, Mom," Mark asked.

I thanked him with my eyes and replied, "The man I married hasn't existed for a long time. The best thing for you to do is continue your plans of going to Madison."

Cal's body was at the Nicolet City funeral parlor that Catholics used; Rachel had been so devastated that two solicitous nuns were supporting her in the funeral parlor rest room when I entered. One of them handed Rachel more Kleenex, which she put to her red nose and eyes that matched her Raggedy Ann red hair. I'd seen Rachel often, of course, over the years, while picking up the kids at Cal's, and at Jenny's and Mark's school affairs. And before that, I knew of Rachel from St. John's Catholic School. She was two grades behind me. Rachel had skinny legs and freckles, the kind of girl Norman Rockwell liked to paint. When she married Cal, she was working as a receptionist in his office during the summer when she wasn't a teacher's aide at St. John's. Our relationship had been remote and polite; I had nothing against her except the fact that she'd married Cal and was the stepmother of my children.

After an uncomfortable silence while I stared at large pictures of seagulls, Rachel sobbed, "He's—he's probably looking down and laughing at us right now." I nodded and read the comforting sayings under each of the several huge pictures of freewheeling seagulls hung in gray frames with wide mats.

Cal had married her, I thought, because she was respectable, hadn't been married before, and had no kids of her own to contend with. He would have seen her as untouched, and, since she was a Catholic, used to taking orders and being properly subservient. "A sweet woman," Aunt Hester said about her. She was also a member of the Daughters of Isabella, a Catholic women's group that Aunt Hester belonged.

"Someone who makes life simpler for me," Cal had said.

And as far as I knew, that had been true. She and Cal appeared to have a good marriage. But there's a saying about what happens behind closed doors, that nobody knows what goes on, and I'd be the last to dispute it. It could be that I didn't hear about anything troubling between them because Mark and Jenny were told not to say anything, or had decided to keep their life with Rachel and Cal separate from the one they had with me. A part of me wanted to know, but common sense told me that the less I knew the better--that the kids had enough difficulties without piling on more.

Cal's father, with characteristic politeness, extended his arm for me to go with him to view the body; his black suit and white shirt reminded me of a penguin. I'd been dreading that moment. I could feel Cal's sneer all the way down the red carpeted aisle. Mark had been dispatched to get Cal's glasses, to make him look "more natural."

Cal's bluish mouth was wider than I remembered, and I couldn't help but recall the dream I'd had of being raped and pulling worms out of my mouth afterward. The worms were all sizes and kept coming. I would pull them, and they'd break like string beans and wiggled in my throat.

When his father said to me, "They did a good job on him," I had to stifle a smile, because it sounded as if he was looking at a paint job on an Oldsmobile car.

Cal's sneer was even more pronounced in death than in life, and I still feared it; it had often prefaced a cutting remark. His nose still flared like he smelled something bad, but his skin looked chalky, stretched, until I realized it was because it had lost its customary oil. I bowed my head to avoid looking at him, to overcome a desire to shake him the way he'd shaken me — the way Uncle Walt's dogs shook rabbits. I breathed through my mouth so I couldn't smell anything, counting the gold dots on the red carpet that resembled the one in Nicolet City's movie theater.

Stepping back, I clenched my teeth until I was afraid they'd snap. Finally, his father extended a penguin wing to me. Gratefully, I took it and made myself look at those watching us as he led me away, determined to let them see I wasn't sobbing.

When we'd returned to the lobby, Cal's father said, "Do you think you'll get married again?" I felt my right eye flutter like it sometimes did; an optometrist said it was a nervous tic.

"I don't know," I said, wanting to say that being married to his son sure as hell hadn't made me eager to remarry.

The Queen Anne table in the hall held a box of Kleenex and a ceramic mallard duck. The painting over the table, a Monet water lily, reminded me of going to an Ithaca Arts Council show of impressionists with Mitchell. It now seemed so long ago, but I remembered exactly what I'd worn when I asked him, "Tell me that good exists."

A shadow behind Cal's father reminded me of when I first saw my shadow on the wall at Uncle Walt's when I was a toddler. It was my earliest memory and I realized it had to be me because it moved when I did. I was very puzzled, but thought I'd surely understand it when I grew up.

I heard Cal's father say, "You could get married in the Church now that Cal's dead." So, the old penguin thought I hadn't remarried because we hadn't been married in the Church. When I didn't reply, he said a few more comments about new Oldsmobiles before going to ask a funeral attendant something.

Aunt Hester, whose shoes were always too narrow, limped over, checked the names of newly arrived flowers, and said, "The casket cost $4,499 and flying the body to Carrefour Island is expensive."

I said, "It would've been better spent on the kid's education."

When she looked at me, I knew which one of her eyes was glass. The fake one didn't show resentment when she said, as if it were a pronouncement from God, "It's what Cal wanted."

Uncle Walt was crying when he joined us. "By God, Cal was like a son or brother to me," he sobbed, and I felt my eye flutter out of control again. Then he leaned back and snapped his suspenders beneath his suit jacket, his head cocked at a jaunty angle. I followed his eyes to a woman who he'd often said he "sure as hell wouldn't push out of my bed." As he approached her, he said, "What's the name of that new hair-do?" He then must have commented on what she was wearing because her eyes fell to her dress. He'd usually pick the best-looking women at a gathering to make comments at like: "You trying to make all the women jealous wearing nylons like that?"

***

The next day when I woke up, the birds were singing and I hoped that Cal was at peace somewhere.

The kids were staying at Rachel's. When Jenny came to pick up some clothes, I gave her some money, and for the first time felt the full responsibility of being the sole biological parent. She was still very pale and said, "It'll be strange coming home now."

Cal had moved out of the house when I quit my job in Rhinelander and returned to Nicolet City in order to retain split custody of the kids. I only hoped that the coworker at Rhinelander was right. The one who'd said, "They won't make you sell your house like they used to. You won't starve."

Before he'd gone to stay with Uncle Walt and Aunt Hester, waiting until his house was available, Cal had handed me a box wrapped with a bow. I blinked away my tears, thinking maybe things might work out between us after all. The kids were huddled together watching. "Open it," Cal had said.

Before carefully removing the bow to save it, I smiled at him. The smile he'd returned was just like before things had gotten bad between us; perhaps all he'd wanted me to do was to give up my job and come home and we'd be a family again. Maybe he'd given me the locket I'd always wanted. But it was a brown leather wallet with initials branded in gold.

When I had looked up again, his sneer had returned and he'd said, "Now let's see you put anything in it," and left. I use it as a tie to the ways things once were and also out of defiance. I rub leather preservatives on it faithfully, although the gilt initials have long faded and duct tape keeps the change compartment together.

I copied Mark's acceptance letter to the University of Wisconsin at Madison and put it in a frame. After dinner, when I was sitting at the dining room table looking at the sunset in the direction of Carrefour Island, Aunt Hester called and said, "Cal's casket was very heavy. They covered him with a comforter before closing it. Your uncle and I are having a High Mass said for him."

I'd remember Cal's death as being between the time of crocuses and tulips. Death held little dread for me—it'd just mean being done trying to understand and no longer would I need to wake up each day like a punch-drunk fighter to fend off sharp jabs of panic.

Listening to Mark's soundtrack of the movie, *The Big* Chill with Smokey Robinson & the Miracles, Aretha Franklin, The Temptations, Marvin Gaye, and others, helped. With no one around, I turned it up loud and played it over and over until songs like "I Heard It Through the Grapevine," "You Make Me Feel Like a Natural Woman," "Joy to the World," "A Whiter Shade of Pale," and "The Tracks of My Tears" became a part of me.

When I let Maize out there was a tiny white feather caught on an uneven edge of the doorframe; it was as if the Cal with whom I'd fallen in love wanted to tell me he was all right and still loved me. The one who'd said there was something mysterious about me that he found attractive. The pure white feather shivered in the palm of my hand until a current of air carried it off. I knew somehow it would drift in the direction of Carrefour Island, and when it did, a part of me went with that never returned.

Giving Birth

I sighed with relief when I saw the sign for Exit 136. It was eleven years since Cal had died and I'd moved to White Water. Halfway into the cloverleaf, I saw a white cat crouching on the roadside and familiar panic flooded me. It was what I'd been afraid to see all along. I wanted to stop, but an exit ramp wasn't the place, it was late at night, and even if I could catch the cat, what could I do except have it put down somewhere? I knew I had to keep going even though the vivid dream about Cal dropping off a white kitten by an expressway came back, and with it the familiar panic and urge to rescue.

Scott had called me after midnight to say he'd taken Jenny to the hospital. I'd been dreaming about Uncle Walt. We'd been at a bar where he'd gotten drunk, so I brought him home, pulling him in a wagon. He was naked, so I threw a jacket over him.

As soon as I entered the building, the awful hospital smell that no amount of air freshener, bouquets, air vents, or smiling nurses could mask greeted me. Patients pushed IV's down white corridors, trying to keep their gowns closed. The inevitable institutional large round black clock read 3:45. On my way to Birthing Room 103, I saw people glued to television sets and prayed the white cat I'd seen by the exit was okay, that I'd done the rational thing.

Room 103 looked like a motel suite except for the bed and the track lighting. Jenny was glad to see me, and I felt better when she joked, "I told the baby it had to wait until you got here."

Scott's hair was sticking up like Woodstock's in a Charlie Brown cartoon, and I knew he wasn't really seeing me when he said, "How was the drive?"

"It was fine," I said, trying not to see the white cat.

Jenny looked fairly comfortable in bed, with Scott holding her hand. When I pushed back her blond hair, I saw my own face.

When the contractions began, Jenny tried not to show pain. She'd never been through this before, so I said, "Don't be afraid to scream when it gets bad. Let it out, just scream and scream."

A nurse came in to check her dilation.

The contractions abated then, and after a while Scott nodded off and Jenny closed her eyes. I knew that rest was the best thing for her and it could be a wait, so I turned my chair to the television screen.

Gone With the Wind was on without the audio. Perhaps I was preparing myself for when the contractions began again, because instead of watching the scene when Scarlett sees Ashley off to war, I fast forwarded to where Rhett said to Scarlett on their honeymoon, "I brought you to New Orleans to have fun and I intend that you shall have it." I thought about the scene of him walking out on her in Atlanta, saying, "I wish I could care what you do or where you go, but I can't. My dear, I don't give a damn."

"How are we coming along?" The nurse asked when she came in to check dilation as if she was testing potatoes on the stove. Jenny looked paler, and Scott was still holding her hand.

Through my tears, I saw it was dawn when the movie ended; the movie never failed to make me cry. Playing the sound track also made me cry. In many ways Scarlett wasn't a good person, but it was her strength I admired. I recalled *Gone with the Wind* stamps in a tattered paperback I had, and an old *TV Magazine* cover of Vivien Leigh and Clark Gable. And I knew that most of the characters in the movie were dead now. Leslie Howard had been the first to go, killed when his Royal Air Force plane went down in World War II.

I'd recently watched a documentary in which a German woman recalled that twelve to fifteen Russian soldiers had raped her during World War II. She said, "I went numb." A smiling Russian veteran said, "It was heroic for soldiers to sleep with women or girls. The more the better. It was natural." The interviewer asked, "What do you think about this now?" The man's eyes faltered and he said, "The officers allowed it."

The trees were beginning to take form outside, and I thought about the fact that before it got dark I'd have a grandchild. A new life would begin, and life for Scott and Jenny would never be the same. They didn't know it now, but they'd never be without nagging worry, guilt, and a host of other emotions connected with parenthood. Still, children brought positive emotions equally unanticipated. I couldn't see much of the sky, and was trying not to feel the cold irony that it was Uncle Walt's birthday.

I recalled telling Dr. Schackmann after one my uncle's birthday parties, "I feel such a fine mesh woven around me and doubt my sanity at times."

He'd smiled and said, "You're more of an adult now and it's much easier to talk with you, but you have a block in your thinking about Uncle Walt—he's a magical being for you. You're an individual, you do things yourself. When you pick out nice clothes, when you do your group work, you do it yourself as an adult. I'd like to make a contract with you, to set a date at which you function on all levels as an adult."

Somehow, I had sensed that what he meant by adult would threaten my world, that functioning as an adult would mean seeing

Uncle Walt and Cal differently, and, no matter what else they'd been, they were my life.

"I suppose I'll have no peace until I do," I had finally said, though still trying to grasp what it'd mean to function independently of others.

"You do realize this," he'd asked, as if not sure if I really was aware what it meant to be an adult. And when I hadn't replied, he'd added, "Will you believe in your own feelings?"

"As much as I can."

"As I said before," he'd went on, "because of your parochial education and your uncle and aunt, you were never given permission to think for yourself, even if you were sent to college."

I couldn't grasp what he meant, but nodded anyway.

"You have no concept of yourself as a person. You're able to detect motivations in others, but you can't detect them in yourself."

Again, I wasn't sure what he'd meant.

"It was a setup," he'd said. "Your aunt and uncle could still be regarded as good parents, but they had to control everything."

"But being an adult to me means being concerned with dull stuff," I had interjected. "Math and science have always seemed too pat, ignoring the big picture. I need space to breathe, to see beauty."

He'd smiled and looked at me for a while before saying, "I'm on the same channel. Businessmen mostly function as adults." Then, as if clearing something away, he had stopped smiling and said, "But we all must function as adults, and you do it more than you give yourself credit for. Was it your uncle who gave you a scholarship for college and maintained it by keeping on the dean's list? Was it the church that awarded your undergrad and grad degrees?"

No matter how hard I'd studied, it still hadn't made me feel good about myself, that I measured up, or that I'd paid Uncle Walt back.

When I looked up I saw the hospital room again. I wondered, if Dr. Schackmann were around, would he consider me an adult now? Perhaps I was, but I could also see the advantages of not being one, because, as I'd suspected long ago while in counseling with Dr. Schackmann, it had indeed turned my world upside down. Since that time, I'd gotten another degree and had contributed solid research, but it was as if it'd happened to another person--a fluke, a mistake that would soon be discovered, and I'd be revealed as the fraud I really was.

I smelled bacon and toast. The carts in the hallway rattled and a new nurse entered chirping, "It's going to be a bright, sunny day."

"Calling Dr. Crane, calling Dr. Crane. Report to Room 204 immediately," came over the intercom.

A deep voice demanded, "I need this sent to Admitting." Things were livelier now.

The deep voice reminded me of Dr. Jenkins. I remembered coming out of the anesthetic after my hysterectomy and how awful it was until they gave me a shot. Aunt Hester and Mark were there, and the nurse had told me to settle down. I'd bit my hand to muffle my screams, but was afraid the pain would last, as it had when I'd had Jenny. The distant whistle of the train leaving Nicolet City wailed like an animal trying to escape.

I heard a scream. Jenny's contractions were stronger, but the dilation stayed the same and she was getting weaker. A nurse was in the room all the time now, and I was getting very worried. Aunt Hester said that the daughters of Eve were supposed to suffer which never made much sense.

"Why don't you just induce labor," I asked the nurse, who looked at me but didn't reply.

"When my daughter was born," I said, gesturing at Jenny, "I had it induced." When the nurse still didn't say anything, I added, "Maybe it's hereditary." Then I fell silent, feeling foolish. I tried not to think that I'd be punished for rebelling against pain by having Jenny die or give birth to a malformed child.

When I was in the hospital after my hysterectomy, I dreamed that Aunt Hester's head was suspended in clear Christmas tree bulbs all over my room, although the size of her mouth varied. She was chanting, "Your kids will go to hell if they're not baptized" in each bulb. She and Uncle Walt came after having mass said for my parents, and scolded me for smoking and being cranky. I recalled her saying they'd saved me from being an orphan. I saw *Jane Eyre* in grade school, and was afraid I'd be sent away to an awful institution and die like those girls.

Watching Jenny now, laboring with such difficulty to give birth made me go back in time.

***

I saw the large mailbox with matching eagles grasping arrows in sharp talons that stood in front of the house I was raised in. On one side of the drive there was a slab of limestone bearing my uncle's name, 'Walter Augustus Alger.' Next to it was a bust of some Roman emperor on a cement pedestal, bearing my uncle's address. There was a huge American flag in the center of the yard, and deer antlers stacked around the pole and floodlights. Cal had an even larger flag installed in our yard, and, like my uncle's, when the wind was strong the flapping drowned conversation.

Inside, Aunt Hester's life-size statue of the Virgin Mary in the foyer was opposite a coat rack elaborately carved with acanthus leaves. A large painting of Christ knocking on a door was hung on the wall, and a jade plant in a large Chinese bowl stood on the highly polished faux marble floor.

When I helped clear the table after dinner, Uncle Walt rolled back the sleeves of his reindeer sweater and said, "Jenny, come here." Something in his voice made my heart race. "Put your hands in my pockets," he said, motioning to a front pocket as he leaned back in his chair stretching out his legs. "There's candy in there for you." He jerked the wooden sulfur-tipped match in his mouth, grinned, and folded his hands behind his head as he waited. He looked at me as if enjoying my discomfort and said, "She looks just like you when you were that age."

I moved to intercept Jenny who was walking toward Uncle Walt carrying her new doll. Then Cal said, "Jenny has to put her doll away."

Cal didn't seem to see my appreciative look. Although Cal and Uncle Walt appeared to get along well, during our last few visits I'd begun to sense that he understood my uncle in a way I didn't. I attributed it to the way men bonded to each other that excluded me.

Aunt Hester quickly said, "Do you use Roman Cleanser when you wash clothes? There's nothing like it to make clothes really clean."

Over the years, I'd often wondered what she knew about Uncle Walt. Appearances meant a lot to her; her respectable position as the leader of St. John's Altar Society and Mrs. Walter Alger "wasn't to be jeopardized," as Dr. Schackmann had said in one of our sessions. But though I knew she was in the habit of hiding her feelings and reactions under pieties, how could she not know about Uncle Walt? At that moment, before Cal had turned Jenny aside, her one good eye stared as if trying to dissuade Uncle Walt's dog from muddying her carpet.

When I was a girl, the pocket thing for me had stopped by the time I got my period, which Aunt Hester called "the curse." But the cuddling on my bed, Uncle Walt pinning me down, increased as if he was angry with me; instead of Dolly, he began calling me Mortimer Snerd, the name of Edgar Bergen's stupid puppet. Afraid of saying anything, of appearing ungrateful, I would freeze. It was often like that, too, when we were alone and he'd circle me, breathing heavily, while I was sitting or standing, as if itching to spring, his frustration permeating the air. It was only recently that I'd made a sickening connection with him and a man who'd circled me in a store before exposing himself.

***

Finally, labor was induced through Jenny's IV. But after a welcome respite, her pains became worse. Why, why, was she taking so long?

I kept checking the clock, and finally at 1:05 p.m., when she'd dilated enough, nurses and doctors appeared in scrubs, and lights blazed as if a director had said, "Lights! Camera! Action!"

They'd decided to use a suction cup to help pull the baby out, and the doctor tried to grab the baby's head as each contraction crested. A trainee had come to watch who looked like she was in high school. She began listing toward me but she couldn't keel over because there wasn't enough room.

When I'd given birth to Jenny, delivery had been a private thing, and afterward I'd sent embossed Hallmark announcements, properly addressed with a fountain pen, illustrating a pink bundled baby carried by a smiling white stork in a hat and tails. Now, I saw a scrub wipe a blob of bowel movement with a bloody towel under the glaring lights before my view was blocked.

"Take a deep breath," the nurse said. "Hold it. Hold it. Push, push. Harder, harder...I can see the head...I want a deep breath. Hold it...Hold it...I want a good, hard push...Harder, harder. Give it all you got. Come on now...that's it, that's it! Good girl, good girl. That was a good one. Rest a little...."

A nurse blotted Jenny's face with a wet cloth. By now I was cursing Scott under my breath for getting her into this mess, and didn't look at him for fear he'd read my mind. Instead I stared at the nurse, who said to Jenny, "You're doing a great job."

After a few minutes, it started over again: "Take a deep breath. Hold it. Hold it." The room had already been uncomfortably warm, but with all the lights glaring over the delivery area and so many people, it became hot. I clenched my hands harder in my resolve not to copy the trainee who was now using me as a prop. I decided I preferred the old delivery version of smiling white storks.

Scott was leaning over the bed, helping Jenny breath. A shiver shot through me and I stiffened—seen from the back, Scott resembled Cal. I recalled then the last thing I heard him say before I lost consciousness having Jenny: "It isn't that bad. Think of what the pioneer women went through." And yet I really wished he was with us now. He'd be still older than me; probably his mouth would form a perpetual sneer by now. Yet a part of me still loved him—perhaps it was like with the larger-than-life-Uncle Walt; they'd been such dominant forces in my life that, even after their death, I was trapped in the vacuum created by their absence.

Finally, when Jenny's screams became unbearable, I heard, "It's a boy!" Tears of gratitude filled my eyes. Jenny would be less likely to remember any bad memories of her own childhood as a girl that way; a boy would have an easier life. Even in this day and age, I still heard the saying about it being a man's world.

The baby was rushed to a table, and I took pictures of the child's first cleaning. It looked like a doll that could cry, like the one I'd wished for on Christmas Eve as a child—with blond hair, a big tummy, and extra long legs and arms. Thank goodness, nothing seemed wrong with him. He looked around as if he'd seen everything before as he was weighed and his feet were inked for an ID. Then he was wrapped in a blanket and placed on Jenny's chest like a loaf of bread.

Where did that dark red mass and white snakelike thing come from in that pan? It was like some primitive memory. Then a shiver ran through me and when I realized they were the umbilical cord and the placenta, I reached for a Pizza Hut flyer on the windowsill to fan my face. The red mass wobbled and my heart skipped a beat. It brought back a dream.

> My liver fell out and flapped like a big tongue. I'd held it tightly to my stomach to keep it from drying out and asked people to help, but they laughed. I tried telephoning, but the dial wouldn't stop spinning. People began laughing in groups when they saw me coming, and when I took the liver away from my stomach, I saw it was dusted with flour, salt, and pepper—ready to be smothered in onions and cooked. The dream ended with me too weak to stand, and Cal relating how students in his human anatomy class used intestines as jump ropes.

Jenny's stitches made blood run down in bright jagged streams. She was told not to be alarmed by blood when she went to the toilet. Then, when everyone began to leave, I looked again at the red mass on the tray. Did they flush the placenta down the toilet? And what about the cord? Was it ground up in a special disposal? Or were they both

carried off in bags along with opened single-serving boxes of
Wheaties, uneaten Jell-O pudding, and *USA Today*?

Scott and Jenny were exhausted, so after taking more pictures and
holding the baby, I left. They asked me to pick up a copy of that day's
Madison Herald for its memorabilia book. I agreed, telling myself not to
go looking for the white cat I'd seen off the exit ramp of the highway.

Another life had been born, an extension of me, who'd try to get it
right. I tried not to remember those fishflies circling the streetlight in
Nicolet City before dying below the light on the road. Every year they
did it: fishflies had to follow the way things were even if their order
was named after the mythical Ephemerides because of their brief life—
it's where the word, "ephemeral" comes from. I learned in class that
some adult species lasted less than two hours, although their fossils
went back millions of years.

I knew Scott and Jenny would be good parents. They were both in
their thirties, had wanted a baby, and had good jobs. As I walked
toward the red exit sign in the white corridor, passing patients
pushing IVs while trying to keep their gowns closed, I realized that
description had also applied to me thirty years ago.

Getting A Tooth Out

A tooth had been bothering me for some time and sensitive toothpaste wasn't going to be the solution. I thought it'd mean another crown or root canal, but when I saw the dentist again, she said it was a wisdom tooth that should've been removed long ago. She referred me to an oral surgeon.

My previous dentist in Nicolet City had said that having a lot of work done on your teeth amplified the anxiety in your mind about having more dental work done. It made you think of all the visits before and enlarged the amount of worry you experienced. What he said was true. Still, having it out would, hopefully, end the pain.

On the way down, I saw an animal on the road and slowed up to try and see if its guts were spread out. If it were smashed enough I wouldn't have to worry about it being still alive. The worst was when there was an animal next to it the following day. It could be its mate, and the thought brought tears. But before I could get close, a county road truck picked it up with some sort of invisible scoop. It was unexpected; I'd never seen it done before.

Why do medical offices have those sliding windows that have to be opened and closed all the time like in some prison? I saw a husky man in a uniform behind the window and assumed it was the oral surgeon.

The receptionist had me do the paperwork. There was an aquarium but I didn't look at it—I heard a motor so it probably was okay since it had an air pump. The waiting room was full. I took a well-thumbed *National Geographic* to steady me, then asked where the restroom was. It was down the hall; the receptionist gave me a key. I kept my eyes on the carpet and didn't look at the skylight indoor garden for fear of seeing plants running out of room under the glass roof.

The article I selected in the *National Geographic* was about how old the earth was and had pictures of animal teeth which helped date the evolution of life. It said that the age of the earth was continually being pushed back; that if you reduced the earth's four and a half billion years to a day, that humans didn't arrive until two seconds to midnight. Wrapping my mind around that was as impossible as it had been in high school.

After another wait, I was duly given a shot. The swab helped numb my cheek, then the oral surgeon shook it before the needle went in. All I saw was his eyes behind glasses above a mask, and gray hair under a cap. He wasn't the husky man.

Gripping my purse and the *National Geographic* on my lap, I had to say, "Give me all the shots you can. I have a hard time getting numb."

"You women and your purses. All I have is a thin wallet." Was he talking about something else because he knew no matter how much he gave it wouldn't numb me?

The chair-side assistant said, "We need to have things with us, don't we? My purse is full of all kinds of things." Ah, she was probably in on the conspiracy. I was in for it and should've asked to be put under and just wake up when it was all over but I'd have to have had someone drive me home.

The oral surgeon said, "I don't understand how you women can lug that stuff. I tell my kids to give me composite pictures of my grandkids instead of one picture for each of them."

I chuckled, and it helped wondering how many grandkids he had and if they were as healthy as mine. After another shot that I didn't feel as much he said, "You carry three pairs of glasses!"

Another chuckle. He must've seen I was worried but I didn't think he'd want to hear about avoiding bifocals, that it was an advantage sometimes not to see things too closely.

The chair had been adjusted so I didn't have to read on my back while waiting to "get a fat lip." The *National Geographic* said that the oldest rock yet found on earth was over four billion years old. I could see why people were upset when Bishop Ussher's date for the first day of creation, Sunday, October 23, 4004 B.C., no longer worked. I'd read it all before but it was comforting to read it again.

The slick paper produced a glare and the white print against the black background made it hard to read. I looked out the window to rest my eyes, but afraid of seeing a stray, I switched my stare to the ceiling. I wondered how wisdom teeth got their name, while trying to grasp whirling on a planet inwardly boiling capped with ice at opposite poles.

My lip was getting numb. Lately hygienists were saying, "For a woman of your age it's uncommon to have all your teeth."

The article said that the brighter the stars look, the nearer they are. The universe is about thirteen billion years old, so it said. To see if my mind still worked, I figured that it took the earth eight and a half billion years to form after the universe began—not that it made it any easier to comprehend.

Seems like dentist chairs always encourage a need to go to the bathroom.

When I returned, the chair had been lowered. I sat and resumed reading. I read that the first forms of life, four billion years ago, resembled blue-green algae. That it's now thought that life began on seafloor vents in mid-ocean ridges instead of pools of water. I stared at the picture caption, LIFE BEGINS, willing it to give up the secrets just like I had when I had first been fascinated with geology. I saw hollow tubes, looking as if they were made of birch bark, with red tubes growing from them by a vent, a gaping blackness like the void I dreaded falling into when things resurfaced that sent me into panic. What looked like a spider could be part of the hollow tube; it looked like a spider I'd found in my sink that I'd put outside.

It was too exasperating not to be able to tell what was alive and what wasn't in the picture, so I went on reading. The first great extinction on earth was caused by the oxygen from capturing energy from sunlight (photosynthesis) that killed off other life forms. I put the magazine down, remembering the inscription carved in stone over the entrance of a natural history museum: "Failure to Adapt Brings Extinction."

The word, 'forms', brought to mind *Godey's Lady's Book*, that popular nineteenth century monthly with engravings of women with sloping shoulders, pinched waists, cupid lips, displaying only tips of tiny feet. The poems and stories, edited by Louis A. Godey, extolled the woman's role as wife, mother, or daughter, the self-effacing Christian life, with illustrations of caged birds and guardian angels.

I shook my head, took up reading again. In the Late Precambrian there were two giant continents; during the late Cenozoic, primates abandoned trees and humans developed within the last ten million years. It was familiar but still fascinating and I read on. Unlike other forms of life, humans are of the same species; at Peru's Pyramid of the Moon, the Moche people practiced human sacrifice. When I looked at pictures of ribs with gashes (thought to indicate they took the flesh off victims), I wondered if it'd been a woman skinned alive.

The next article was about a game preserve where an elephant matriarch unlatched the enclosure gate with her trunk and stood aside to let the antelopes escape. There wasn't a picture of the old matriarch, but I imagined her eyes full of wisdom and blinked back tears.

I was beginning to worry that by the time the tooth was pulled the anesthetic would be worn off when the oral surgeon returned. "You'll only feel a little tug," the masked man said, leaning over. It helped picturing him as Zorro, or the Lone Ranger.

I took a deep breath and all I felt was a bit of discomfort. Gauze was stuffed where the tooth had been.

"That's it?"

"Yes. You must've expected it to crumble."

After a deep sigh of relief it didn't need to be dug out bit by bit, I said, "That's really great! Wow! I can't believe it went so fast and I didn't feel anything."

After a moment I made a request. "I'd like to keep the tooth if I could." I didn't care if they thought I was being silly. It just seemed a shame to leave it behind after all these years.

My chair was adjusted. "Just stay there a minute for some postoperative instructions," the masked man said. He patted my head and was gone.

It was over! After all that worry, waiting, and hoping the ache would go away. I was grinning as much as I could with the gauze in my mouth when a girl came in to tell me to keep applying a little pressure with my teeth on the moistened gauze for fifteen minutes. She gave me a prescription for pain medication along with more gauze in case the bleeding continued. The postoperative instruction sheet said to drink lots of liquids, but not to "use a straw for 24 hours so the blood clot in the socket wouldn't be disturbed."

A few days later I looked at the tooth. It was bigger than I thought, and shaped like a fat curved candy corn, tipped with metal and was white except for the blood. I moved it with a piece of paper. Funny, after being a part of me, I didn't want to touch it. In vain did I look for the nerves with a magnifying glass, those thread-like things , wondering if they'd all come out or if they died in the gaping hole. How long would it take to fill that hole looming in my mouth like that seafloor vent in the *National Geographic*? It could be the tooth next to it that was the problem. So I just had to wait and hope for the best.

I scooped the tooth back into the blood-specked envelope. Perhaps it'd be the only proof I'd lived a million years from now since I'd requested cremation. Assuming, that is, we hadn't obliterated the planet.

War In Iraq

The War in Iraq had begun, so in the evening I turned on CNN. The coalition efforts were called Shock and Awe. I wasn't sure what relationship it had with the 9/11 attack. No one knew the consequences of this war, but flags and decals on cars sprouted up, making me feel unpatriotic, worse than a slacker. Two marines had been killed in action. Someone was talking about the Iraqi home court advantage. The phrase, Operation Iraqi Freedom. Bent men in gas masks. A report on Patriot PAC3 Anti-Missiles. Fifteen hundred bombs and missiles were to strike in the first twenty-four hours. It was the next morning in Baghdad. Earthviewer.com, a digital globe, showed Iraq, and I recalled what Tim O'Brien said about being in the Vietnam War: "You can't tell where you are, or why you're there, and the only certainty is overwhelming ambiguity."

The next evening the Iraqi were blamed for not following the Geneva Convention by showing dead soldiers on television. The NCCA scores were on the bottom of the screen: Syracuse 68, OK St 56. News of a British plane downed by a US plane. On the bottom of the screen: Butler 79, Louisville 71. Saturn Ion. Call 1-800 TERMINIX. Twenty-five dead so far. Tougher going than expected, but I wondered if the media put it that way to make it more competitive and keep viewers. Reporters embedded with troops. Laptops with night time keyboards. US prisoners to be treated humanely or else those guilty would be considered war criminals. Burning US Flags in Afghanistan. Fighting in Basra, Nasiriya.

The next day, a local restaurant had a sign: "Thank you soldiers, You Keep Us Free."

Reporters looked like they knew more than they were reporting. Wall Street tumbled. More debate about whether Saddam was alive. More emphasis on how bombs were aimed at targets to avoid civilians. US troops handing out food. It was 4:30 in the morning in Iraq and calls to prayer were heard. On the bottom of the screen: In WWI and WWII, 1 in 15 soldiers were killed or injured; in the Persian Gulf War, 1 in 1500.

The radio that day had said that many Iraqi people were returning to Iraq to defend it from Operation Iraqi Freedom. Over 75 billion, the projected cost for a thirty-day war.

The next day, a sandstorm complicated fighting and an Iraqi in civilian clothing was shooting at US soldiers. Red and green night shots made natural light unreal. A tense interview aboard an aircraft carrier. Fear of chemical weapons if US troops cross the line around

Baghdad. BBC News fear of suicide bombers. People pouring French wine down drains to protest lack of French support. Television reported that at no other time had so many people seen war unfold in real time. A poll said more people on the East Coast were against the war than those in the Midwest. Finger pointing because it was thought it'd be over by now. Backup troops are still in US because Turkey didn't let them enter; equipment has been on ships for weeks. Iraqi people scrambling for food boxes.

The next time I watched, it sounded like the war might last a year; 215 war protesters arrested in NY in die-ins. Daniel Ellsberg, the Vietnam War Peace Activist, spoke against the war and said that Bush wouldn't listen to the protesters. Hotels.com; Lycopene is now in Centrum. Tank crushing a picture of Saddam; 27 US, 20 British dead so far; 7 US POW's. The war a week and a day old. The tank again crushing Saddam's picture. No weapons of mass destruction had been found yet. Bank of America. GMAC Real Estate. Someone concluded that fewer casualties would result if the war went slower.

Writing notes down helped make what I was seeing and hearing believable.

The train whistled when I was in the bank looking at *Newsweek* covers while waiting for coins to be counted. I'd sorted in bags the pennies, nickels, dimes and quarters, collected from White Water Humane Society canisters. The *Newsweek* March 10 issue was on how faith shaped President Bush's life and presidency; March 17 was on biological weapons and urban warfare; March 24 was about why America scares the world with a picture of MOAB (Mother Of All Bombs); March 31 was on "Shock and Awe," Baghdad on fire. The bank had 'Support Our Troops' US flag posters for sale, yellow ribbons were on lampposts and tree trunks. The train whistled but I couldn't tell what direction it was going.

In July, there was talk about impeaching President Bush.

Articles came out like the one about Don Rumsfeld, responding before the war on questions about terrorism, "As we know, there are known knows. There are things we know we know. We also know there are known unknowns. That is to say, we know there are some things we do not know. But there are also unknown unknowns, the ones we don't know we don't know."

Where were all those tons of deadly weapons that Iraq was supposed to have? A *Christian Science Monitor* article reported there were about 230,000 U.S. troops in and around Iraq, including about 150,000 inside Iraq; that troop morale had hit bottom from the danger, heat, and uncertainty of the occupation. How many had combat trauma? They, and their families, would have to deal with post-traumatic stress disorder for the rest of their lives.

By early September, it was reported that hundreds of billions of dollars would be needed to rebuild Iraq. That postwar cost was going to be much more than anticipated; the infrastructure wasn't known when the war began, nor was it anticipated that looting and sabotage would occur. Thousands of rare museum pieces had been stolen and archaeological sites looted. It was the same after the Gulf War, and the wars in Cambodia and Bosnia.

In October, Senator Robert Byrd remarked on the Senate floor that people in the US had been led to war like spectators admiring "The Emperor's New Clothes" when he really wore none. "Taking the nation to war based on misleading rhetoric and hyped intelligence is a travesty and a tragedy. It is the most cynical of all cynical acts. It is dangerous to manipulate the truth."

An article in the *Cleveland Plain Dealer* by columnist Connie Schultz, began: "The war in Iraq, like all wars, has left us women behind," and went on to state the fact that "Men declared this war. Men planned, or failed to plan, this war. Men misled the public to wage this war."

Tying Up Ends

Fall, when the slant of light in the sky has changed imperceptibly until one day you sense it is no longer summer. Fall, when you close basement vents and secure the windows, when you hear ducks heading south in their wedge formation and wonder again how they know the direction to fly and when to depart. Fall, when you look more closely at your house and wish for a fireplace. A contemplative season, a reckoning of accounts, when "dust thou art and to dust you shall return" seems as real as the dry leaves scattered by the wind.

***

One September day, after it stopped raining, I went out on the deck of my home in White Water to lose the feeling of being trapped. The freshness of the air reminded me of my dreams of flying with my arms outspread like Superman's. And I once again wondered why the flat sky and flat land in White Water were so oppressively near one another. The trunks of the downed trees were almost black. Fear suddenly washed over me when I thought they'd moved and I'd jumped from my chair before I realized that the deck just presented them at a different angle from how I usually saw them.

In the evenings when the frogs croaked, I thought about dinosaur ancestors and wouldn't have been surprised to have seen cavemen dragging prey in one hand and women in the other. After all, in the scheme of things, it was just a blink of an eye.

White Water was a place where high wind came up quickly, as if the lack of big trees permitted the wind to have its way with the land. When I saw green leaves that had fallen, toppled by the wind, I wanted to put them in water or in the loamy ground—but either way, they'd die.

In town, things slowed down on weekends. People in dresses or suits gathered at the many churches. One Saturday, through a vast glass window of one of those modern churches, I saw people crowded around a bride. Something about the long white dress made her look like a ghost in the middle of all those guests; it probably had to do with being given away by her father to her husband—to give up one man's name and take on another's, though times were changing and perhaps this bride would become one of those hyphenated "Smith-Johnsons."

She stood out among the well-wishers, as brides always do at weddings. Jenny, I recalled, had certainly been radiant and glowing at her wedding. Before Mark accompanied her down the aisle, I'd told him to walk very slowly, to make the walk last as long as possible, because never again would she be such a center of attention. Weren't virgins once given much adulation before being sacrificed to the gods? Given the best food, clothed in finery, decked with flowers, and then … tossed into a well or down a cliff? Hadn't priests blessed them and bestowed new names upon them?

And yet, afraid as I'd become when I thought of marriage, I'd probably marry again if I could. Be like those birds in *The Thorn Birds* that sang the sweetest just before impaling themselves on thorns.

Whenever I entered the hardware stores I always felt I'd come in at the middle of something, because men would stop their conversation or lower their voices, shifting their weight while giving furtive glances. A clerk would slowly disengage himself and bare his teeth in a smile. It was silly in this day and age for me to react like this, but inevitably I became helpless, smiling, apologetic, seeking the expertise of a male—afraid, perhaps, that if I didn't I'd be accused like Scarlett in *Gone With the Wind* of unsexing herself by not following the accepted role of dependency for women while fending for herself. If I did see another woman, she seemed to give me a pitying look and edge closer to the man with her.

As I drove home, buildings looked flatter and had a disposable/interchangeable look, as if they'd decided the constant flux of students was best handled by conformity, or as if the Wisconsin Continental Glacier was still leveling all things in its path. My new house also had this flatness, and the ceilings were lower than my old house. There were few old buildings in White Water to lend a sense of continuity, to what had happened before.

The next morning, unable to sleep because of a plant I'd seen in the library in a pot too small for it, despite my having dropped a note in their suggestion box, I saw the impersonal, ever-widening stare of dawn through the blinds. It seeped in so slowly...if I hadn't kept my eyes on it, I wouldn't have seen it. As the blackness outside my window was replaced by gray, as on a film negative, I wondered how many were seeing the night creep in windows on the opposite side of the earth.

That night a television show said seventy percent of the earth was covered by oceans and it wasn't known until the 1960's that the largest geographical features on earth were the mountain ranges underwater; that there were creatures living underwater independent of the sun; that new life was constantly being discovered; that probably life began around warm underground vents; that all the water on earth eventually passed inside the earth through black smokers, I tried imagining the wonder the scientists felt when first seeing the black smokers in 1977 on the East Pacific Rise crammed in a submersible vehicle. Black smokers resembling erupting volcanoes are formed when superheated water from below the Earth's crust comes through the ocean floor. The minerals from the crust dissolved by the hot water precipitates when hitting cold ocean water, making black chimney-like formations around the ocean floor vents, hence the name, black smokers. I knew that an organism has been discovered that uses the faint glow coming from the black smokers, the first found in nature to use light other than sunlight for photosynthesis.

I always wonder, when collecting rainwater for my plants and Kitty, where it has traveled, and wish I could see the clouds as well as the depths of the earth where it has been. The water is transparent and yet is so heavy to lift in pails.

***

In a documentary, the announcer said that in the 1930's, after millions had died, mass arrests in Russia were no longer necessary because terror itself kept the people in line. There was footage on concentration camps, and, seeing it, I once again couldn't believe such horror could've gone on without my knowledge while I was growing up as a child. "Only when you learned to cope with atrocities," the narrator said, "could you see what you'd repressed"—but he didn't say how. Records weren't released about how many soldiers weren't able to adapt and ended up institutionalized. The Jews hadn't believe places like Dachau existed because it was too inconceivable; when they had been warned about the camps, they had usually thought that the bearers of the news had lost their minds.

The documentary helped focus things for me. Being abused, it seemed, and being terrorized were not much different. I'd begun sensing similarities, for instance, between myself and Mary Elizabeth's father, Uncle Will, who'd served in World War I. He could never sit still, like Uncle Walt's hunting dogs trying to get rid of porcupine quills—the more they tried, the deeper the barbs penetrated.

Uncle Will did a great job reciting "Casey at the Bat." He'd go through an elaborate windup after carefully adjusting an invisible hat, and then strike out. I remembered mimes placing their hands so convincingly that you were sure there were walls in front of them instead of air; people liked to laugh at others who were uncertain if things were real.

Mary Elizabeth had once brought an 8mm movie showing her father turning a hat at odd angles, clowning around as he paced like the footage of the caged lion at the zoo that preceded him in the same movie.

Uncle Walt was in the home movie, on his stomach, target shooting. When he picked up shells that lay alongside him on the blanket, he grinned in his confident way. When his hair fell over his eyes, I couldn't watch anymore.

When Uncle Howard used to visit, cans of beer appeared in his hand like magic as he paced like a shark forced to keep moving because that was the way it breathed.

Now that Uncle Howard was dead, I wished I could've comforted him by saying I knew what it was like to never be at peace and to always feel pursued. Had he hoped by marrying and having children that things would change, that time would help? But I suspected it didn't, and that Uncle Howard never talked to anyone about it. He didn't seem to really notice his daughter, Mary Elizabeth. She got her affirmation from being a Catholic and managing to maintain a fashionable appearance.

The rare times Uncle Howard looked at me, it seemed he never really saw me, but now I knew that his rage and sadness didn't have anything to do with me. Had he been warned about his drinking? I'd never seen him drunk, even if he had died from cirrhosis of the liver—to stop would probably have meant that he'd been institutionalized. I wondered what he thought when his son left for World War II. Was he one of those soldiers who couldn't wait to forget war? I'd noticed that after 1918 writers seldom used superlatives such as the most, the highest—or wrote as if they were sure of anything.

Had he ever connected his shell shock with the trenches? Was it seeing comrades skewered as bait on barbed-wire fences, or was it staring at a familiar sky hearing "Twinkle, twinkle, little star" while covered in the body parts of his comrades that pushed him over the edge? Was it then that he'd written "Not Before," to tell how things were and what they'd become to help him tell what was real?

"Not Before" were the words I carried around in my purse to help me fight the panic of obsessions. Dr. Schackmann had said my trench was dug by being brought up by a seductive uncle, and it had deepened after marrying Cal.

I'd read that enough similar symptoms had been observed in World War I soldiers to coin the term shell shock; after World War II, the Korean War, and the Vietnam War, it was called post-traumatic stress disorder. I related to what Tim O'Brien wrote about being in the Vietnam War: "The bad stuff never stops happening; it lives in its own dimension, replaying itself over and over." Vincent never had to join the service.

***

When I was going through my divorce, Vincent had said, "With Uncle Walt and Aunt Hester behind Cal, what can you do? But the Lord knows I did not think much of Cal staying at their place before he moved into his new house."

I told him, "Yes, we had shelter with them as adopted children, and they fed and educated us. But what about love and respect?"

"You have always expected too much," Vincent replied. "Then you go off in your own world and refuse to see things."

"See things?"

"Why we need the teachings of Holy Mother the Church."

My grin must have indicated my reaction. He didn't give me a chance to reply. "Whatever you think is wrong with you would look small if you read the lives of the saints. No one is free. It is imperative to have order."

"A patriarchy?"

"A hierarchy," he said. "I have to follow those over me in the church. Since you have no husband to obey, you must follow Uncle Walt."

Even if I hated to admit it, I thought it simplified things, and that Cal could've been right, too, when he said you had no choice but to follow your script. Hadn't Nietzsche advised, "Be careful lest in casting out the devils you cast out the best thing that's in you."

Still, I said to my brother, "I think women form their beliefs from what they see rather than from theories, because we have closer ties to the rhythms of the earth than men. Women are more practical. We have more of a feel for what's important, what's real, and workable." Then added something that'd been forming my mind, "Women have to be stronger because they don't have many myths to follow—the heroes men have like Odysseus and Paul Bunyon. Yet that very lack of inclusion frees them from being constricted by traditional thought, and allows them the freedom to find meaning that works for them."

Vincent tried to rub some lint off his sleeve, but it went back as if it'd been magnetized. "Why invent something when everything is figured out for you by trained men in Holy Mother the Church? Questions just bring more questions which cannot be answered by untrained people. Do you see where that dangerous and foolish thinking has gotten you? Where is your community to belong to, your support?"

He had a point--to forget what he said about not belonging, I recalled telling Mary Elizabeth's husband that when I mowed the grass when it was so dry one summer in Nicolet City, "I'd never seen clouds of dust like that before." And when he said, "It's never been so dry before," the logic, the mere acceptance of saying things the way they were, seemed crude, unfeminine, impolite, non-Catholic.

***

Being free was something I'd wanted ever since I was a child, and now that Uncle Walt was dead, I had to explore a new world in White Water where I wasn't Dr. Hyde's wife or Walter Alger's daughter.

Though I'd gone to some incest survivor group meetings, I hadn't seen a counselor since Rebecca had said that she was looking for a playmate; it could have meant nothing but I no longer felt comfortable continuing sessions. Now, in my daydreams, I pretended my mother was there, somehow captured in her quilt that I often touched for reassurance.

"So your obsessions have become worse," my mother softly inquired.

"Ye-es, I'm afraid they have."

"Why do you think they have, my child?"

"Probably it's because my daughter had a baby triggered things. It was after she was born, when I returned to Nicolet City where I was raised by Uncle Walt. Untangling things is like watching one of those *Columbo* episodes where Peter Falk figures who did it after it was done."

I'd begun worrying about a neighbor's shrub, which was in a small pot, because shrubs belonged in the ground with plenty of room for roots. The thought of it not having enough room left me feeling suffocated, and I woke up in the morning wanting to rescue it.

"I must feel trapped," I told her, "and I can't get away. It wasn't this way when my son's daughter was born and now I turn fans on at night to lessen that trapped feeling, even after having central air conditioning installed."

Her voice was a caress when she said, "Why did you return to Nicolet City?"

"Uncle Walt told Cal about an opening, and my husband wanted to leave Detroit after the race riots."

"You were there when they happened?" Her gray eyes, the color of early morning fog, quickly darkened with alarm.

I nodded. "They started when Cal and I had gone out for the first time after Mark was born. The James Bond movie was stopped and everyone was told to go home because rioters were advancing down Grand River from the inner city. The ride home through empty streets seemed forever not knowing what would happen or what we'd find when we got home."

"How awful," she said in a velvet voice.

"When I got Mark from the neighbor's, I was afraid. I moved his bassinet into our bedroom and peeked between the drawn curtains, afraid of seeing the disaster coming closer, like Scarlett O'Hara in the burning of Atlanta. And the news blackouts left me feeling isolated."

"You were such a lovely baby. I loved you every minute I had you, my Lily. You're my loveliest lily, the fairest of them all."

I often wanted to ask her if she went back into their burning nursery not to save a strain of lilies she and my father had been perfecting, but because she felt her life was over since it was only a week before that my father had been killed. But I never could.

One time she asked, "How do you think Cal got the way he was."

"I think the door to other possibilities was still ajar, though he was born into a Calvinist-type family. He loved playing the piano, you know, and there was a lot of good in him. The door was closed when he became a surgeon, with the demands that profession brought. And then it was locked when he realized my childhood relationship with Uncle Walt, after we moved to Nicolet City."

The soothing voice said, "Do you think Cal fell out of love with you?"

"In court he said he believed couples should stay together for the sake of children." Why did she have to remind me that Cal had never told me he loved me—it was a word he didn't say lightly and I'd admired him for it.

I said, "I saw a television documentary about black holes that was beyond anything I've ever seen. Nothing can escape falling in a black hole once it reaches a certain proximity to it, not even light. Nothing can come out of the gravitational field. It absorbs all light so is called a black hole. It can be detected by studying stars that orbit a region in space that looks empty." I had to share it with her because the stark fear they engendered was like getting close to what really happened in my past.

Sometimes I conjured up my mother with an Aladdin-shaped vase I'd bought as a child in a secondhand store. Her concerned gray eyes would always appear, but my joy was often overshadowed by my anger at her leaving me as if she'd started the fire that took her life.

***

How long would it be before I no longer heard Aunt Hester repeating like a Greek chorus, that if I didn't have my kids baptized they'd go to hell? How long before I no longer feared seeing Uncle Walt's outline hovering in my bedroom door? Long ago, Dr. Schackmann had told me, "You were set up."

I no longer wanted to be the sacrificial goat chased from the village with a red mark on its back to appease the gods. But I also learned in folklore class that, traditionally, women have been grouped either as good and quiet, or knowledgeable and evil. Giving a name to something that isn't understood makes it less frightening; that people wrongly treated in life have ghosts that will not be quieted.

A Magazine Survey

On the way to a dental checkup, to stave off seeing strays, I recited one of Mrs. Stoke's holy card verses she'd said my mother had liked: "The Lord bless you and keep you, the Lord shine His face upon you," and, since I'd forgotten the rest of it, continued with "The Lord is my shepherd, I shall not want." I pictured my mother's girlhood friend saying her rosary, the worn beads rattling like bones against pews once been living trees. I was grateful she kept in contact with me because she was a link to my mother.

In the waiting room, I read a request in a magazine for volunteers to take part in a study about child incest survivors. The two other women in the room were discussing how cleverly Julia Roberts had faked her death to escape an abusive husband in *Sleeping with the Enemy*. The magazine included articles like: "Be His Very Best in Bed" and "What Men Won't Tell You," and models portraying the latest look.

For weeks afterward I debated about participating in the incest survivor survey. My family was the only one I'd ever had and wasn't the illusion of a good family as necessary as breathing? Yet shouldn't the kind of things that happened to me be stopped in order to end churning out people like me? But then, wasn't it human nature? Men are stronger than women, and the strong have ruled the weak from the beginning of time. And doesn't the Bible admonish wives to obey their husbands and honor their fathers? But wasn't there a wider truth that was corroded by silence, that encouraged things to keep happening? Didn't an obligation to tell the truth extend beyond my own family, a larger duty?

Muriel Rukeyser had written that if a woman told the truth about her life, "The world would split open." But I feared that if I spoke up, I'd be lucky to even get a response such as: "So what? Abuse is as common as chicken pox, and like the poor, it'll always be with us. You think you can fix the world? Think again, lady."

Still, why not do myself a favor and get rid of the burden of carrying it around? But wouldn't I always so what difference would it make? Why taint myself even more? But didn't abuse flourish as a fungus while it was hidden away? Why not expose it into the light of day and help stop victims being viewed as contaminated? Wasn't the long tradition of silence protecting widespread abuse, the heavy silence as bad as abuse?

Mrs. Stoke's priest had said, "Accept things the way they are because it's God's will." At times I thought it was solid wisdom; at other times, the easy way out. Didn't the Greeks have the Three Fates deciding birth, life, and death? Other major religions held similar beliefs. In class it had popped up in Alexander Pope's, *Essay on Man*: "Whatever is, is right." The women in Mrs. Stoke's church, reciting rosaries to accept things, were probably different ones now than when I was there. Still, would they be there on their knees if their mothers hadn't opposed things? Wouldn't I be doing a greater good to my children and their children by telling the truth? Vincent had dismissed what I was trying to escape as of my own making. The last present he gave me was a mug with a cartoon of a woman driving a bicycle in the wrong direction on an expressway.

And wouldn't I be a snitch, and speaking ill of the dead as well, if I spoke up? And if no one cared, wouldn't that make it worse? My hopes of how things would be transformed leaving me without even that? What if no one would have anything to do with me? Wasn't I unrealistic to hope that things would ever become better, and only still 'poking my head through the clouds' as Cal said? One Greek had said that the unexamined life wasn't worth living, and yet another gouged out his eyes after finding the truth. And even after I told, it wouldn't mean the end of all my symptoms—a magic wand wouldn't have waved them away like I so desperately wished. I'd also have sullied the Alger and Hyde names, and all for naught.

Why did I now remember the mole I'd caught in Nicolet City? The one in the humane trap that let things go free once they were opened? When I came home from work, it was dead in the fogged trap, as if it'd tried very hard to escape. For hours after, I felt I couldn't get enough air.

And yet, if I didn't face the past, the symptoms wouldn't lessen, because they were attempts to get things right—to rescue and thereby feel rescued; to make sure animals had a home and plants had enough room, light, and water to grow. Things partially consumed by fire lacking air will smolder and smoke until energy is expended through fire.

When I got enough courage to ask a physician during an annual physical in Nicolet City if I could have post-traumatic stress disorder, he dismissed the possibility. It was what soldiers got, he told me— predisposed soldiers, because not all of them returned traumatized. He said it with certainty because at the time it was accepted by the medical community to be true.

I wondered how much to tell Mark and Jenny. If they knew, wouldn't it ruin the image of Cal and Uncle Walt? What right did I have to do that? Wouldn't I be angry with them for not taking my side, and feel guilty if they did?

It had been like finding a hidden picture in one of those children's puzzles—once you knew where it was, you couldn't believe you hadn't spotted it immediately. Yet, like those pictures, it was disconnected from what was considered real. Whenever *Indiana Jones and the Temple of Doom* is on TV, I can't watch the scene with the snakes because it triggers something even it wasn't real. Still, it isn't known what composes dark matter making so much of the universe.

Tool Bag

At my next session, Dr. Bradford gave me a pep talk: "How many people have your string of research work. Look at what you've accomplished!"

I did have that. Through the years, it was something I knew I could do and had done—and was still doing—no matter what, that provided me with credibility, a sense of grounding, and acceptance in the wider world of my profession. My last work was for the Geological Society of America but it seemed by another person.

"You've supported yourself and your children with no help," Dr. Bradford went on, "and they've turned out well. You said they are excellent parents and are leading steady, good lives." I nodded. "And you'll agree that bringing them up with your husband and uncle was like Odysseus' passage between Scylla and Charybdis."

He knew I was taking English classes so he probably thought it was a fitting comparison. Still, it could have been because he was a college psychologist. There was a poster on his door with a saying by Eugene O'Neill: "Obsessed by a fairy tale, we spend our lives searching for a magic door and a lost kingdom of peace." I smiled at his odyssey allusion, but was thinking about how I could have been a better mother, and that Mark and Jenny turning out well had nothing to do with me.

The sun highlighted Dr. Bradford's bald head as he said, "You haven't been put in a mental hospital, and you've managed to contribute a great deal." When he said, "As I told you before, Lily, children blame themselves in cases of abuse because the only reason they can think, of why caretakers would act that way, is because they, the victims, are bad. So they try harder to please." Dr. Schackmann had said that no matter how hard I tried to please, I would never feel it was enough.

Dr. Bradford in another session had told me to keep a tool bag to use when a new drive to rescue arose, so I carried this list:

TOOL BAG
Take care of yourself
Write it down
Pray
Swear
Read about post-traumatic stress
Not Before—it always wasn't like this
This is just another one—there have been many

Your brain isn't the same
Things are seen through the eyes of the perceiver
Avoid being drawn in whirlpools—they're like children's tantrums that feed on themselves

I'd refer to it so often that every few years the paper would fall apart and I'd rewrite it, adding any tools that would help, deleting those that no longer worked.

A student in one of my classes had recently given a presentation about Native American clothing and had brought a dress with uneven fringes and crooked beading. The student explained they made their clothing that way purposely to illustrate their belief that one shouldn't compete with the perfection of the Great Spirit. It left me thinking, again, about what Dr. Schackmann had observed: I was afraid of uncovering my soul. He'd also said, "When you choose, you can look at things straight as an arrow."

There was Winnebago blood on my mother's side, though no one would talk about it so I never knew how much. When Dr. Schackmann brought up the subject of Native Americans, I identified with it.

Dr. Bradford said, "Give yourself credit for managing a job, since you were brought up in a time when it was held that a woman's place was in the home. You've done very well. Your panic hasn't driven you to getting into trouble, like being arrested like you said you feared, thus confirming the rumor that you'd gone to Ithaca to be in a rest home."

I nodded. I was still having a hard time, though, trying to wrap my mind around his advice: "If your relatives think it's day when it's really night, go ahead and let them believe it."

"As long as you resent your uncle," Dr. Bradford advised, "he has a hold on you. You can't forget, but you can forgive."

I said, "When I began using some of my uncle's swear words, I realized he'd learned them from someone, that he was the result of other influences that I didn't know about. For all I know, his parents could have done terrible things to him. Aren't we all products of our environment?" Had Uncle Walt been driven to find acceptance from me that he hadn't from his mother, his other wives, or Aunt Hester?

"Not all of us chose to inflict ourselves on others, though," he said.

"Then how can I forgive him," I asked a few moments after digesting his words.

"It will take time."

I shook my head in disbelief and for some reason recalled the pyramid sand pile on the Nicolet River, the largest in Wisconsin that would continue to stay there because it cost too much to remove. And *The Emperor's New Clothes*: how crowds of people cheered in admiration for the emperor's clothes when they didn't exist.

On my drive home I remembered asking in an English class, "Don't writers have a harder time now? The social restraints which writers like Edith Wharton wrote about no longer exist."

"You've just described post-modernism," the professor said. I'd jotted what he said down to hide my blank expression although I knew post-modernism meant coming after modernism which was generally accepted to have ended in 1945 with the atomic bomb.

Post-modern was explained as multi-views: no two people see things the same way. Young students in class accepted it without raising an eyebrow, or as one said, "I have no trouble with it." The professor, in her thirties, was raised on post-modernism but I felt stuck between modernism and post-modernism. One part of me believed in an accepted canon of literature, another rejecting it as the world of white males while my mind twisted back and forth as if watching some tennis match.

Uncovering The Dream

Dr. Bradford began the session with a question. "Have you been able to remember any more of that dream you gave to Dr. Schackmann?" He'd asked me this more than once before, and told me to consider trying to recall it. He assured me I could just remember what I could handle and could stop anytime.

Fear clamped my jaw shut.

"The one that begins in the basement?" he said, prodding me.

Why did I again recall the rescue worker on that television documentary I'd seen? The part where he'd related, "When a person falls between a passing train and a train platform, the body gets twisted like a corkscrew from the ribs down. When they're moved, they die because their guts fall out."

Dr. Bradford said, "I think, in some respects, that you're holding yourself back. What I mean is, I believe that now that you've been considering telling those closest to you that you were abused, you might be ready now to face that dream, and the fear it engenders. I'd like you to try."

When I didn't reply he said, "Why not close your eyes and see if you remember anything. Nothing can hurt you here."

"You really think it'd help?" I said, even though I knew he thought so, and had been building myself up to do it.

"Yes. As I said before, your uncle and husband are dead and you no longer live in Nicolet City. You are free here and can move on. They are no longer around to hurt you. Your children are grown up, married, and are doing well. You've proven that you are strong, and remember, you are free to stop any time."

I gulped air, nodded, tried to relax, taking in details of Dr. Bradford's office to remember things secure and ordinary, as if departing not unlike a child taunted to go underwater for the first time. The box of Kleenex was in the same spot on his desk with a tissue ready for students who could cry—students I envied.

I'd come to have confidence in Dr. Bradford and wanted to show him I was willing to help myself. I owed it to him to try. What he'd said in the past showed me he was a very sound, ethical psychologist I was very fortunate to have come across the best one and the most experienced at the university counseling center. I was coming to the end of my allowed number of appointments as a student so it would be wise, if I could now, to remember. He'd never shown any physical interest in me; I was older than when I'd seen Dr. Schackmann and Dirk, but still—I couldn't close my eyes with anyone, so I studied my purse. I heard Cal telling me on the way to a medical association dinner about one of his colleagues taking advantage of women under anesthetic but all of the cases had been tossed out of court because he used a sharp lawyer. When I asked why the members didn't stop him, Cal had laughed and said, "If the women get pregnant, they'll end up with more intelligent kids."

A deep wave of rage that nothing had been done about the surgeon even though it was years ago, suddenly spurred me on. I felt strength rising in me, welling up to surmount my terror. In a voice without emotion that sounded very far away I said, "It is damp, musty," steeling myself against unfathomable dread to descend, telescope, and drift as I fixed on the my purse through narrowed eyes. Taking a deep breath, I say, "There's stone walls and sand. There's a heavy silence, muffled, the kind you hear only underground. Dim light is coming from the small window just above the ground."

I sought Dr. Bradford's benevolent presence, to provide needed security, and made myself continue with downward eyes again as if telling him a story.

"It's as if I've dropped to a deep murky unknown abyss I'd always feared. There's a heavy timelessness, a feeling of falling—free falling in the dark, of suspended time, things closing in, of everything gray or black. Everything's heavy, muffled, isolated; snakes writhing--I can't get away, I can't breathe. Uncle Walt's hair tumbles over his eyes."

I paused to try and stay my racing heart, clenched my purse tighter before continuing, "Words won't come out of my mouth no matter how hard I try. I don't exist."

It was impossible to tell how much time had gone by, or how much Dr. Bradford could tell from a voice that had no resemblance to my own.

"Go on," Dr. Bradford said softly, "you're doing fine. Remember, if it gets too much, just stop."

"I...I keep struggling for air. I watch the dust flutter in the narrow beam of light coming from the basement window turn into tiny pink butterflies, and I flutter with the pretty pink butterflies out the small window in the stone wall. They are such delicate dancing butterflies, so free, so happy, like fairies in one of my books. We fly in the sunshine. Gradually I can breathe without fighting and the deafening silence doesn't weigh so.

I paused and heard Dr. Bradford gently say, "Yes?"

My voice continued, "Uncle Walt says, 'You are my own Dolly. You hear?' You'll never get away. Nobody will want a bad girl, you hear?' He shakes me until I go as limp as my oilcloth doll, pockets his jackknife that'd fallen out.

After hearing Dr. Bradford's reassurances, my voice sounded like it was coming from a long tunnel when I said, "I don't know how long it was before I rose from the sand. I never cried."

I stared at my hands clutching my purse, as if coming from being submerged under water deep and murky with primeval age. After a few moments, now aware of warm blood in my mouth from where I must've gashed it, I was able to say, "What does a dream prove?" trying not to gag as if pulling worms out of my mouth that kept breaking.

Dr. Bradford's eyes didn't reflect disgust. "You're doing very well, Lily."

I shrugged. My shoulders felt heavy while the room blurred, as I fought to forget the shouting silence, the mustiness, the suffocation, the heavy timelessness.

It took a lot of effort to shake my head and say, "Dreams aren't reality."

After a pause, Dr. Bradford said, "Do you remember anything else happening around this time?"

I opened my purse and got some Wendy's yellow napkins. Clutching them in my fist, I recalled going up the basement stairs knowing part of me was left behind. "It was around that time that I kept putting my underwear out on a chair for Aunt Hester to wash."

"You wanted her to know."

"I don't know," visualizing Aunt Hester's thin lips form an even tighter line.

"But you know you put your underwear out like that on a chair."

"I changed them so often, I'd run out."

"Why?"

With a racing heart, I said slowly "I felt dirty." It raced faster when I wondered if that could be why I still changed my sheets and towels after using them once. And how I always felt cleaner when Vincent, in saying mass, wiped his hands on white linen after the altar boy poured water over them. Staring at my hands, I added after a deep breath, "It was also when I started stuttering."

Warm blood slipped from my nose, and, blotting it with the yellow napkins, I heard Cal remind me what pioneer women went through. The red against the yellow glared like something from a circus, or sand that swallowed so quickly. In psychology class, I'd learned that Rorschach included anatomy in each inkblot, but I never saw any; to avoid having anything else fall into place like dominoes, I pictured a princess and was deciding on the shade of her gown when Dr. Bradford broke in: "It will take time to internalize what you related."

I was glad to be with Dr. Bradford, someone I trusted, when I'd finally been strong enough to dig down to retrieve the dream, grateful for the security that Wendy's napkins provided when I'd lost all concept of time. He had me stay overtime until I was steady enough to drive.

On the way out, a poster in the lobby of the sculpture, *The Thinker*, hunched over with one hand on his chin with words about the importance of thinking for yourself seemed mockery. Even if in a semi-dazed state, I remembered that the Greek word 'psyche' was the same for soul and butterfly and shook my head. When I went out the door, the essence of the dream stayed closer to what was real than the parking lot.

When I got home I decided if things got too bad, I'd daydream about Mitchell, buy some new perfume with a lovely name. Estée Lauder was always coming out with something like SpellBound, Beautiful, or Tuscany Per Donna, that had notes of jasmine, honeysuckle, and tuberose. The glass bottles for each had their own distinctive shape and were well protected by beautiful boxes in muted shades that begged to be kept after the perfume had gone.

Sharing The Past

I'd kept my past a secret because I didn't know what had happened to me when I was little for sure, and because to say anything would've been disrespectful to my aunt and uncle who'd I been taught to believe were God's representatives on earth. Dr. Bradford had urged me to share my past to my children and wider family. "The main thing," he said, "is you will no longer have to carry the burden of secrecy. You will have freed yourself to go forward. Like I've said, you can be anything you want to be. People don't know you here in White Water--they could believe you're a deep sea diver."

I'd written first to my oldest relative and told her about Uncle Walt. She wrote back advising me to ask God to forgive him. Another relative wrote, "We all have crosses to bear." Two others to whom I revealed my past never replied.

I wrote to Aunt Heidi, too. She didn't believe what the counselors had said, writing back that she didn't know "how I could have believed such a thing." She didn't answer any of my questions, but did say, more than once, that her parents had never abused her and Uncle Walt. It never occurred to me that they had, though I was always a bit afraid of my distant and reserved grandmother, dubbed "the ice queen," who didn't show emotions. Was Uncle Walt the way he was because his mother hadn't given him the nurturance he needed?

Aunt Hester was the first relative whom I told in person, though I dreaded it. She had been there all those years, and, as a little girl, I'd reached out to her, only to be rebuffed in her cold, religious way. I debated bringing it up now, but knew I had to for my own sake, as Dr. Bradford had said.

I said to her, "I've wanted to tell you many times about Uncle Walt. He didn't treat me as a child but as a female, and I've been told it was incest."

We were at lunch after shopping at Marshall Field's. I suppose I thought that would make her feel more comfortable, although maybe I was trying to comfort myself. But as I'd expected when I'd rehearsed telling her, Aunt Hester's mouth and eyes narrowed. But she didn't interrupt me. Instead she got an embarrassed look, as if what I'd told her was in bad taste. When I said I'd wanted to tell her the truth for years, her embarrassment changed to an expression I'd never seen before and couldn't define. I ended with, "Uncle Walt showed no consideration for me as a person."

"You never wanted for a thing," she chided, "and we provided you with clothes and an education." And added in her hushed church voice, "We always took you to church."

I knew what it meant to be in denial, so her reaction shouldn't have surprised me; I hoped she might now that Uncle Walt was gone. She asked no questions.

She looked at her watch and said, "I want to go and buy that Hummel figurine, the one with the girl carrying the broom." She insisted on paying the bill and when she said in her tight-lipped church voice, "I'll request prayers for you from the St. Joseph's Indian School apostolate of prayer. They do so much good work for poor Indian children," I knew the topic was closed.

I don't know if I would've told Mark when I did, if not for the fact that I was afraid to visit him and his wife in their new house. I'd feel compelled to re-pot all his plants in larger pots and worry about whether his children's pets were getting the right care. I could now see how post-traumatic stress disorder was self-perpetuating: I feared seeing something that wasn't getting the right care, but by avoiding situations, like not seeing Mark, it made me feel abandoned.

I wrote to him. He e-mailed saying that my past was insightful and that I was coming up with conclusions that "employed a lot of psychology."

In high school, when he was taking psychology, Mark said, "Mr. Olds said he'd known a woman who people started calling nuts and she became nuts."

I'd nodded and said, "I can see how that could happen."

"He also said if water was thrown on your face when you were very thirsty and couldn't get any, it could drive you nuts."

I could also see how that could happen.

When he visited me, and we were in the kitchen as I washed the dishes and he dried, he said, "I remember Dad pushing you around and yelling at you. There are always two sides to things."

How much more hadn't I uncovered yet? Was I still confusing Cal and Uncle Walt? Should I have waited until I was clearer about everything? But I couldn't wait, because I was about their age, in my thirties, when my time bomb went off and the symptoms of post-traumatic stress disorder began. If I died now and they had to face trauma from the past without the benefit of my knowledge, they'd be at a disadvantage. I settled on the cliché "knowledge is power." It was better to know, because if they didn't, they could conjure up even worse things if the past caught up with them. They'd never stop resenting my filing for divorce and I could understand that.

I told Jenny when we were returning after a shopping trip and probably wouldn't have spoken so freely if I hadn't been driving and able to keep my eyes on the road.

She listened closely and then said, "Did anyone else believe it happened?" When I related what Caroline and Susan had said about Uncle Walt and Cal—"They're out to crack you"—and that when I'd told Cal, he'd agreed that Uncle Walt could have done such a thing, she merely stared ahead. Out of nervousness, I went on to tell her some of what I'd read about abuse. As I did, I became angry, and it bubbled over into red hot rage with swear words she'd ever heard me say that surprised both of us. Was this what Dr. Bradford meant when he said that most incest victims experienced depression which was largely repressed anger?

It was hard telling her because I remembered how necessary it was for me as a girl to have a good opinion about those who were family. The irony could be that I'd done too good a job of hiding things, and I shouldn't be surprised that people didn't believe what had been hidden. The way I was perceived, as a result, no doubt made me sound less credible now. When my children were growing up, Mark had once asked me what it meant to be schizoid after I picked him up at Cal's, during that period after the divorce when we had split custody; no doubt he'd heard his father call me worse than that. After the divorce, they, like everyone else, saw me as the one who'd destroyed the family. As Uncle Walt termed it, I was "not running on all cylinders." And yet part of me resented not being believed now— that perhaps just imagining what the support would've been like would have been better than the reality. Survivor organizations warn support from family isn't to be expected but it was easier not to accept that.

I wondered what life would have been like if I hadn't stayed in Nicolet City to be with them, even though when I made that decision, I swore I'd never hold it over their heads—it was mine alone. Now, I just hoped it'd helped more than hurt them, that the final irony wasn't that I'd only heaped more trauma on them, as well as myself, by staying. At the time, I couldn't leave them, and now know it was because I'd be repeating abandonment and that parochial school guilt/putting others first, reinforced it.

Jenny's husband, Scott, said when they came for a visit, "Jenny told me about your uncle. It must've been awful." After a few moments, he added, "Jenny and I wondered about things, like why you wouldn't go certain places, and this clears things up. I'm glad I was born a man." Yet, on following visits, there was a constant need for me to believe he wasn't thinking about my past and that he didn't think the less of me.

***

I'd accepted my kids couldn't help but see me as a mother, not as a person. That was just the way it was; they weren't gnawed by unrelenting symptoms, so how could they understand? Wasn't it natural that they wanted to keep the world they'd known? And yet, if the time bomb of the vicarious trauma they'd experienced would be triggered some day by their children, a sound, a smell, some image, they'd have more of a chance to diffuse it using the past as tools. It was something I had to tell them even if it put a wedge between us that could never be removed. I realized even if they read Mary Shelley's, *Mathilda*, they couldn't understand being, "struck off from humanity," that Mathilda experienced because of her father's desire.

There was, however, a persistent, unnerving fear that I hadn't spotted all the hidden pictures yet—not unlike watching Judy Garland and Fred Astaire in *Easter Parade* appear they were going down the street realizing it was just the scenery moving. Even though I knew on a whole I had it much easier than most, there's a fear of not being on solid ground--being pulled into a black hole. Black holes are where space and time are mixed up, and are so bizarre they are difficult to understand—all equations break down, time and space are woven together. Since the gases in the Earth's atmosphere blur our vision, infrared imaging was the first to detect black holes. There's so much being discovered in my lifetime: perhaps the human species that sent a satellite explorer beyond our solar system will develop compassion for their own species as well as the millions of others on earth closely related to us.

I keep pushing aside the fact that there are covert and overt types of incest, dismissing that something happened to me because I can't remember anything with certainty as defined by law, still not fully accepting that damage happens in both types. In some states the law terms the overt type as carnal knowledge, statutory sexual seduction, 1st, 2nd, 3rd degree sexual assault, and other names. Why I relate to Kitty's crouching near the ground to hide. Why, when someone asked me the reason for my divorce, I was dismayed to have no ready answer and then concluding it's related to John Muir's observation:

"When we try to pick out anything by itself, we find it hitched to everything else in the universe."

The last help I sought was a psychiatrist Dr. Bradford recommended in case he could prescribe medicine. After looking at my records, the psychiatrist got a similar expression that Father Teiresias in Nicolet City had over thirty years ago--a seer looking into the future and said perhaps it was society I should look to for explanations. The prescription he gave me, like the others just resulted in severe headaches, diminished ability to think, and insomnia.

My journey will probably continue like soldiers in the dense jungles of Vietnam, fighting what they couldn't see. With my breast cancer outcome uncertain, I'm sustained by the beauty in common things, the honesty of animals. Blind to my own weaknesses, my travel companions continue to be the ever popular see-no-evil, hear-no-evil, speak-no-evil ceramic monkeys Aunt Hester dusted so faithfully.

About the Author

Carol Smallwood's work has appeared in *English Journal, Michigan Feminist Studies, The Yale Journal for Humanities in Medicine, Journal of Formal Poetry, The Writer's Chronicle, The Detroit News,* and anthologies. She 's a 2010 Short List Finalist, Eric Hoffer Award for Best New Writing; 2009 National Federation of State Poetry Societies Award Winner, and appears in *Contemporary Authors; Who's Who in America. Lily's Odyssey,* her first novel, is her 22nd published book.

Other Publications by Carol Smallwood

Contemporary American Women: Our Defining Passages, All Things That Matter Press, (co-ed.), 2009. *Writing and Publishing: The Librarian's Handbook,* American Library Association, (ed.) 2010. *Librarians As Community Partners: An Outreach Handbook An Outreach Handbook,* American Library Association, (ed.) 2010. *On the Way to Wendy's,* Pudding House Publications, 2008. *Thinking Outside the Book,* McFarland, (ed.) 2008.

Publication Credits

"Death in the Family" first appeared in *Best New Writing 2010*, Hopewell Publications, 2009.
A revised passage in "Cal and Dr. Schackmann" appeared as a poem in: American College of Chest Physicians, *CHEST*, June 2009.

ALL THINGS THAT MATTER PRESS ™

FOR MORE INFORMATION ON TITLES AVAILABLE
FROM
ALL THINGS THAT MATTER PRESS, GO TO
http://allthingsthatmatterpress.com
or contact us at
allthingsthatmatterpress@gmail.com

www.ingramcontent.com/pod-product-compliance
Lightning Source LLC
Chambersburg PA
CBHW030542030726
47495CB00004B/1099